"I just finished reading R.I.P Sheriff Will by Glynn Amburgey. I was very impressed. The story was very plausible, and the path had many twists and turns. I liked that Glynn humanized the characters, it made the story more believable. As a former Sheriff and supervisor of a drug unit that conducted many high profile cases with the DEA and FBI, Glynn's book returned my mind to those days where drugs, corruption and murder were all intertwined.

As for the criminal investigations of both the murder and the corruption, Glynn conveyed the failings of people who are placed in positions of public trust. Also, the lengths family members will go through to protect their own."

Former Sheriff Pat Perez, County of Kane, Illinois

D1207295

Kevin !
Hope you enjoy
my book -
Glynn Amburgey

R.I.P
Sheriff Will

by Glynn Amburgey

JUKE BOX BOOKS LLC

ISBN:978-0-9840728-2-8

Juke Box Books, LLC
St Charles, IL

To Donna,

Because of you this exists, without you I couldn't.

Chapter 1

*Hum, what size is it? Should I just guess or take several sizes with me?
I mean it's about 7 steps from the tool box to the car, don't want to
waste that kind of effort going back and forth. Ok, it should be one of
these three.* Dave thought as he took three hex key sizes out of the box.
It was only a small coolant leak, around the thermostat housing, but
completely unacceptable at a cruise night or car show. The '40 Ford
was by no means a perfect show car, but he did have his standards. The
housing bolts took hex keys instead of the normal wrench or socket,
one of the small detail features that add to the custom look of a street
rod.

His Ford Tudor, as the two door sedans were called in 1940, was a
favorite of the many cars in the collection. This one was his alone,
unlike most of the other cars in which he shared ownership with his
brother and sister from Dad's estate. But he loved them all and
continued to maintain them just like he, his brother and father did for
many years.

Dave also owned outright a 1966 Chevy Impala Convertible, a 1931
Model A Ford Coupe and a 1971 Oldsmobile Cutlass Convertible, but
the rest of the thirty some cars were from Dad. Dad began the hobby
when Dave's brother, Kent, was about fourteen. Dad always enjoyed
the time he and Kent spent together working on the cars even though
Kent never really got the bug. Little brother, on the other hand, was
always fascinated by cars and anything mechanical. So the collection
just fell naturally to Dave to maintain. It also made sense since Dave is

here and Kent lives outside of Chicago where he is chief surgeon in a suburban hospital.

The collection is housed in an outbuilding on the family farm. There are several barns and out buildings on the farm. The farm house has been rented out since Dave's mom died a couple of years ago, but all of the other buildings and the farm itself are run by Dave. In addition to housing the car collection, this building also contains the farm workshop. It has an area large enough to bring in the farm equipment for maintenance. The shop is heated so that work can be done though out the winters.

Yep, it was the hex key he thought it should be, but he was also sure that if that had been the only one he had brought over from the tool box, it would not have been. The two bolts, though tight, were not a problem to get loose. As he removed the second one his cell phone rang.

"Sargent, this is Dan Muscovy," he heard when he answered. "I've got tragic news. The Sheriff has been found dead of an apparent suicide at his lake house." Dave dropped the hex wrench and grabbed the side of the tool box. He felt a wave of shock, panic, despair and grief, almost at once. The voice on the phone continued, "I need to go up there, and understand that you've been there many times. Can you go with me?"

"Sure," Dave said, with a voice that sounded foreign. "It'll take me about forty minutes. I'll meet you in the station."

"Sorry, Dave, no time, you home?"

"I'm at the farm."

"Get home and throw on a uniform. It's on the way; I'll pick you up in ten."

"Ok, on my way, see you in ten."

Suddenly, the thermostat housing leak seemed trivial. H e headed home.

Dave's house was only a quarter mile down the road. His parents had given him and Joyce the property to build the house as a wedding present. In reality, it was a part of the family farm that was not very conducive to farming, but it made a lovely home site. It was along a creek bed in a wooded area. It had been used as a small pasture when his dad ventured into livestock many years ago, but it was too far away from the barn to make real sense.

As Dave pulled in the drive he flashed back to how he felt coming home after his brother called him when his dad died. His dad and Sheriff Willard Lewis had been best friends since grade school. Uncle Will, as he had always known him, was as much a part of Dave's childhood as any other adult. He would have to wait to deal with that. He needed to get focused, and in control. Grieving would have to wait.

Buttoning his uniform shirt, after a quick wash up and hand scrub, he heard the siren as the squad turned from the highway less than a mile up the county road. He figured he had less than a minute before Major Muscovy, head of the investigations division for the Lincoln County Sheriff Department, was there. He pulled on his trousers, shoes and was buckling his gun belt as he heard the car slide into the driveway. As he ran out the door, he grabbed his jacket. He wasn't sure how long he was going to be gone. It could be a long night.

"We'll take your squad," Muscovy yelled as Dave was locking the house. "A marked cruiser will be more visible than my unmarked."

Muscovy was locking up his car after pulling his evidence kit and brief case from the trunk.

Dave popped the trunk of his County Sheriff squad with the remote after unlocking the doors. The squad car was parked where it most always was when Dave was off duty: at the end of the drive past the four car end loaded garage. He got in the driver's seat, fastened his seat belt and waited while Muscovy put his stuff in the trunk and climbed into the passenger seat.

"Let's go," Muscovy grunted as he strapped himself in. "We'll talk after we get on the interstate."

Dave knew the meaning of that. He was being told to get there as fast as possible, all attention to the high speed driving. He didn't say a word as he flipped the switches for all the lights and siren, emergency pursuit mode for the seven miles to interstate highway.

In just over five minutes, Dave reached up and switched off the siren as he wheeled the heavy cruiser onto the north bound entrance ramp to the interstate. He left the flashing lights on and accelerated as he merged into the left lane for the roughly sixty mile trip to the exit for the lake house. He switched the radio over to the state police channel and checked in with their dispatch.

"Ok," Dan said, "let me tell you what I know." His tone was all business, but Dave sensed an underlining emotional level that he knew they both shared.

"The sheriff went up to the lake for the week end," Dan continued. "He told Cheryl on Friday that he planned to do some work around the place and would be back last night."

Cheryl was the office secretary and more or less functioned as the office manager.

"When she got into the office this morning and noticed that the sheriff had not been in, as normal, she called him. His cell went to voicemail, so she got worried and got me involved. I had a unit swing by his house. They found his squad there but no sign of his personal car. The house was locked up. I called his wife and daughter but neither of them had heard from him."

Dave was intent on his driving, but the traffic was light and even at over ninety five mph he was confident that there was little danger as he listened to the events of the morning.

"I placed a call to Sheriff Allen, up in Arlington County and he agreed to have a deputy stop by Will's place," Dan went on. "The cabin was open, and they found him." Dan hesitated, took a deep breath and said, "Shotgun..... To the head."

There was silence in the car other than the road noise and the swoosh sound made as they flew past other vehicles that were driving nearer the speed limit. Dave was confused; he had last talked with "Uncle Will" as he was going out the door at noon last Friday. It was a normal, common conversation, like they had had thousands of times. Yes, Will was under stress, as he was constantly lately with all that was going on in the county. But he loved what he did, as was evident by continuing to run for reelection well into his eighties, and he loved life. Dave could not believe he would shoot himself.

"I let Bob know that you were going to be with me this afternoon," Dan changed the subject after a couple of silent minutes. Major Bob Cooper was Dan's counterpart on the patrol side, and was Dave's direct supervisor. "He said he will cover your roll call today and assign someone to fill in for you till you get back."

Dave glanced at his watch. It was 2:30, still several hours before his normal shift start. He normally got into the station about six pm on his normal shift days of Monday, Tuesday and Wednesday. This normally gave him time to get up to speed on things before he provided the assignments and direction to his patrolmen before their twelve hour shift at the seven pm roll call. The three twelve hour days and the four hour Friday morning administration time made up his forty hour work week. But, it normally took more than forty hours to get the job done right. This was accepted and understood, as in the case this afternoon, but today was not just the job. It was much more: tragic, emotional, personal and most of all unsettling.

"I know you and the sheriff were close," Dan said. "I've heard that he and your dad were best friends."

"Yeah, dad and Will were best friends since grade school," Dave said. "The story goes that after high school, dad stayed on the family farm and Uncle Will joined the sheriff's department. He and dad continued to best friends as he worked up through ranks. I think he was first elected sheriff about forty years ago. He was like an uncle to me and my brother and sister. Our families have always been intertwined."

"You continued to be close after your dad passed?"

"Oh, yes," said Dave. "He and his daughter were never really close so I guess I was like a son to him, or nephew, at least. He, Dad and I had a lot of the same passions: fishing, hunting and cars. Hardly a week went by that we weren't doing something together. It was like we were family. And after Dad died four years ago he also filled some of that void for me. I think in some way I did that for him too."

"He got you into the department?"

"Yeah," Dave replied. "The summer after I got my Master's, I came home while trying to decide which offer to take. I got busy with dad on the farm, and the next thing I knew harvest was over and I was still here. Will suggested I join the force as a fall back till I moved on. So I went to the academy and after a while on the job, realized that I liked the work. There was also lot to be said for being back around the farm with dad. So, eighteen years later, dad and mom are both gone and now Uncle Will, and I'm still here."

"You say you got a Master's, what in?" Dan asked.

"BS and MS from Purdue, both in Electrical Engineering, with a minor in Mechanical," said Dave.

"Do you feel the degrees are wasted on the force?"

"No, not really. Dad was a believer in higher education. He could afford to put us through school, and it was important to him that we go. Both my brother and sister are doctors, and like mine, their education was fully paid for by dad's farming. It was probably the most important thing he felt he could do for us. I think if he hadn't been able to afford it, he would have gone into debt for it. He always said he wished he could have gone to school, so I guess we were living his dream. Anyway, my education was a big help on the farm keeping everything operational and gave us the knowledge to do some things other farmers have to hire out. I designed the sprinkler control system, the security system and energy management system. My computer skills were also a great help in setting up data bases to manage the farm operation. My education may not be needed in the department, but it doesn't hurt and the job gives me an income and the flexibility with hours that allowed me time to assist with the farm. As far as income, if I was working as an engineer I would probably make less than I currently do from the force and the farm income."

"How many acres are you farming?"

"A little over three hundred. My two sons' help a lot and I hire additional help if I need to. We grow corn and soybeans, rotating crops as needed."

They were now approaching the exit for the county road to the small town near the cabin. Dave slowed and took the ramp. There were two cars on the ramp that pulled to the shoulder and stopped as they approached, giving them the right of way. Dave turned east toward the small town of Grifford, according to the sign, four miles away. The cabin was six miles north of there on the shore of Lake Mallard.

The four miles to Gifford, population 465 according to the town limit sign, passed too fast as far as Dave was concerned. He was not looking forward to what he would soon see. He turned north at the main intersection in the middle of Gifford in front of Pop's Gas, an old style gas station that still pumped gas for patrons. As was nearly always the case Pop was sitting on his lawn chair under the canopy keeping track of all the happenings in Gifford. Dave accelerated out of town as his stomach muscles tightened and began to churn.

Chapter 2

As Dave and Dan approached the cabin property they saw two Arlington County sheriff cars off to the left side of the road in front. On the dirt drive to the cabin was another sheriff car, a state police cruiser, a sheriff's van and a county coroner van. There was also a late model Chevy parked across the road. Dave parked off the left side of the road behind the two squads and turned off the flashing lights as he shut off the engine. Parked next to the cabin, in front of the small garage that was used for winter boat storage, was the Chevy pickup Dave recognized as the Sheriff's personal vehicle. Strung from tree to tree about thirty feet out from the cabin, and running around it, was yellow "crime scene" tape. The taped perimeter also encompassed the garage and the pickup. Standing just outside the tape was a group of seven people, four in uniform and three in civilian clothes. One of the non-uniforms was a woman.

As they walked up the drive, two officers turned toward them.

"You must be Major Muscovy," said the taller of the two, as they approached. "I'm Sheriff Allen. Sorry to meet under these circumstances."

"Yes, call me Dan" answered Dan. "And this is Sargent Dave Harbinger."

They shook hands.

Sheriff Allen turned to the officer with him. "This is Corporal John Davidson; he was the first on the scene." As Dave and Dan shook hands with Davidson, Sheriff Allen continued. "When Davidson approached the cabin, he saw Sheriff Lewis through the window. He found the front door open so he went in and checked for vitals. Finding none, he retreated outside and reported. He secured the area and no one but our evidence team has been back in the crime scene, except for Janet from the coroner's office who confirmed the fatality."

"Dave was a close friend of the sheriff," Dan offered. "He was up here often. He may be able to tell if anything seems irregular."

"Good idea," the sheriff said. "Let me see if the evidence guys are ready for us to take a look." He walked toward the cabin, dipped under the yellow tape, but did not go on the porch. "Pete, I have a guy here who knows the place," Sheriff Allen called. "Do you want him to come in?"

"That may be helpful," came a voice from inside. "But just him for now, we'll need another ten minutes or so before all is secure."

The Sheriff motioned, Dave swallowed hard, took a deep breath, and moved toward the door.

He walked in the door and stopped just inside. Everything looked just the way it had when he was there fishing about a month ago, except for Uncle Will. His body was sprawled out on the floor by his reloading desk on the west side of the room. His face, or what had been his face, was a dark mass. A shot gun was clamped in the vice on his reloading desk with the barrel angled upward at about thirty degrees. The desk chair was upside down a few feet away. *Focus*, Dave thought. *This can't be as it seems. He wouldn't have done that. There has to be something.*

"I'm Pete Jacobs, evidence tech," a voice said next to him.

"Dave Harbinger," Dave answered as he shook the extended gloved hand.

"If you don't mind," Pete said as he handed Dave a pair of surgical type rubber gloves.

"My prints are probably all over this place already," Dave said, as he snapped them on. "My sons and I were up here about a month ago fishing."

"So tell me," Pete asked, "does anything look different, or out of place?"

Dave slowly looked around the room. *Be careful*, he thought. *Make sure you see and register what is there. You are under stress and when under stress a glance may cause you to see what you think should be rather than what is really there or not there. I must concentrate to register what I see rather than what my memory has recorded in the past.*

The cabin was typical of a lake retreat. The general orientation was south to north along the south bank of the lake. It had a great room that ran the length, front to back, on the west side, with two bedrooms and a bath along the east side. The roof beams were exposed and there was a loft area, accessible by a wall mount ladder, above the bedrooms. The loft contained additional sleeping area; there were three double beds up there. Just inside the front door and to the left were two overstuffed sofas and a matching chair arranged in a rectangle with a large round coffee table in the middle. A large TV was sitting at an angle in the far left corner. Most of south wall between the door and west wall was taken up by a large picture window.

Along the west wall of the cabin, from the edge of the TV for about ten feet was a tall book case with ten shelves full of books. Next to the book case to the north was the work bench with a desk across from it that was used as a work desk and reloading station. Uncle Will also used this desk to work on and maintain his firearms, thus the reason for the vice that now held the shot gun. There were several canisters on the desk with gun powder, primers, bullet casings, shell casings and various sizes of bullets and shot. The desk also had scales and presses for reloading different bullets and shotgun shells. There was a large desk lamp on a swing arm clamped to the south end of the desk. The lamp was positioned such that it was over the rear center of the desk. The lamp was on.

The rest of the west wall was part of the kitchen area with cabinets and a stove before turning the corner along the north wall. There was a counter with a sink under the window and more countertop to the refrigerator which was next to the back door. The rest of the kitchen area was taken up by a large round table with chairs around it. There was a hanging light over the table with three globes. The light was on.

After his slow, very deliberate, look around the room, he said, "I see nothing out of the ordinary. I've been in this place several times a year since I was a toddler. It has never really changed, and that is true today. I've got nothing to offer."

"Ok, take your time and look around the other rooms," Pete replied. "Let me know if there is anything."

"Sure."

With that he proceeded to very carefully go through the entire cabin. Then out to the garage, down to the dock and over the property. He found nothing. As much as he wanted to find the smallest scrap of evidence that would point to some other explanation for what had happened, he could not. He just couldn't believe it. Uncle Will was not that type. *He would have never done that, would he?*

Long before Dave had completed his search, Pete had released the crime scene and Dan, Sheriff Allen and the others were able to go into the cabin. The coroner was given the ok to remove the body. Pete and his crew had gone over the scene with the finest toothed comb that could be bought. They had bagged and tagged every dust mite and anything bigger. Finger prints were lifted from every surface and cataloged for future reference.

The shotgun was given special attention and would be analyze to see if it could be positively tied to the fatality, although there seemed little doubt at this point. But, in truth, there is little that can be determined from the gun since rifling does not exist with shot as it does with bullets. There was a spent shell in the gun and other than finger prints that is really about the only evidence that could be expected.

Sheriff Allen, Dan, Pete and the rest of the team methodically processed the evidence to reconstruct the events leading up to the shotgun blast. Photos were taken, angles measured, distances measured, things were marked and cataloged. Although it remained an Arlington County investigation, the State Police and Lincoln County would be listed as assisting agencies. Dave, having spent all his time on the patrol side, had no real experience as a crime scene investigator so he simply observed, answered questions, and tried to stay out of the way.

Sheriff Lewis was a big guy, over six feet tall. His arms were long enough to reach the trigger of a shotgun held in front of his face by a vice. But to add to the possibility, there was a yard stick on the bench, where it could have fallen if it had been used to extend his reach. So the preliminary determination from the team was suicide. However, as is always the case, it was assumed to be a homicide as far as collection of evidence was concerned. So the team continued the work of collecting. Anything could turn out to be a clue.

As they got back into his car after over four hours on the scene Dave was thinking the evidence seemed to point to suicide but was torn by a single question, *why a shot gun, a service revolver would have been much easier.*

Just before getting onto the interstate to head south, Dave and Dan pulled into a fast food chain to grab a bite. After getting their burgers, fries and drinks they sat a small table by the window. Nothing was said for several bites into the meal.

"Yes, he was an old man," Dan reflected, "but man was he on the ball. He was sharp, full of energy, and always available with advice and direction. He had the uncommon ability in managers to correct or even reprimand without making it feel personal or belittling. I really enjoyed working for him. I don't think I have ever known anyone in this field more respected at all levels. He was a true man of integrity, maybe even to a fault."

Dave looked across the table into eyes that were full of emotion. But he still kept the air of complete professionalism and control.

"You know," Dave agreed, "as far as the, integrity to a fault is concerned, I think his wife and daughter may completely agree. Even after almost ten years of separation, they continued to complain that the department, and enforcing the law, meaning more to him than they did."

"Family life is often a problem for us," Dan offered. "I believe you have had similar issues, as I have heard."

"Yeah," said Dave, "My wife and I have been separated for about five years. Our schedules worked well to allow one of us always being available for the kids when they were growing up, but not so well with keeping the magic alive. We hardly ever saw each other with me on patrol every night and working the farm when I wasn't, and her working every day. When we were together we just couldn't get along. If I'm perfectly honest, I was more interested in working on the farm, or my cars, than spending time with her. One day she decided to rent a place in town. She and the boys moved in there closer to her work and the school, and I stayed in our place."

"I'm afraid that story is not uncommon," Dan replied. "I guess I'm one of the lucky ones. But my wife has never worked, so we've always had time to be together when I am off. I think that has really helped."

"So, what happens now, in the department?" Dave changed the subject. "Will was sheriff for as long as I have been in the department."

"Well," Dan began, "I would guess the County Board Chairman will select someone as acting sheriff until the next election. He would need the full board to approve his selection but I would guess that to be automatic. Since we don't have a Chief Deputy position, which would be a natural acting appointment, it could come from any level. My guess is he will select one of the command staff, but I really don't know. We may hear something tomorrow, but I expect the acting appointment no later than the county board meeting next week."

"So you, Bob or Major Jackson will be acting sheriff and whichever one of you is selected someone will be moved up to acting in that command position," Dave said.

"That would be my guess, but as I said, it could be anyone. It could even be someone from outside the department, but I would be surprised at that."

"It's going to feel strange without the Sheriff around," Dave said in a low tone almost to himself.

"We all feel the same way," Dan reflected.

They were quiet for a time. Then they talked about other things, unrelated to the events of the day, for the rest of the drive back to Lincoln County. Both men knew they would have to deal with the emotions but wanted to delay those thoughts for a while longer.

Chapter 3

It was after 9:30 pm when Dave and Dan got back to Dave's house so that Dan could pick up his car.

"Do you want to take the rest of the night off?" Dan asked as they pulled into the driveway. "I appreciate your help today, and have no problem if you want to call it a day. I can tell Bob I gave you the night off. I'm sure he'll have no problem with it."

"No," Dave responded, "I appreciate the offer, but getting back into the routine would be best, I think."

"I understand," Dan said as they got out of the car, "I'll keep you informed of any developments, and thanks again."

Dave helped Dan transfer his stuff to the unmarked and they headed for the station in both cars.

In the station Dave checked in at dispatch to get up to speed. All activity logged this shift so far was routine, with nothing out of the ordinary. Dave would normally have gone into his office to check on the shift paper work and review future manpower assignments. But due to the events of the day, being alone in his office in the middle of the night was not appealing to him. Dave decided to get out of the office.

Major Cooper had assigned Corporal Brian Rodriguez to acting supervisor in Dave's absence. There were four corporals on Dave's team. The county was divided up into quarters with a corporal assigned to each quarter on each shift. The corporals supervised the deputies working their respective quadrant. There were normally six deputies per quadrant on the midnight shift and eight on day shift.

The responsibility of an acting supervisor was to assign tasks at the roll call and be in charge when events require. After roll call, with no unusual events, the acting supervisor would revert back to his normal duties. Rodriguez was out on his normal patrol duties.

The dispatcher informed Dave that Rodriguez was providing assistance to the city police at an accident, with injuries, scene on the west side of the city. Dave asked the dispatcher to inform Rodriguez that he would meet him at that location in about ten minutes.

Dave flipped on the flashing strobes a few minutes later as he parked his squad car along the curb behind the Lincoln County Sheriff car with number thirty seven on the rear by the tail light. There were also two city patrol cars and a city command SUV on the scene. Car thirty seven was the issue of Corp. Rodriguez.

Brian and Dave had been friends since high school. Brian's parents had migrated to the south end of the county from Mexico shortly after they were married. They were farm workers in the vegetable farms. By the time Brian was in high school his dad had proven himself and was the farm manager for one of the large corporate operations. Brian went to junior college for an associate degree in criminal justice and then joined the department. Brian had been in the department for about four years when Dave joined.

The Ford F150 pickup had been broadsided by an older Honda Accord. Now it was being loaded onto a rollback tow truck as another tow truck pulled away with the Honda. A medium height deputy sheriff with two chevrons on his sleeve was walking back from the center of the intersection toward the two sheriff cars.

"Tough day, huh," Brian said, as Dave got out of the car to meet him.

"You know it." Dave responded, "Are you clear here? Got time for a cup of joe?"

"Yep, all clear, it's city paper work. Apparently the Honda blew the light, but no serious injury. Let's hit Cliff's."

Dave nodded, and they got in their cars.

Cliff's was a twenty four hour 50s style dinner near the interstate. It was less than a mile from the accident scene. The diner had aluminum looking panels on the outside and was shaped similar to on old street car. Inside there were bright red vinyl booths along the outside wall with white table tops. There was an old Wurlitzer juke box that still worked, with remote wall boxes at each booth. A long counter ran the length of the dinner opposite the booths with red vinyl stools. There was chrome everywhere and mirrors. Pictures of old movie stars and classic cars adorned the walls.

Dave and Brian took a booth just inside the door. There were only two other customers at this late hour and both were at the counter.

A waitress behind the counter, dressed in the frilly 50s style dress, smiled and nodded as Dave said, "Two coffees," as they sat down.

"Anything going on tonight that I need to know about?" Dave asked.

"Nope, all's pretty quiet."

"Good, there's something we need to talk about," Dave said slowly. "I don't know how much you've heard, but the facts seem to point to suicide."

"But you're not convinced," Brian interjected.

"Well, it just doesn't feel right to me." Dave looked down at the table as the waitress put two cups of coffee in front of them.

"Thanks," Brian said to the waitress. She smiled as she walked away.

"I'm probably wrong, and I probably need to just accept it and move on, but....,"Dave's voice trailed off as he took a sip of the hot coffee.

Brian waited.

"Have you talked with your cousin lately?" Dave asked as he looked up.

"Oh," Brian's face flushed as he grasped the reason for the question. "Not for a few weeks, but are you thinking there could be a connection?"

"I don't know," Dave said, "But Uncle Will was really coming down hard on their operation, and I was just wondering"

"Wow," Brian interrupted, "they would certainly be up for something like that, and wouldn't hesitate if they thought they could get away with it. But how did it happen? Is it feasible they could be behind this?"

"It was a shotgun to the face. There doesn't seem to be evidence against the initial conclusion, but I'm thinking a service revolver would have made more sense," Dave answered. "If it was a homicide, I think the drug cartel would be high on the list of suspects due to the pressure they were putting on the sheriff to get him to back down. I understand he was on the verge of turning it all over to the feds, and they really didn't want that."

"Do you want me to check up on Bobby? Find out where he's been and what's been going on?" Brian asked.

"No," Dave responded, "I may do that, but I need to let things settle for a while and see how I feel after I've had some time. You know I wouldn't want to bring attention to Bobby without cause. That could be really bad for him. But I wanted to let you know what I was thinking, run it by you, so to speak."

"Understood," Brian said. As he started to continue, his shoulder radio speaker barked with a call from dispatch. A car had struck a deer on county sixteen near Seaward Crossing, unit fifty five was being dispatched, but Brian was closer so he responded that he would take the call.

Dave waved him out of the booth. The job comes first, even when friends are in deep conversation. Dave took another drink of coffee as the diner lit up with the reflection of the flashing lights outside and he heard Brian hit the siren pulling out of the lot.

His thoughts turned back to Bobby Hernandez, Brian's cousin on his mother's side. Bobby had come from Mexico to stay with Brian's family after his parents were killed in an auto accident when he was 14 and Brian was 17. It had been a hard adjustment for Bobby and he never really fit in, not speaking English, knowing no one and dealing with the grief of his loss. Bobby got pulled into a Mexican gang that had set up a drug distribution operation in a small farm just across the county line into Williams County.

Dave had known Bobby since he came to live with Brian's family. As strange as it might seem, the relationship with Bobby changed little after Brian and Dave were in the department and Bobby was in the gang. Bobby was nineteen, when his interest in the gang was developing. He was drawn by the group of Mexican guys about his age that seemed to always be having fun and to have money. Brian and his parents objected and tried to convince him that it wasn't right. Bobby rebelled and left. After about a year in the gang, Bobby was the one that reestablished contact with Brian's parents. He stopped by for a visit one Sunday afternoon and became part of the family once again, acknowledging and accepting that Brian and his parents did not, and would not, support his gang ties, but that he was family.

Brian, and Dave, developed a no-questions-asked type of relationship with Bobby that seemed to work. Brian and Dave never asked about it or discussed Bobby's gang connections when they were together. Bobby visited with Brian's folks regularly and was always welcomed. Most importantly, Bobby always treated Brian and his parents with respect. Dave didn't think that Bobby had ever lied to them, maybe because they had never asked anything to require it.

It was suspected that the drug farm run by Bobby's gang was a processing center for large shipments from Mexico and South America. From there the drugs would be divided up into smaller quantities and transported to cities around the east coast and mid-west. The amounts were a point of significant debate, but everyone seemed to believe it was a profitable operation.

The size of the gang varied from time to time with people coming and going from Mexico, but it was generally thought to be from ten to fifteen in number. The structure was a gang leader with three lieutenants. The leader was a mid-fifties guy by the name of Juan with a reputation of being a bad dude. He was thought to be a blood relative of one of the Mexican Cartel bosses. He had a big house on the property next door to the farm. Ownership of the farm was an offshore corporation. All the gang members drove high end luxury cars or SUVs registered to the farm. Their favorite brands seemed to be BMW, Porsche, Mercedes and Audi. Juan had a green Bentley and other cars.

The Federal Drug Enforcement Agency (DEA) had been watching the drug farm for several years. DEA had raided the property several times but found no evidence of drugs. The DEA suspected that the drug gang was being advised of when a raid was about to happen. The suspicion was the source of the leaked information was the Williams County Sheriff's Department. This did not set well with Sheriff Lewis and created a rift between him and Sheriff Alexander in Williams County. Sheriff Alexander had assured Uncle Will on numerous occasions that there were no payoffs and that his department was diligently pursuing the drug ring. This did nothing to convince Will. His animosity toward Sheriff Alexander and his department continued to grow. This not only created problems between the two sheriffs but also a real problem between Sheriff Lewis and his daughter, Megan. Megan's husband, John, was a Major in the Williams County department.

About two years ago, Dave had been asked to hang around for a special meeting after his shift ended one Tuesday morning. The meeting included Dave, two other sergeants, Bob Cooper, Dan Muscovy and the sheriff.

"Sergeants," the sheriff began the meeting, "we are going to implement a traffic safety program in the county. One part of the program will be highway safety checks. We intend to set up road blocks, on selected county highways at various times, to look for seat belt violations, uninsured vehicles, drunk drivers and general vehicle safety checks. We would like for you three to take charge of these road blocks when one falls on your shift. The command staff will determine when and where a roadblock will take place. You will discuss with Bob the manpower required for each at the time it is set up. Any questions?"

There were several questions and the discussion continued for about twenty minutes before the meeting broke up. The following Monday Dave got a call at home from Bob asking him to come in early so that they could get ready for the first of the road blocks.

The first road block was to be on county road 6, just north of the County line. County road six became Williams County road eighteen as you crossed the county line. Less than a mile across the county line, in Williams County, on county road eighteen was the drug farm operation. Bob told Dave to pick three of his deputies to man the road block with him.

"And," Bob continued, "Corporal Kowalski has also been assigned to your team. Judge Robins has agreed to be available all night if the need for a search warrant should arise."

Corporal Kowalski was the handler for the department drug sniffing dog. Dave was instructed to run the road block for the entire shift. As Dave headed out of the station to pick the spot on CR six for the road block he suspected safety might not be the whole reason for this venture.

About forty minutes later Dave had selected a spot in a dip in the road to set up the road block. His four man crew was all in place and ready to check and inspect. Coming from either direction someone would be within a couple 100 yards before they saw the road block. There was plenty of time to react, slow, and stop, but once visible to a motorist there was no way to avoid the inspection. It would be possible for someone to make a three point turn and go back the other way after seeing the road block, so Dave posted a patrol car facing in each direction for pursuit if that should happen. Cones were set up, and flares prepared for after dark. Traffic was always light on CR 6 so the crew was expecting a long boring night.

Long and boring it was. By two AM the next morning only about fifteen cars total had come by their location, with most of those in the first couple of hours. At a little after two a pair of headlights came over the hill to the north and noticeably slowed as the driver saw them. Then the vehicle stopped and sat for a few seconds before proceeding slowly toward them. As it came to a stop next to them they saw that it was a late model Chevy van, white in color with Texas plates. It appeared that there was only the driver in the van. As he opened the driver side window Dave noted that he appeared to be of Mexican heritage. As one of the deputies instructed the driver to shut off the engine and checked registration and insurance, Corp. Kowalski and his dog, Simon, walked around the van. As Simon reached the rear of the van he began to bark. Kowalski turned to Dave and nodded.

"Sir," Dave said as he approached the driver's window, "would you allow us to search your vehicle?"

The driver subconsciously glanced over his shoulder. "A, no," he hesitated and continued in broken English, "I don't think you can do that, can you?"

"No, sir we can't without your permission," Dave informed, "not without a search warrant. But, we can hold you here until we obtain a search warrant. And, we will if you will not give us permission."

"I will not give you permission," the driver said.

As he had previously been directed, Dave called dispatch, gave them the description of the vehicle and the probable cause of the reaction of the drug sniffing dog and asked them to send the closest unit to Judge Robin's residence to have a search warrant issued and brought to the road block location. The whole process took just over an hour. During that time the van sat in the middle of the road with the driver inside. With search warrant in hand Dave instructed the driver to get out of the van. He complied, and the search began.

It wasn't a long search. Simon went right for four large suitcases in the back of the van surrounded by furniture and household goods. The suitcases were somewhat buried under stuff, as if to make it look like they were just part of a household move. Inside the cases were various drugs, including methamphetamine, OxyContin, and a full case of cocaine.

This was the first of several such road blocks set up by Sheriff Lewis with the main intention of making life difficult for the drug gang. He never expected to stop the flow, but once he began the road blocks the drug gang had no choice but to avoid the Lincoln County roads when shipping product. Since the most direct route to the interstate was through Lincoln County, the diversion added time and inconvenience.

Bobby later told Brian his gang buddies blamed Sheriff Lewis for having to change their operation. Brian had passed this information along to Dave. Sheriff Will laughed when Dave told him what Bobby had said. "Step one in getting them shut down," he said.

"More coffee?" asked the waitress at Cliff's, jarring Dave from his thoughts of the drug gang.

"No, thanks," he said as he finished his second cup of coffee, dropped five dollars on the table and headed back to the station.

As he was turning into the station lot he heard a call on the radio of a multiple vehicle accident on the interstate about 4 miles north of town. He turned back out of the parking lot and hit the lights as he accelerated and keyed his mike to inform dispatch he was in route with an ETA of five. Traffic was light at this time of night, so the siren was unnecessary. In just under five minutes he was approaching the scene from the south. Ahead he saw a semi jack knifed in the south bound lanes and several cars crashed across the lanes and into the center grass. He was the first officer on the scene although he saw what he assumed to be a state police car with lights flashing about a half mile north coming around stopped traffic along the shoulder in the south bound lanes. He pulled into the grassy median between the north bound and south bound lanes and began to do his job of providing assistance. In truth, although he hated the misfortune of those involved, the distraction was welcomed.

Chapter 4

At shift end Dave headed home. He was so tired he just dropped his gear and clothes on the bedroom floor. But when he got in bed he couldn't sleep. The bloody scene at the cabin filled his mind. It was almost eight am. He had been up for about twenty hours. Just about the time his eyes finally closed, the phone rang.

"Dad," he heard as answered, "Are you ok? Mom told us about Uncle Will last night. I'm so sorry."

"Yes, D, I think I'm still somewhat in shock, but I'll be fine. Thanks."

Dave's oldest son was Dave Junior, but everyone called him D. He was about to begin his junior year at Arizona State. He was on a baseball scholarship and would be heading back to school in a couple of weeks. Dave was very impressed with his ability at shortstop, as was his high school and college coaches, but Dave tried hard to keep him from getting his hopes of a pro ball career too high. D seemed to understand this and was majoring in sports journalism in school.

"Chris and I are planning to come out later, if that's ok," D said, "when do you think you'll be up?"

Chris was Dave's other son, who would be starting his senior year at Springfield High School soon. Chris was also a good athlete. He played high school football and basketball but didn't have the passion for sports that D showed.

"I've got the alarm set for four," Dave said. "But instead of you guys coming out here, how about we meet at the Outback for dinner about five?"

"Ok, that sounds fine, see you then, have a good rest."

"D," Dave said before hanging up, "I really appreciate the call, say hey to Chris."

Surprisingly, Dave slept soundly until his alarm clicked on the radio to the 4 pm news on the local Springfield station. The lead story was about Sheriff Will. All indications were that suicide was the case of death, but the investigation was continuing. The county board chairman has indicated that he will propose the appointment of an acting sheriff at their meeting tonight. The board will also discuss whether to hold a special election or wait for the regular election in November to elect a new sheriff.

Dave showered and dressed before he picks up the phone to place a call he needed to make.

"Hello," said the voice on the other end.

"Aunt Dar, how are you?" Dave asked.

"Oh, Davie, I guess I'm ok, how are you?"

Her name was really Doris, but Uncle Will always called his wife Dar. So it just seemed natural that everyone else would as well. Will had married late in life; he was into his late thirties when he met Doris. She was fifteen years younger, and impressed by an older man in uniform.

"I guess we don't know what to say or do," Dave said. "It's really hard, isn't it? Is there anything you need me to do for you?"

"Thanks, Davie, you have always been so sweet." Dar answered. "Megan is here and we are coping together, but I'll be sure to let you know if we need anything."

"I'm off on Thursday evening; I'll stop by to check in with you then, if that's ok."

"That will be fine, sweetie, see you then, and thanks for calling."

Dave headed out for a Blooming Onion and a steak with his sons.

After a nice dinner with the boys, Dave got into the station a little later than usual. On his desk was a note to call his supervisor, Bob Cooper. Dave dialed Bob's cell phone.

"Dave," Bob answered on the second ring, "I have been asked to fill in as acting chief. I'm going into the county board meeting now. If the board approves my appointment, I'm asking you to step up to my command position. Are you ok with that?"

"Well, Bob, I haven't thought about it, but I guess I can do that." Dave responded.

"You know it will mean moving to straight day shift, eight to five Monday through Friday. I know how much you like your current schedule."

"I understand that, Bob, but I'm sure I can adjust. It's only till the election, anyway. Unless,… are you planning to run for election?"

"Relax, Dave, I have no problem filling in, but have no interest in the job long term," Bob consoled. "I'm sure I'll get enough of the politics in the next couple of months."

"Ok, then," Dave said, "and congrats."

"Keep this confidential for now," Bob directed, "but be ready to assign a replacement for your position after the board meeting tonight. I will call you with the results of the vote. Your replacement will be expected to move into your position immediately, and you will go off duty at that time. You will report to the command staff meeting at 9 AM in the morning."

"Ok," said Dave, "I'll be in my office until you call. Thanks, Bob."

The conversation ended there. Dave started to think about what had just happened, but realized he needed to get the assignments done for the roll call meeting in 12 minutes. It normally took about 15 to do that, so thinking could come later, the job needs to be done.

After roll call, as the team was heading out for their respective patrols, Dave caught Brian Rodriguez attention and motioned toward his office. Brian followed Dave in.

"Brian," Dave began as he sat down at his desk, "I wonder if you could plan to come back in sometime between 9 and 9:30 tonight. I may want to continue our discussion from last night, but first I want to collect my thoughts. It's been a whirl wind of a week already."

"Sure," Brian said. "I'll bring coffee and donuts."

"Good, thanks." Dave said as Brian turned and walked out.

The next hour flew by as Dave worked to clear up paper that had accumulated on his desk. He really had no time to just sit and think about what was happening. He was right in the middle of a quarterly manpower assignment sheet when the phone rang.

"Acting Major Harbinger, this is Acting Sheriff Cooper," the voice said. "See you at staff meeting in the morning."

"Ok," Dave replied and he was promoted, temporarily anyway.

As Brian came into Dave's office about ten minutes later carrying two cups of coffee and a Dunkin Donuts bag, Dave got up from the desk and motioned Brian to take his chair. Brian did so, with an inquiring look on his face. Dave sat down in one of the visitors chairs, turned back the top on one of the coffees and retrieved a donut from the bag.

"Thanks for the coffee and donuts, acting sergeant," Dave said with a smile.

Once Brian was up to speed Dave headed back home. Brian had filled in for him on several previous occasions, as had the other three corporals, so Dave had no concerns. His new position, however, would be something else, not so much from the responsibility or doing the job, but from the complete change of his routine. The times he had filled in for Bob in the past were only brief periods, like a day or two, or a week at most. He was now looking at an extended period of eight to five daily, as Bob had pointed out.

It was just after ten when Dave got home. He set the alarm for 6:30 and got back into bed only about six hours after getting up.

"This is going to really screw up my system for a while," he mumbled to himself as he shut off the light.

Sleep did not come easily. Dave tossed and turned for most of the night. His body was used to being up all night on Tuesday nights. He really did not feel rested when the clock radio clicked on at 6:30 Wednesday morning. But what could he do? He was about to establish a new routine, so he needed to get to it.

At 7:45, Dave walked into the station. As opposed to his normal route entering the side door, by dispatch and into the patrol section, he walked straight to the main entrance.

The door was locked. He used his key and went inside. Just inside the door was the receptionist desk, which would soon be occupied by a young girl and relatively new hire, named Angela. To the right, along the outside wall were the offices of the three majors. In the rear was the sheriff's office. The large open area in middle was occupied by the desks of the various clerks and administrative staff.

"Good morning," he said to Cheryl as he walked to the rear of the office area where her desk was just outside the Sheriff's office.

"Hi, Dave," she responded, "I thought I might see you in here this morning. There was speculation yesterday that the board would appoint Cooper acting Sheriff and I assumed he would select you as his replacement."

"Really," Dave quizzed, "why me?"

"Just a hunch, knowing how much they think of you," she said.

As she was speaking, Bob Cooper walked in the front door, closely followed by Dan Muscovy. They were in deep conversation.

"I think we should chase down anything we can find on the drug guys," Bob was saying, "Let's be damn sure they had nothing to do with this."

Bob and Dan nodded and said good morning to Dave and Cheryl.

"Cheryl," Bob said, "I'll just bet I don't have to tell you what the board did last night, do I?"

"They made you acting sheriff and you assigned Dave acting Major," Cheryl quipped.

"And, I'll bet you knew it before I did," Bob laughed. Turning to Dave he said, "Let's go into the office."

"I'll bring in coffee," Cheryl said getting up from her desk.

"Thanks," Bob said as Dave followed him into the space he had always associated with Uncle Will.

Chapter 5

In the hour before the staff meeting, Bob walked Dave though what he could expect. He was quick to point out that, even though Dave was now fully in charge of his division, Bob was always near and available. Bob expressed compete confidence in Dave's ability to handle the job, and assured him that he had the full support of the command team. He also said he was sure Dave could expect the same support from all of the administrative and support staff as well, as soon as they were informed of the changes.

The command weekly staff meeting began promptly at 9 AM in the conference room. Bob, Dan, Dave and Cheryl were present. Also present was the fourth member of the command staff, Major Craig Jackson, head of finance and administration. Although he was a sworn officer of the department, Craig Jackson had never really functioned in an enforcement roll. His career had always been in finance and accounting. Sheriff Lewis had hired him about ten years ago when it was becoming clear that the department needed someone on staff who understood how to budget and track expenses. Craig was brought in and soon became an indispensable part of the command staff.

Bob began the meeting by asking Dan to discuss all he knew about what had happened to Sheriff Lewis. Dan told the story in detail and finished up by stating that he continued to be in contact with the Arlington County Sheriff's office, the Arlington County Coroner's office and the State Police investigations branch. All reports from each agency will be sent to him for his review as soon as they are completed and ready to file. He was not sure when the reports would begin to roll in, but would continue to follow up. Dan also said that he and his team had searched the sheriff's apartment here in town and a report of what they found was in the works, but nothing seemed out of the ordinary.

After Dan had completed his report, Bob asked if there were any outstanding investigations, of which Dan was aware, that could have been a factor in the sheriff's death if it was not suicide.

Dan said he was still working on the list of felons that have been released from prison after being put there by Sheriff Lewis. He provided a list of recent and current, on going, investigations that the Sheriff had been directly involved with. First on this list was the Williams County drug farm.

"I'll continue to research and follow leads," Dan concluded. "If the reports continue to indicate foul play was not involved, all of this becomes moot."

The meeting continued with discussion of all of the normal activities that it takes to run a sheriff's department. As the meeting progressed, budgets, necessary unbudgeted expenditures, manpower, and other such things were all hashed over. But, Dave couldn't shake from his mind the "if foul play was not involved" concept from Dan's report. He was trying to get a grip on what he really thought about that. Did he have reason to believe that Uncle Will could not have done it, or was it just emotion? However he tried and whatever he did for the rest of the day, this was on his mind.

Shortly after five pm, Dave headed home. He was tired; the change in routine would take some getting used to. It would be pleasant to be off work every evening for a change. It will open up more opportunities to spend time with his sons. After getting home, he called D and filled him in about the temporary promotion and the schedule change. D was glad to hear Dave would be more available in the evenings and said he would tell Chris.

Dave thought about how to spend his first evening as a normal eight to five worker. It struck him that he could now enjoy opportunities he had not often had on past Wednesday evenings. In particular the cruise night at Cliff's which he normally was only able to drive past, or at most stop in on a brief break. Tonight, he could take a car and be part of the activity.

He called D back. "Do you and Chris want to go to Cliff's for the cruise night and dinner?"

"Let me ask Chris, but I'm in for sure."

"Great, I'll meet you at the barn in about a half hour."

"Sounds good," D said, "see you shortly."

Dave headed for the farm.

Since the '40 was out of commission, Dave thought he would take the 1956 Buick Convertible. He picked out the 1970 Chevelle SS454 Convertible for D, since it was one of his favorites. If Chris came with D, Dave knew he would want to take the 1969 Camaro Z28. Dave had the Buick and the Chevelle out of the barn and was wiping them off when the boys pulled up in D's Malibu.

"Great idea, Dad," Chris said, as he got out of the car. "Do I get to drive the Z?"

"I thought you'd want to," Dave answered, "I was just going to get it out, here, you finish wiping down the Buick while I get it."

Ten minutes later they were on their way in a three car caravan headed for Cliff's.

When they arrived at Cliff's, they parked the three cars together in the lot which already had about twenty other classic and muscle cars. They walked around the lot together looking at the other cars and talking with the owners they knew and the one they didn't know as well. Most of the talk was about the cars, but some who knew Dave asked about the Sheriff and what Dave could tell them. Dave thought he sensed a degree of skepticism from those who asked concerning the suicide aspect, which didn't help him come to grips with what the evidence seemed to show.

After about thirty or forty minutes Dave and his sons went into the diner for dinner. They all had burgers and fries which seemed like the only meal that fit with classic car cruising. D and Chris always liked the cars and being around the car people, especially with their dad.

When dinner was finished they went back out into the lot and caught up on the cars that had come in since they had gone inside. Then they sat together in folding chairs behind the cars and watched as people came by to check out their cars and talk about them. As the sun began to set they headed back to the farm to put the cars away.

As Dave was walking back into his house his phone rang. He looked at the caller I.D. and recognized his wife's number.

"Dave, it's Joyce," she said after he answered. "Have you got a minute? We need to talk."

Dave knew the tone of voice well and sat down at his kitchen table. "Sure, what's up?"

"I heard about Will and the boys told me about your promotion. I know you've been going through a lot this week, and I probably shouldn't do this now, but I just can't wait longer," she paused. "I want a divorce."

"Geez, Joyce," Dave complained. "Why now?"

"Well, to tell the truth, with D in college and Chris going off the school next spring, I've been thinking I don't want to be alone. I don't want to be with you, so it's time for me to free myself for the future."

"So you've found a guy," Dave said, cynically.

There was silence. "Oh no, I'm right. She has," Dave thought.

He waited.

"No," Joyce said finally, "I have been asked out several times, but it didn't feel right accepting, being married to you and all, so no."

Dave thought it sounded like she was trying to convince herself that she was in the right.

"Several times by the same guy?" he questioned.

"A…" she stammered. "It doesn't matter. Are we going to fight over this?"

"No, Joyce." Dave knew he had nowhere to take this conversation. "If you want a divorce I won't fight it. Do you have an attorney in mind?"

"I don't know," she hesitated. "Maybe."

"Are we splitting up as we are, or are you going to force me to sell the house and everything, and take half of everything I have?" Dave asked.

"No, I don't want the house. How about you keep the house, everything left in it, the cars and the farm and I get what I have here, including my car, and the savings account?" she offered. "I also think you should pay for the boy's education."

"I'm ok with it except, how about you get half of the savings account," Dave countered.

"Three quarters?" she asked.

"No," Dave said. "Half is fair, unless you pay for Chris' education and I pay D's.

"Okay," she said.

"So we're clear? I agree to pay the education for the boys; you keep what you have at your apartment, your car, and half of our savings account. I keep this house and all the furnishings, my cars, and my interest in the farm. We both have our own checking accounts which are not subject to the settlement."

"Agreed," she said.

"If this is what you want, you go ahead, get an attorney and have it prepared," Dave said. "We'll split the cost of the attorney and the filing. I don't see a reason for me to pay an attorney as well."

"Ok," was all she said and hung up.

Dave sat alone in his kitchen, the phone still at his ear with the dial tone humming, anger growing within him for several minutes. Then it dawned on him that he had no reason to be angry. He had given up on the marriage himself years ago. It was something that should have happened then, but neither of them wanted to hurt the kids so they just moved apart using the excuse that it would be easier if she and the boys lived in town. He got up and headed for bed, surprised by the relief he felt.

Chapter 6

Dave was working at his desk about two the next afternoon when his phone rang.

"Major," said Angela, the receptionist, "I have Mr. Keller on the line for you."

"Ok, put him on."

There was a click, and Dave said, "Dave Harbinger."

"Dave, this is Jim Keller," said the deep baritone voice on the phone. Jim Keller was the President of the bank and had been a good friend of Dave's dad and Uncle Will. Based on the discussion with his wife the previous evening, Dave was wondering what Joyce had done with his bank accounts.

"What can I do for you, Jim," Dave asked hesitantly.

"In short, you can run for Sheriff," Jim responded. Jim was also chairman of the political party of Dave's dad and Uncle Will.

"What?" was all Dave could think of to say.

"I think you heard me, Dave," was the response with a slight chuckle. "The committee met last night and think you are the best candidate to replace Will Lewis. We would like for you to run. We aren't sure who the opposition will put up yet, but we don't believe they can come up with anyone as well known around the county or as well liked as you."

"My dad was well known, but I'm not so sure I am," Dave countered.

"In politics it's the same thing," Jim responded. "Name recognition is everything, and you've got it in this county."

"But what about Dan Muscovy, or Bob Cooper, they both are far more qualified than I?"

"It's a matter of qualifications and electability. "We think we could get either of them elected, but we know we can get you elected. You are a sure thing in our books, so that's the way we want to go, if you are willing."

"I don't know," Dave said hesitantly.

"Look, why don't you take a couple of days to think it over. Talk with your family and people you trust," Jim said. "I'll call you back sometime next week and we'll discuss it further. I'm sure you will have questions that need answers before you throw your hat in the ring. We want you to run, but we also want you to be fully on board before you make the decision. Do you have any other questions for now?"

"No questions come to mind right now," Dave answered. "We'll talk next week. Thanks for the call, Jim, and the support."

As he hung up the phone, Dave took a deep breath and thought. What else could possibly happen this week? He got up from his desk and walked straight back to the sheriff's office. Cheryl saw him coming and waved him on in. As usual the sheriff's door was open. He tapped on the door frame.

"Come in," Bob said.

Dave walked in the office, Bob was obviously studying a report and motioned Dave into a visitor's chair. Dave sat and waited. Bob continued with his report, made a note on it, put his pen down and looked up.

"Sorry, Dave," Bob said, "what's up?"

"Well," Dave began slowly, "I just got a call from Jim Keller..."

As Dave paused, Bob interjected, "And he asked you to run for sheriff."

"He talked with you?" Dave asked.

"No, but you are the logical candidate for the position," Bob said. "It's a political position, Dave, you are by far the best possible choice."

"But I thought you were, or Dan, not me," Dave commented.

"Cheryl," Bob raised his voice, "could you please ask Dan to join us?" Then turning back to Dave he said, "I won't say I wouldn't like to keep this job, but I also realize that I am not well known and would have to work hard to get elected. I don't think I am ready to do that. You on the other hand, will not have to work hard to get elected since the whole county knows the Harbingers."

Dan walked in the office and took the seat next to Dave.

"Dave has been asked to run for sheriff," Bob said to Dan.

"I am not at all surprised," Dan said. "Are you going to go for it?"

"I haven't decided. I hadn't thought about it."

"Dave," Bob said, "you have my full support, if you decide to run."

"Mine too," Dan said, "I think you would be great at it, and I'm not just saying that, I really mean it."

"I don't know," Dave still hesitated, "I thought it would be one of your two, not me."

"Dave," Dan said. "You've been a member of the department as long as we have. Everyone knows you, likes you and respects you. You have been directly exposed to the sheriff's office, by way of Sheriff Lewis, for your entire life. I don't think anyone has a more complete understanding of the entire department than you do. I honestly believe your long term exposure to the department makes you the logical candidate. If you asked me, I would tell you to run."

"Hmm," Dave said, "I understand what you both are saying, but I just don't feel like I am qualified."

"Well, one thing is sure," Bob spoke up, "at least two of your command staff will do everything in their power to make sure you are the best sheriff in the state, qualified or not. But, I think you are far more qualified than you think."

"It would be an honor to work for you, Dave," Dan agreed.

After getting back to his office, Dave found it hard to concentrate on the work he had to do. His mind naturally kept going back to the idea of being sheriff, the replacement for Uncle Will. *Is that something he wanted? Could he really do the job? Could he really get elected? What about the farm, could he continue to run the farm and be sheriff?* All of these thoughts, and many more, ran through his head repeatedly for the rest of the day as he tried to concentrate on his new duties. He felt drained, mentally, as he walked to his car at the end of the work day. At least tomorrow is Friday he thought, and the week will be over. "Next week can't possibly throw as much in my face," he said out loud as he opened the car door.

Later on that evening as Dave sat watching the news program he always recorded with his TIVO the caller I.D. showed Joyce was calling again.

"Hello."

"Dave," he heard Joyce say. "I talked with a lawyer, she is putting the filing together as we discussed last night. She expects to have it ready by the middle of next week and would like to meet with you then to go over it with you and confirm you are in agreement."

"That was quick," Dave said, "kind of makes me think you had talked with her already."

"No, Dave, I just met her today," Joyce quipped sharply. "Have you got a pen and paper, I'll give you the number?"

Dave picked up a pen from the end table next to his chair, "Ok, I have a pen," he said as he prepared to jot the number down on the edge of a Hot Rod Magazine.

"Her name is Ms. Thomas," she said and she gave him a phone number.

"Got it. What firm is she with?" Dave asked, after he had written down the name and number.

"Whitman, Wallace and Sherwood," she said, "call her and set up and appointment."

"Ok," Dave said, and the line went dead.

Just before going out to lunch the next day, Dave pulled out the piece of paper he had torn from the magazine cover and placed a call to the number he had written on it.

"Whitman, Wallace and Sherwood," the pleasant female voice said, "how may I direct your call?"

"Ms. Thomas, please."

"One moment," he heard and then there was music in his ear.

"Jan Thomas," said another pleasant female voice after a few seconds.

"Hello, this is Dave Harbinger," Dave said, "my wife, Joyce, said I should call to set up an appointment to talk about our divorce."

"Yes, Mr. Harbinger, thank you for calling," she said. "How about next Wednesday afternoon, say one thirty?"

"Ok, that will be fine," Dave said as he jotted down a note on his desk pad. "I can take a late lunch."

"Our office is at 337 East Main," she said.

"Yes," Dave said, "I know your location, I'll see you then."

"Ok. See you then, good bye."

"Good bye." Dave hung up the phone and thought to himself, *I'm going to be divorced.* He headed out for lunch.

Later that afternoon, Dan Muscovy came into Dave's office and sat down in one of the visitors chairs.

"I've been working on the idea of the drug gang being involved with Will's death," he began, "but it's hard to figure how they would know about his place up there, let alone where it is located. I guess they could have followed him, but it's hard to believe Will wouldn't have made a tail on that trip. Have you got any ideas?"

Dave flashed back to a time that he and his dad had taken Brian and Bobby with them on a duck hunting trip up to Uncle Will's cabin. That was a long time ago, but could Bobby have been the source for the information Dan was looking for? Could Bobby remember where the cabin was after all this time? Maybe just the knowledge of its existence and the general area was enough for them to find it?

"I hadn't thought about that aspect," Dave responded. "Let me think on that a bit."

"Ok," Dan said. "Let me know if you come up with anything," and he left.

Dave wondered if it was time to tell Dan and Bob about the relationship he and Brian had with one of the drug gang members. It had never come up as an issue until now, so Dave was relatively sure no one else in the department was aware. He needed to think about the impact on Bobby if the word got back to the gang, but at the same time if they were involved then Bobby was as guilty as the rest of them and Dave would have to help to take them all down.

Chapter 7

The following Wednesday a exactly one thirty in the afternoon, Dave walked into the offices of Whitman, Wallace and Sherwood Attorneys at Law on East Main in downtown Springfield. Sitting behind a large counter with a tasteful marble looking top was a twenty something woman with dark red hair.

"Dave Harbinger for Jan Thomas," Dave spoke as the red haired woman looked up at him.

She looked down for a second, and then said. "Yes, Mr. Harbinger, please have a seat and I'll let her know you're here." She motioned to a group of leather chairs to the left of the entry door. Dave picked a chair against the wall and sat.

In about two minutes, an attractive woman approached Dave and held out her hand as he stood.

"Mr. Harbinger, I'm Jan Thomas," she said.

Jan Thomas appeared to be in her late thirties. She was about five foot five, or six, and dressed very tastefully in a light green dress. The dress length was to just above the knee and showed well shaped legs. She had shoulder length blonde hair and appeared to be very fit. Her makeup was light and she had no jewelry other than a small gold neck lace and a Rolex watch. Dave was instantly drawn to look at the fingers of her left hand which had no rings of any kind. He followed her as she motioned back toward the way from which she had just come.

They went down a corridor with offices on the outside wall and a large open area filled with desks to the inside. The desks were occupied by people Dave assumed to be clerks and paralegals. There were ten or fifteen of them by a quick scan. About half way down the corridor Jan turned into one of the offices and Dave followed.

"Have a seat, Mr. Harbinger," she said as she sat behind the desk. Dave sat down facing her across the desk. On the desk was a walnut and gold name plate with Jan Thomas, Partner engraved on the front.

"Your wife tells me that you do not intend to hire counsel," Jan began. "And that you have agreed to pay half of our fee. Is that correct?"

"Yes," Dave answered.

"Ok," she said, "I have prepared the filing according to what your wife said." She handed a document across the table which appeared to consist of ten to fifteen pages. "This is your copy, I request that you review it and let me know if there is anything different from what you have agreed. I plan to file with the court early next week, unless you identify any issues. Does that sound fair?"

"Yes," Dave said. "That should be fine. What happens then?"

"Once it has been filed, the court will put it on the schedule for hearing," she said. "It normally takes four to six weeks after filing to get before the judge. You and your wife will appear and the judge will review the filing and most likely approve the dissolution."

"And that's all there is to it?" Dave asked.

"Yes, pretty much, unless you find a problem with what I just gave you, and even then, it's just a matter of the time it takes to come to an agreement. Any other questions?"

"I just have one other question, somewhat unrelated?" Dave said. "Have you known my wife long?"

"No, she and I just met the other day. Our Managing General Partner asked me to handle the case for him. Why, do you have a problem with me?"

"Oh no, I have no problem with you at all," Dave responded and smiled, "I was just curious."

"Good, I want to make this as easy as possible for you. I know this is hard. Please feel free to contact me any time."

"Thanks," Dave said, "I'll let you know if I have any questions or concerns."

"Please call me, either way," she said, "I will hold off on the filing until I get the go ahead from you."

"Ok, I'll call you as soon as I have looked it over," Dave said as he got up to leave.

"Fine, I look forward to your call," she smiled warmly as he left.

When Dave got back to his office there was a pink "While You Were Out" note on his desk telling him that Jim Keller had called and would like a call back at his office in the bank. Dave dialed the number and Jim answered on the second ring.

"So, what do you think?" Jim asked after the normal pleasantries.

"I'm still not convinced that I could be elected.

"Believe me, not only can you get elected, it will be a landslide. All you have to do is say go and our machine will kick into gear and your campaign will hit the ground running. My only caution to you is to be sure you want it before you say go, because it will happen if you want it or not."

"Ok," Dave said, "I do want the job, but mainly because I want to continue what Sheriff Will Lewis was doing, and to assure his legacy is a good one. I want to make sure that everyone knows how much Sheriff Lewis did for this county. That's what it means to me."

"I hear what you're saying," Jim said. "The committee is meeting tonight so we will get things moving. I think you have made the right decision, Dave, and I think you'll do great things for this county. Will Lewis and your dad would be proud. We'll talk tomorrow about the process from here on out," he said as he hung up.

Dave sat for a moment contemplating the potential life changing event he had just set in motion. However, before he could begin to grasp the magnitude, Dan came into his office and sat down.

"Any ideas about the drug gang topic we talked about last week?" Dan asked.

"As a matter of fact, I do have something to tell you about that," Dave said. "I would prefer to keep my source confidential at this point, but am able to tell you that a member of the gang has direct knowledge of the sheriff's cabin and the location."

"Would your source hold up in court as reliable confirmation?" Dan asked.

"Without a doubt," Dave responded.

"Good, I don't know if there is anywhere to take this, but knowing that puts one piece of the puzzle in place. Thanks for your help," Dan said.

"Any word from Arlington?" Dave asked.

"I talked with Sheriff Allen. He's still waiting for the report from the medical examiner. He thinks it may be in early next week. His team has about finished with the crime scene report and there is apparently nothing in there to indicate foul play."

"Does it feel right to you?" Dave asked.

"No, it really doesn't," answered Dan. "But feelings are only good in police work if they lead you to evidence to prove those feelings. In this case that hasn't happened, so far."

"Yeah, I guess you're right," Dave agreed, "but…" They were quiet for a minute, both wondering if there was something they were missing.

Dave broke the silence. "Changing the subject, I want you to know that I have decided to run for Will's job."

"That's great!" said Dan enthusiastically, "I'm all for it. What can I do to help?"

"Well, I'd appreciate your vote," Dave said, "but other than that it would not be appropriate for you to do more. You need to keep neutral in politics involving the department, you know?"

"Of course," Dan smiled, "rest assured you have my vote, and I will ask my wife to vote for you too. Have you told Bob?"

"Not yet, I just got off the phone with Jim Keller when you came in," Dave said, "I'll go do that now."

"Ok," Dan said getting up, "I'll get out of your hair, and thanks for the info on the gang."

Dave went down to Bob's office and filled him in on his agreement to run for sheriff and the information he had passed on to Dan about the drug gang.

"If the gang was involved I would think there would be some evidence," Bob thought out loud. "They never really seemed that smart to me, but maybe I have misjudged them. What do you think?"

"I haven't had much direct contact with the gang leaders nor do I have knowledge of the gang make up. But I know Sheriff Lewis was constantly studying anything he could find on them. Is there any information in his files that would help?"

"I have found no files related to the drug gang," Bob said. "Cheryl tells me that sheriff kept detailed notes on them, but she doesn't know where his notes are. She thought he may have had them with him. I'm waiting on the crime scene report from Arlington County to see if they found them up there. If not, we will ask his wife for permission to search his house again on the chance that we missed them."

"Do we need her permission?" Dave asked. "She didn't live with him, and hasn't for many years."

"That may be true," Bob said. "But according to the law, she is still his next of kin. Everything goes to her and his daughter. So technically his stuff is now theirs."

"Of course," Dave said. "Well, let me know if I can help, I know his wife fairly well."

Dave went back to his office and got back to work. He had plenty to do and decided that he would put in a little extra time this evening. There were two reasons he wanted to do this, first to get the work done and second to be around when Brian came on shift at seven, so they could talk. He walked over to dispatch and left a message for Brian to come to his office when he had time.

Shortly after six pm, Brian walked into Dave's office. They exchanged greetings and talked a little about all the things going on for several minutes.

"Brian," Dave said. "We need to talk about Bobby. I don't know if the gang was involved in Uncle Will's death, but we are going to be looking into that possibility. If it turns out they were involved I'm afraid Bobby is going to go down with the rest."

"Yeah. That's the way it has to be. I know there is no way we can, nor should, protect him. He chose to be a part of the gang, and if they go down, so does he."

"I think I'd like to talk with him," Dave said. "Can you set it up?"

"I suppose. "What do you have in mind?"

"See if he can come by the farm some evening next week," Dave said. "Just let me know the day and I'll be sure to be there. Say seven o'clock."

"Ok, I'll let you know."

After Brian left his office Dave worked on a few more things and then headed home. He stopped on the way at a fast food kabobs place and got dinner to take home. As he was eating, he thought about Jan

Thomas. *"Why not"* he said to himself, *"I'm about to be single."* He thought she seems to be single as well, very intelligent and very attractive. He was wondering if she was really as nice as she seemed. There must be a reason she's single. Or maybe she is married but doesn't wear a ring. "Do women do that?" he was thinking when his phone rang. *Joyce*, the caller I.D. told him.

"Dave, have you looked over the papers?" she asked as he answered.

"How do you know I even have them yet?" he asked.

"My attorney said you were in today."

"You talk with your attorney every day?" Dave questioned.

"That has nothing to do with anything. Have you looked at them?"

"No, I have them, but I worked late and haven't read them yet. What's the hurry?"

"I want to make sure you don't just throw them in a corner somewhere and in a month I am still waiting."

The lady doth protest too much.

"Ok, I promise I'll look over them and get back to Jan by Monday," he said.

The line was quiet for a moment.

"Jan?" she asked.

"Yes, your attorney, you do know her name, don't you?"

"Of course," she shot back, "I just didn't expect you to call her by her first name. Ok, see that you get it taken care of." She hung up the phone.

Dave wondered what was going on. But at the same time understood that it didn't matter. It would soon be over.

Again, the phone rang, *Keller* the I.D. told him.

"Hi, Jim," he answered. "What's up."

"Sorry to call so late, Dave," Jim said. "But I learned something at the meeting that I couldn't wait to share. We have intel that the opposition party met last night and they apparently have not put anyone up. It may be that they're waiting to see who we put up, or it may be that they don't have anyone that they think is viable."

"So, what does that mean, Jim?" Dave asked.

"Well, it may be something else," he answered. "But if it is one of those two choices here's the way I see it. If they're just waiting to see who we have, I think that means they don't have a strong candidate. When they see your name they will know they don't have a chance. If they don't have anyone viable they don't have a chance, either. So, if it's either one of those the result is you are running unopposed."

"Yikes!" Dave exclaimed, "then I'm sheriff."

"That would be my guess, right now," Jim said. "I would guess we'll know what's going on by the middle or end of next week. I just don't think the opposition wants to use up any political capital without at least a chance of some return. They haven't had the sheriff post for so long that they don't spend effort working people to be prepared to run. If they don't have someone in the wing it really makes it hard to get the voters attention. They were probably starting to work for the next election, but Will's sudden departure didn't give them time."

"So, I don't really have to campaign?" Dave contemplated. He was a bit confused.

"Not very much," Jim answered, "at least this time. Sheriff Lewis was just beginning the second year of his four year term. You would be elected to fulfill the remainder of his current term. So in about two and a half years you will need to run for re-election to a full term. My guess is the opposition will have someone ready to run against you then. I'll be in touch when we know more." He hung up.

Chapter 8

Saturday morning Dave met D and Chris at the farm at seven. They had planned to take three of the cars to a car show in Redford, a small farming town about fifty miles away. Dave had been to the Redford show in years past. The draw was that the car show was part of a sauerkraut festival. This particular car show was for 1948 and older cars so Dave and the boys were taking three street rods from the collection to the show: a 1940 Ford convertible street rod, a 1932 Ford coupe street rod, and a 1934 Ford pickup street rod. The plan was to trade off vehicles whenever they stopped somewhere. They would drive for about thirty minutes before stopping for breakfast. Dave started out in the '40 Ford, D in the '34 pickup and Chris in the '32. All three cars were show quality street rods and were attention getters everywhere they went. Dave also liked them because two of the three drove so well on the highway.

Dave particularly liked the bright red '40 coupe because it had been one of his dad's favorite cars to drive. It had a 351 Ford engine that had been modified enough to give it plenty of power but not so much that it wasn't drivable. It had a four speed transmission, air conditioning, killer stereo and very comfortable bucket seats.

The '34 Ford pickup was royal blue with a chopped top. It had a 292 Ford Y-block with three duces, a loopy cam and three inch exhausts. The interior was all leather and very comfortable. It had a five speed manual transmission, air conditioning and a stereo that could be heard over the engine if the cutouts were closed.

The yellow '32 Ford coupe was like the one John Milner drove in the movie American Graffiti. It had a chopped top and a big block Chevy with dual quads and a hefty cam. Of the three cars, the '32 had the hardest ride due to the short wheel base and the stiff suspension. It was also the least comfortable inside with a rather cramped seating style due the top chop and the way the body was channeled over the frame rails. But, Chris thought it was the most fun to drive.

The route to the show, including the stop for breakfast took about two hours. They parked the three cars together, wiped them down and then walked the show grounds looking at the other cars. At lunch they sat at a picnic table under a large oak tree and ate what they had collected from various vendor booths. Dave was enjoying a day with his sons and cars. What could be better.

"How do you feel about the divorce, Dad?" Chris asked Dave as they ate.

"I guess it has been coming for a long time," Dave answered, "I'm ok with it, I guess. How do you boys feel about it?"

"I don't like it much," D spoke out, "it just doesn't seem right to me. But, if it's what you guys want, who am I to object?"

"You have every right to object, D," Dave said. "You're part of this family. But as you probably know, objecting is not going to change things."

"Oh, I just think Mom is only thinking about herself," Chris said. "She thinks when I'm gone she would be alone and doesn't like it. I tried to convince her to move back home, but she wouldn't hear it."

"Don't get down on your mom, Chris. We really haven't had a good relationship for many years."

"Did you know she has a boyfriend?" Chris asked.

Dave answered slowly, "No, I didn't, how would I know something like that?"

"Well, I don't know if they've gone out or anything," Chris continued, "but I know she has lunch with him a lot. He's my friend Steve's dad. Geez, Dad, he's been married three times, and Steve says every time they get younger. I think he's like seventy years old."

"What's his name?" Dave asked.

"Steve Sherwood, I think his dad's name may be Randy. He's a lawyer, and has his own firm, I think." Chris said.

"As in Whitman, Wallace and Sherwood, Attorneys at Law."

"Yeah," said Chris. "That could be it. Have you heard of them?"

"Yes, I have," Dave said. "That's the firm your mom hired to do our divorce."

The ride back home seemed longer to Dave. He was feeling a bit of jealously, and betrayed. She didn't have to lie. She could have said: Dave, I've found another guy and want to dump you. *At least that would have been honest.*

Shortly after getting into his office on Monday morning, Dave pulled the business card he had taken from the holder on Jan Thomas' desk and dialed the number.

"Jan Thomas."

"This is Dave Harbinger, I've gone through the filing and have a couple of minor corrections. When can I stop by to go over them with you?"

"Let me see," Jan said, "I have a few minutes at eleven this morning if that works?"

"That will be fine see you then."

"My pleasure," she answered.

Shortly after nine Cheryl stuck her head around the door and said, "Bob wants to see the command staff in his office."

He headed for the sheriff's office. When he got there Dan was already seated in one of the visitor chairs. Bob was at the desk looking intently at the computer monitor.

"Morning," Dan said as Dave sat in the visitor chair next to him. Craig Jackson came into the office and sat in the remaining chair.

"We got the preliminaries from Arlington," Bob said without preamble. "I'm passing copies along to each of you for your review. It includes the crime scene report and the medical examiner report. Let me know if anything jumps out at you. They still think suicide, but Sheriff Allen says they are keeping it open until we have had time for review. So let's get on this and see if we can find any reason to hold on closing this case. We'll talk about it again at staff on Wednesday. Any questions?"

There were no questions and everyone headed for the respective offices. Each hesitant and anxious at the same time. They didn't want to go through the details of the sheriff's death, but they wanted to find the clue that they had missed, if there was one, to prove it had not been suicide.

Dave opened the file and printed it out as soon as he sat down at his desk. He pulled the printout from the printer and started to read and study every detail. He started with the crime scene report. One by one, he went through detail after detail, looking to see if there was something that was not as he remembered, out of place or just didn't make sense. He was about two thirds of the way through the crime scene report when he noticed it was time to head for his meeting with Jan Thomas. He put a sticky note on the page he was on and closed the report and put it in his desk.

As he walked into the offices of Whitman, Wallace and Sherwood, Attorneys at Law the receptionist looked up from her desk and smiled and said, "Mr. Harbinger, isn't it?"

"Yes," Dave said. "You have a good memory."

"Not really," she answered. "Ms. Thomas just called and asked me to just send you on back when you come in."

"I'm sorry," Dave said, "I didn't hear, did you say Mrs. Thomas?"

"No, Ms. Thomas," the receptionist corrected. "She's not married."

"Oh, thanks," Dave said as he headed for the single lawyer's office.

"Come in," Jan said as he knocked on the door frame of her office. She smiled as he walked in, "Mr. Harbinger, please sit down."

Dave sat in the visitor chair and took out the file he had reviewed since they last met.

"The errors I found were minor," he began. "But I know how important accuracy is in legal matters. First, the address of my farm has two digits transposed."

They discussed the items Dave had found in detail. She made the notes for each correction. After they finished she said it would only take her about thirty minutes to make the corrections and print a new copy.

"Would you like to wait, or just have me mail it to you?" she asked.

"I have a quick stop to make up the street," Dave said, "I can come back, or maybe you would like to bring it and meet me for lunch at O'Malley's?"

O'Malley's was an Irish Pub about a block up the street from her office.

"Well," she thought for a minute, "I guess I can do that, sure, I'll see you in about forty minutes."

Dave left and headed up the street to the bank where Jim Keller was President. The entry to the bank was made to look like a stately mansion of the old south. Dave wondered if that was supposed to make people feel better about leaving money.

Dave walked passed the teller cages toward the back of the bank, where Jim's secretary sat at a large desk. She was a mid-fifties woman whom Dave had know most of his life.

"Hi Helen," Dave said, "is Jim available?"

She turned and looked in the office behind her. "Sure is, go on in," Helen said.

As he walked into Jim's office he motioned at a visitor chair. "Have a seat, Dave, I wasn't expecting to see you, but always a pleasure."

"I'm meeting someone for lunch at O'Malley's and have a few minutes, so I thought I'd run a couple of questions by you, if you've got time?" Dave said.

"Sure, no problem, what do you need to know?" Jim asked.

"This is all happening so fast," Dave began, "when is the election?" "We're working on the paper work right now to get your name on the November ballot," Jim said, "normally it would take petitions, and so forth, but to fill an open post we can do it the easy way. And, filing dead lines don't apply with an open post."

"Ok. If elected, when would I become sheriff?"

"Normally it would be in January after a November election. But in this case, since you would be filling a vacant post, it would be soon after the election. I would guess the county board would certify the results at their meeting following the election and you would be installed at the same meeting," Jim explained.

"So, sometime in November," Dave commented, "I may be sheriff."

"That would be my guess," Jim said. "We'll need you to sign the forms when they are ready, and you will need to file at the county clerk's office, but other than that it's underway."

"Thanks, Jim, for believing in me," Dave said. "I won't let you down."

"I'm sure you won't, Dave. It's a pleasure to help," Jim said.

Dave left and headed for lunch at O'Malley's. He asked for a table with a view of the door so that he could see Jan when she came in.

Mainly so that she wouldn't have to look all over the restaurant for him, but also so that he could watch her walk toward him. He had only been there a few minutes when she came in. She was wearing a white blouse and dark skirt. The blouse was rather loose and the skirt was rather tight. *A good combination* Dave thought, as she walked his way.

"I'm so glad you agreed to have lunch," Dave said as he stood to greet her. He pulled a chair out for her and she sat. She handed him a legal size envelope.

"All corrected, Mr. Harbinger," she began.

"Dave. Call me Dave."

"I don't think I should, Mr. Harbinger," she said, "I am representing your wife in this legal matter. She is my client and until the legal matter for which she has hired me is completed, I must insist that we stay on a professional basis only."

"The legal matter for which she has hired you will be over when the judge bangs the gavel, correct?" Dave asked.

"Yes, I have only been hired to handle the divorce and that will be complete, as you say, when the judge bangs the gavel."

"You don't expect my wife will hire you for anything else after that?" Dave asked.
She looked at him, smiled and said, "I wouldn't accept another case from her."

"After the divorce is completed, would you go to dinner with me?"

"Mr. Harbinger, I cannot agree to socialize with you while I represent your wife, that is entirely inappropriate," she said. "You should not ask, until after the case is resolved."

"I withdraw the invitation, for now, but I won't forget."

"I hope you don't," she replied.

They ordered lunch. They talked about the weather, the death of Sheriff Lewis, sports, and even some politics over lunch. Nothing personal was the order for the day and they kept it that way. Dave somehow knew that it would not be long before they were discussing personal things but he could wait.

After what turned out to be a wonderfully distracting lunch break, Dave went back to his office and back into the crime scene report. He completed going through the document by mid-afternoon with no success in finding any clues. He moved on to the medical examiner's report. Again, he made an exhaustive detail by detail process of his review.

About five pages into the medical report he came upon a single sentence that made him stop. The sentence read: "88 no.12 buckshot found and removed from the face, skull and internal to the head." Dave reread it and thought, "what about the other 2?"

Dave got up from his desk and went next door to Dan's office. Dan was also deep into the reports, but Dave interrupted him.

"Dan, I found something," Dave began. "The medical examiner's report says they found 88 number 12 shot in the sheriff. I know for a fact that every shell that Will Lewis reloaded had 90 shot pellets. He was very exact in his reloading, using a scale to assure he had exact amounts in every reload."

"You are sure of that?" Dan asked.

"As sure as the day is long," Dave said.

Dan picked up his phone, dialed and after a moment said, "Sheriff Allen, please, Dan Muscovy calling." He listened, then said, "how about Lt Pete Jacobs, is he available?"

There was a pause while Dan waited, after about thirty seconds he said into the phone, "Pete this is Dan Muscovy in Lincoln County. Listen, we've been going over the reports and Dave Harbinger says that Sheriff Lewis always loaded his shells with 90 shot pellets. The report says that only 88 were found in the body, any chance that count can be off a couple?"

He listened to the other end and then said, "if they are that sure there are only 88 in the body, then we need to find a couple of more."

He listened again and said, "I agree, let me know."

Turning back to Dave, Dan said, "they are positive there are no more in the body. Pete is going to go back out and get some shells and do a count to confirm your number. He is also going to confirm that the shell in the gun was one of the same reloads. He says he will go right out there this afternoon and should have something to tell me by noon tomorrow."

"Ok," Dave said.

"Good catch, Dave," Dan said. "That may be a clue."

Dave went back to his office.

Chapter 9

AT two o'clock the next afternoon, Bob called the staff into his office.

"Dan and Dave have uncovered a curiosity or possibly a clue," Bob explained to Craig as they all sat down. "Sheriff Lewis always reloaded his own shells with 90 number 12 buck shot. Only 88 were found in his body. Dan talked with the investigator up there and he followed up."

"I just got a call from Sheriff Allen and he tells me that his guy has confirmed the 90 number. Apparently they have checked about thirty shells and every single one of them has had exactly 90 balls. They wanted to send a team back out, but only one guy is available so we're going to give them a hand to see if we can find the other two balls," he said. "Dan, I want you and Dave to high tail it back up there and fill out the team. He said it would be a couple of hours before they got to the scene so you have plenty of time. It isn't clear if this will take us anywhere or not, but it is something to clear up."

"On our way," Dan said as he and Dave headed for the door.

They took Dan's car this time for the trip up the interstate. In just over an hour they were on the exit ramp to Grifford. They took the same route into town and turned right across from Pop's gas station. Pop watched them turn north from his chair under the awning.

As they pulled up to the cabin, Dave noticed the only vehicle there was Will's pick up, still parked where it had been the day of his death. The crime scene tape was still visible although some of it had torn and was flapping in the breeze. They waited in the car for the Arlington County guy.

In about ten minutes, an Arlington County Sheriff's van pulled into the drive. Dave and Dan got out of the car and said hello to Pete Jacobs.

"Good catch, guys," Pete commented.

"Dave is the one to thank," Dan said.

"Good job, Dave," Pete said, "I don't know if it's anything or not, but I agree that we need to find out. Let's get to it," he said as he handed them latex gloves.

The three of them put on the gloves and headed into the cabin. They moved to the west wall by the desk where Sheriff Lewis was found. Pete set an evidence collection kit he was carrying on the floor and pulled out a roll of blue tape. The shot gun was gone from where it had been clamped in the vise on the reloading desk. He put one end of the tape on the vice, where the shot gun had been. He estimated the angle and direction of the shot gun barrel and pulled the tape to the west wall. They would use this as a reference to begin the search for the two missing balls.

On the wall where the tape ended was a peg board for tool storage above the work bench along that wall. The total distance from the vise to the wall was over eight feet. Subtracting the length from the vise to the end of the barrel, the distance from the end of the barrel to the wall would have been only about seven feet.

"Not much time for shot to spread out in that distance," Pete said.

"Yeah," said Dan. "But we don't know how it may have been deflected by the head. It could have missed him entirely which would put it pretty much on line with your tape, or it could have glanced against the skull and gone anywhere."

"That's true," Pete offered, "but if it was deflected, I would expect a deflection angle of less than forty five degrees. So, we should find them within a circle with a radius of about four feet with my tape being the center. Wouldn't you say?"

"Makes sense to me," Dan said,

Pete took the tape and, using a tape measure, roughed out a tape circle on the pegboard with a four foot radius from where the first tape attached to the wall.

"They should be within this circle," Pete said. "We'll go over every inch as is, if we don't find them we will pull off the peg board and look behind it." He reached into his bag and pulled out three magnifying glasses. They went to work.

They found nothing.

"What if the shot hit a tool and deflected," Dave said, "then they could be anywhere in the room."

"A possibility we will get to if we aren't successful around here," Pete said.

They used a hammer and crow bar from the work bench to pull down the peg board. Once again Pete made his tape circle and they began the process again. Again, nothing was found.

"Maybe my angle estimate is wrong," Pete said. "Let's expand the circle another foot."

This amount of expansion brought the bottom edge of the work bench into play. Dave got down on the floor and began to inspect the pine board that ran along under the bench. The light was not good under the table top so he got a flash light from the work bench and began to trail it along the underside of the bench. As the light trailed along the bench he saw it, not on the bench, but on the back wall under the bench.

"Guys, look at this," he said with a degree of excitement.

Dan and Pete joined Dave down on the floor under the work bench. In the wall they saw two very small holes, less than an inch apart.

"I think you found them, Dave," Pete said.

Pete crawled out and got a camera and photographed the two holes and then took reference photos to show the location. The three worked together to measure and record the exact location of the two holes.

"Doesn't make sense," Pete said. "The angle is all wrong. How could they have gotten there even with deflection?"

"Unless the gun barrel wasn't were we found it when it was fired," Dan said thoughtfully.

The three shared stares at each other.

"Let's make sure what those holes are," Pete said. "Before we go there."

Pete got a knife and crawled under the bench and began digging at the wood around the holes. In about ten minutes he came out with two 12 gauge shot gun pellets.

"I'm guessing the gun barrel had to be pointed in a downward direction to put these pellets there," Pete observed. "Let's see if we can estimate where."

He got the tape out again and the three of them began drawing lines and measuring angles in an attempt to estimate the location of the gun when fired. After about twenty minutes they had an area that they were relatively confident the gun had to be in when fired. It was at least a foot above where they had found the gun in the vise and angled downward.

Pete dialed his phone, "Sheriff, we have a murder," he said into the phone. "No doubt about it. We found the other two shot pellets in the wall below the work bench. We measured the angles and calculated where the shotgun would have to have been to put the shot in that location. It is not feasible that the gun could have been fired from the location it was found. The gun barrel was facing upward and was above the level of the work bench when it was found. Even taking deflection into account it is not feasible."

Pete listened to the phone for a few seconds then clicked it off.

"He wants to see the report, but agrees to move the file to unsolved murder."

After Dan called Bob to let him know what they had found, they began the process of closing out the crime scene investigation. They needed to document all they had found and make sure of their measurements. They double checked and documented every aspect of their conclusion. More pictures were taken from every angle as the new information raised questions that would need answers. Some questions had yet to be asked so their documentation of the scene might be the only way to prove or disprove a fact down the road. They attempted to be as thorough as possible. It took about three hours before they replaced the crime scene tape around the cabin and headed out.

As they headed back through Grifford, Dave suggested they stop at Pop's. Dan pulled into the gas station and they got out of the car. Pop nodded as they walked over to him sitting in his chair.

"You guys aren't local cops?" Pop asked.

"Lincoln County Sheriffs," Dan answered.

"Oh, Will Lewis was Lincoln County Sheriff, huh?" Pop asked.

"Yes," Dave offered, "we're here assisting the local department with the investigation. Would you mind if we asked a few questions?"

"Don't mind at all," Pop said, "fire away."

"Are you aware that Sheriff Lewis died in his cabin a couple of weeks ago?"

"Yeah," Pop answered. "It was on the week end sometime but not sure which day."

"During that week end," Dave asked, "do you remember seeing any foreign luxury cars turn up toward his cabin, possibly Mercedes or BMWs?"

"Nope," Pop said, "and I would have remembered that. We don't see many high end cars around here. Old widow Smith has a Mercedes, was her husband's before he died. She moved back here after he died and brought it with her. She don't go up that way though."

"Did you see any vehicle go toward the cabin that you hadn't seen before that week end, maybe a van, truck or SUV?"

"No, nothing unusual," Pop said. "Cept maybe it was you guys on that following Monday in an out of town sheriff's car, lights on too when it went by."

"Yes," Dave said. "That was us."

"Of course I saw all the cop activity going up that way that day," Pop said, "State Police, too."

"So, you didn't see any car or truck that entire week end that you hadn't seen before going up that way?"

"No one, at least while I was here," Pop said.

"Okay, thanks for your time," Dave said.

"That didn't get us anywhere," Dave said to Dan as they pulled out of the station and headed for the interstate.

"Well," Dan offered. "He isn't there twenty four seven."

"I know," Dave said. "But I can't think of a time during the day that I've come through here that he wasn't sitting there."

"Well it was worth a try," Dan said. "You thinking the drug gang?"

"Number one suspect as far as I can see," Dave said. "They could have come in on him while he was working at his desk, picked up his gun, shot him and put the gun in the vise. If they were wearing gloves there would be no trace. It would only take a minute or two and they would be gone."

"Would he have heard them coming?" Dan asked half to himself.

"Maybe not if they came in through the woods," Dave said.

"No sign of a struggle," Dan said. "Seems to me Will would have put up a fight."

"There is that," Dave admitted. "But we know someone did it."

Chapter 10

The next morning there was a command meeting in Bob's office first thing. After acknowledging the work of Dave and Dan and going over what they had found Bob said, "Now what do we know and where are we headed?"

"We know the shot gun was not in the vise when it was fired," Dan said. "The angle of the barrel, based on the location of the shot we found indicates that suicide is not the probable cause of death. It just is not possible that he could have held the weapon at that angle, fired it himself and put it in the vise after he was dead. There had to be a shooter that placed the gun in the vice after he had killed the sheriff. Our measurements indicate that the sheriff was sitting in his roller chair at his reloading desk. The assailant held the weapon less than a couple of feet in front of his face and about twenty to thirty degrees below horizontal. We know the approximate distance by the amount of shot that stayed in the body, and we know the angle by the location of the two shot we found that didn't enter the body. We believe our analysis is sound."

"What do we know about the who?" Bob asked.

"There was no struggle, so, we speculate that, either he knew the perp or was surprised by him," Dan continued. "There was no evidence whatsoever of anyone being in the cabin that should not have been there. All of the good prints lifted have been processed. His were everywhere, and they lifted several good ones from Dave and his sons

and from Will's son-in-law. There are a few that have not been
identified but we suspect two are of his wife and daughter who do not
have prints on file."

"How could he have been approached without his knowing?" Bob
asked.

"Pete, their evidence guy, says he may have been asleep at the desk,"
Dan said. "Which I think is feasible."

"If he was asleep, anyone could have walked in and did the deed," Bob
said. "Do you agree, Dave?"

"I suppose," Dave said. "There was a book open on the desk which he
could've been reading and fell asleep. There were lights on which
could indicate the crime happened at night, but at the same time the
cabin was always dark and lights on in the day time was not unusual,
especially if he was working at the desk."

"So, our prime suspect is the drug gang?" Bob asked.

"That's the best we have right now," Dan said, "we're still looking at
others but that's our number one. Dave and I questioned the local gas
station guy who sees all goings on up there, but he didn't give us
anything useful. In particular we asked if he had seen any vehicles that
could have been our drug guys. He had not."

"We have the weapon, and no fiscal evidence that they were there,"
Bob thought out loud. "If they did it we have nothing to tie them to it.
Does anybody have an idea how we solve this?"

Everyone looked at Dan. But no one said a word.

"I have a question," Dave spoke up. "Has Cheryl looked over the crime
scene report? There may be something she would know about Sheriff
Will that the rest of us wouldn't."

"Good idea," Bob said, "I'll ask her to look it over."

The meeting broke up with everyone wondering what they could do next. Dave went back to work and tried to get things done, but he kept thinking about what could lead to a solution to the crime.

Just before time to go home, Dave's phone rang. The caller I.D. said Jim Keller.

"Hi, Jim, what's up?"

"I just got word that the opposition are not putting up a candidate," Jim said enthusiastically. "You are unopposed."

"Wow!"

"I need you to meet me at the clerk's office to make it official," Jim said. "What's your morning look like tomorrow? Will ten o'clock work for you?"

"Yes, I'll meet you there at ten."

Dave pulled the mail out of his mail box as he got home. In the mail was an envelope with the return address of Whitman, Wallace and Sherwood, Attorneys at Law. He went inside and sat at the kitchen table and opened the envelope. Inside he found a single sheet of paper informing him that a court date had been set for the divorce hearing. The note was signed by J. Thomas, Partner. Dave checked the wall calendar. The date was just over two weeks away.

Dave had been meaning to go see Aunt Dar, since they talked on the phone after Uncle Will's death. He had called and canceled out on the Thursday that he had initially promised because that was in the middle of his change from patrol to command. He changed his clothes and headed out.

Aunt Dar lived in a modest condo. She and Uncle Will had bought and shared it after their daughter got married and the large house was no longer needed. When she and Uncle Will split, he rented an apartment closer to the station on the opposite side of town. Dave had helped him move out, along with their son-in-law, John, and Dave's sons. He rang the bell and after a few seconds she opened the door.

Aunt Dar was still attractive in her late-fifties. She had a nice figure that indicated a good workout routine. Her blonde hair was medium length and suggested a recent visit to the beauty salon. Her makeup was perfectly understated to the point of almost wearing none. Dave had never seen her looking other than she did now. To some degree it was her business to look good, she had been in the cosmetic sales industry for years. She had reached sales goals repeatedly. The company she sold for gave pink Cadillacs to their top sales people. Aunt Dar was driving her third one.

"Davie," she said, "how good of you to stop by."

"Hi, Aunt Dar, sorry it's taken me so long to get over here."

"No apology is necessary," she said. "And now I hear you may be the new Sheriff. I think that is fabulous. Will would be so proud."

"Yes, it looks like I may be," Dave said.

"You know, if he had known you would be next in line for the job, I think he would have retired years ago," she offered. "He always thought so highly of you."

"That's good of you to say," Dave said as they sat down in the living room, "I always thought highly of him as well."

"So did I," she said. "The old coot, oh how I loved that man. But I just always felt I came second to the law. It was hard for me, and Megan. In a way, I thought if I left him and moved in here that he would see the error in his ways and change, but he never did. And now he's gone, and I'm alone."

Dave could feel the emotion building in her. He wanted to change the subject but at the same time felt a need to just be quiet. They both sat looking at the carpet for what seemed to Dave to be a long time.

"Do you think it had anything to do with me?" she broke the silence.

"No," Dave said hesitantly, "I don't. I think it was all related to work."

"I hope you're right," she said. "I've been trying to figure why he would do that. I had just talked with him the day before he went up there, he seemed preoccupied but not depressed or anything like that. He said he wanted to go up to the cabin and relax for the week end because the next week was going to be stressful. He was one who would face issues, not run from them. It just doesn't make sense."

Again, Dave was silent. He was struggling with whether or not he should tell her what he knew. It was not public knowledge and he was not sure he should let it out, but at the same time it would help her deal with the questions.

"Aunt Dar," Dave said, "I know you have been told it was suicide, but it may not have been. Please keep it confidential, but we have reason to suspect otherwise."

She looked up at him with complete shock in her face, her lower lip quivered.

"What," her voice shuddered. "He was murdered? Who would want to do that?"

She looked like she was about to pass out, all color was gone from her face.

"We don't know who, we're working on that," Dave said, "but it may not have been as previously thought."

"Well," she said as she slowly regained her composure. "I guess that explains a lot. I just didn't see him doing that, the suicide I mean. But, on the other hand, he was so careful about everything, how could someone get to him? The old guy was still as sharp as a tack and wouldn't let someone get the jump on him."

"We think he may have been asleep at his desk," Dave offered. "Someone could have come in on him."

"Yes," she smiled. "He has been caught sleeping at that desk."

"One other thing," Dave said. "There are some finger prints that have not been identified. We think a couple of them may be you and Megan. We would like to get you and Megan to submit to finger printing so that we can confirm, if you don't mind."

"Of course, but I hadn't been up there for a long time," she said. "I'll tell Megan too."

"You can come by the station," he said. "It will only take a minute. Megan can go into John's station and have it done. They can send the print directly up to Arlington County for confirmation."

"Okay, I can do that tomorrow, I'll let Megan know."

Dave hung around for a while as they visited about other things, then he headed back home.

The following morning there was another meeting in Bob's office. The three commanders and Cheryl were present.

"As Dave suggested, I asked Cheryl to look over the crime scene report," Bob said, "Tell them what you told me, Cheryl."

"As I told Bob," Cheryl began, "Sheriff Lewis was still old fashioned in some ways. He used a computer, but only for email. He still had me type letters for him which he dictated on a small tape recorder he always had with him. He also used the tape recorder to make notes to himself, and sometimes he would give me a tape which had his notes on it instead of the letters or memos he wanted typed. I didn't see the tape recorder listed as an item found in the cabin. That seemed strange to me."

"Yes," Dave said, "he always had it in his shirt pocket or clipped on his belt if his shirt didn't have a pocket. I remember him talking into it numerous times while out on the boat fishing."

"So, where is it?" Bob wanted to know.

"Good question," said Dan, "I'll call up to Arlington and check with them."

"There should be a bunch of tapes somewhere as well," Cheryl said.

"We found tapes in his apartment," Dan said. "Probably about thirty of them."

"Okay," Bob said. "Bring those tapes in. Let's find out what's on them. Cheryl, sounds like you've got some work to do."

"I'll get right on it."

Later in the morning, Dave went around the corner to the County Clerk's office. When he walked in Jim was there at the counter talking with one of the clerks. When he saw Dave he waved him on past pointing to a conference room on the right and said, "the paper work is right in there waiting on the signatures of the next sheriff of Lincoln County."

Dave went through the filing page by page. He signed where it had been indicated that a signature was required. In about five minutes it was all complete. He was a registered candidate for Sheriff of Lincoln County.

"All done," he said to the clerk as he handed in the competed forms.

"Alright," Jim said. "We want you to look over the campaign poster design we come up with and the flyers we plan to send to the residents. Can you come by the office?"

"Sure, maybe over lunch, if that works."

"Works fine, see you around twelve fifteen," Jim said as they walked out the door together.

As agreed, at lunch time Dave went by Jim's office and looked over the yard sign and poster design the committee had put together. The general design was a white background with the word "vote" in the upper left corner in script, "Harbinger" in large blue block letters in the center and "Sheriff" in smaller red block letters across the bottom. Dave thought they looked fine. He had not thought much about how effective a sign was but he always had yard signs for Uncle Will when he was running. He also had no idea about the cost of running a campaign.

"How much is all this costing?" Dave asked.

"The party is loaning your campaign the money," Jim said. "Until we can get your fund raising going. It will cost in the range of twenty thousand dollars, I would guess. We're already working on setting up some events for fund raising. As your campaign manager, I've got that under control. I don't see any issues with raising the cash needed."

"So I don't have to pay for this?" Dave asked.

"You will have to raise the funds to pay for it," Jim said, "We will set up a Harbinger for Sheriff account at the bank. The party will loan the money needed to you and you will pay it back with fund raising."

"Okay," Dave said, "but if I'm not able to raise the funds I will need to pay the party back."

"Technically, yes, but don't worry the donors are already on board," Jim said, "you have nothing to worry about."

That evening was another cruise night at Cliff's. It was the last of the season that both boys would be able to go, since D would be leaving for school at the end of the week. The boys met Dave at the farm and he let them pick the cars they wanted to take. D picked the 1970 Plymouth Hemi Cuda and Chris the 1967 Corvette roadster. The three of them headed out with Dave in the 1970 Plymouth Superbird. Once again they had a great time looking at the cars at the cruise night. As they sat down to eat all the boys wanted to talk about was the run for sheriff. They couldn't believe that their dad may be the next sheriff of the county. They went on and on about how great they thought it was and how proud they were. Before they finished eating, for the first time, Dave had no doubt he had made the right decision when he decided to run. The excitement of his sons was enough to make him feel good.

Chapter 11

The next evening, Dave was working in the shop at the farm when he heard a car pull up. He looked out the open doorway and saw a gray seven series BMW with large chrome wheels come to a stop outside. The door opened and Bobby Hernandez got out and walked toward Dave.

"Bobby," Dave said, "how are you? It's been awhile."

"Yeah, Bro," Bobby replied, "what's up, Brian said ya wanted to talk."

"It's good to see you buddy, how have you been?" Dave asked.

"Been okay," Bobby answered, "makin a livin and livin large."

"Been to see Brian's folks lately?" asked Dave.

"Was there Sunday for dinner," Bobby said, "theys good people, treat me right, don't give me grief."

"Bobby, did you hear Sheriff Lewis is dead?" Dave asked.

"Yeah, man, I heard. That's tough I really liked the dude," he said, "we had a great time up at his crib in the woods. I liked the time fishin and huntin duck with yo dad and the Will dude. It was solid time."

"Tell me what your group thought of him?"

"Hey, dude, my homies didn't like the old dude a bit," Bobby offered, "he came down hard on our business, man, that hits home, ya know."

"Did your homies want him dead?" Dave asked.

"Ya know it, dude," Bobby said, "woulda taken out in a breath, could get way with it."

"Did they know you knew him and had been up to his cabin?" Dave asked.

"No way, man, nuff bad vibe on me them knowin bout Bri, ya know," he responded.

"Do you think they had anything to do with his death?" Dave asked.

"Woow, what ya sayin?" Bobby asked. "Thought the dude wasted hisself."

"Just thought I'd ask," Dave said.

"Lookit, man," Bobby said, "don't know nutin bout what ya sayin, me an you go way back an I been straight with ya, but my homies is kin too. Aint crossin no one. Got ma own code, ya dig?"

"I hear you, Bobby," Dave responded, "I wouldn't ask you to cross anyone, but I want you to know that there's nothing I can do for you if you are involved in something. I think you understand that."

"Yeah, man," Bobby said. "You got your bag, an you gotta do what's with it, that's the way it is. I respect that, man, wouldn't expect you to break your code either. Gotta split, dude, stay cool, good to see ya."

"You too, and thanks for coming by," Dave said.

After Bobby left, Dave wondered if he had learned anything. It seemed clear to him that Bobby didn't know anything about gang involvement in Uncle Will's death. But just because he didn't know about it didn't necessarily mean they weren't involved. It could just be that Bobby wasn't involved and they didn't tell him, or he could be lying. So had anything changed?

"A really good investigator I'm turning out to be," he said to himself as he went back to working on cars.

The next day, Bob stopped by Dave's office.

"Cheryl has transcribed two of the tapes so far," Bob said. "They are mostly just his notes to himself about nonrelated things. I'm giving copies to the team so that we can all look for anything relevant, here are yours. There is an hour per tape, so it's going to take her some time to get them all done."

"Okay," Dave said, "I'll take a look. Did Dan get any response back from Arlington about the recorder?"

"They are sending someone out to go through the pickup. I guess that's the only thing that hasn't been full searched. They said they would get back to him."

Bob left and Dave began reading the notes Cheryl had transcribed from Uncle Will's tapes. For the most part they were things he wanted to remember or thoughts he had that he wanted to note for further consideration. He apparently was used to going back over his tapes and wanted to refresh his memory about why he was noting something because he normally would begin each note with the date and time and in some instances his location.

"January 12, 6:30 a.m., paper says the governor will be in Springfield next week, ask Chief if he needs security help," was one such post.

Dave wondered if he needed to go back and review his tapes or if making the note to himself was enough for him to remember to do the task. Some people are visual to the extent that if they write something down it helps them to remember it, others are more verbal in the saying out loud helps the memory. He suspected Uncle Will had been the latter.

Dave read the entire two hours of recordings and found nothing that he felt was a clue or useful in the investigation. In particular there was nothing about the drug gang. He did feel a bit voyeuristic and uncomfortable in delving into Uncle Will's personal notes, but knew it would be worthwhile if it helped nail his killer or killers.

On Thursday evening D stopped by Dave's house to spend a few minutes before he headed back to school. He would be leaving on Friday morning to drive back to Phoenix. It would be Thanksgiving before he would be home again. As they said their good byes and D drove out the drive way Dave thought about what would happen between now and the next time he would see his oldest son. He would be divorced, be elected sheriff and who knows what else? Hopefully, in the "what else" was finding out who killed Sheriff Will.

About two weeks later, on a Thursday morning, Dave found himself standing in the courtroom in front of a judge. Standing next to his left was Jan Thomas, Attorney at Law. Standing to the left of Jan Thomas was Joyce, about to be ex Mrs. Harbinger. The proceedings began by Jan introducing he and Joyce to the judge. The judge asked Dave if he was represented by council, to which he answered, no. The judge asked if he had seen the document filed by Attorney Thomas, reviewed it and in agreement with it, to which he said yes. And, that was pretty much all there was to the proceedings, the judge banged the gavel and he and Joyce were no longer married.

Dave didn't feel much different when he got back to his office. He went straight back to work and was immersed in a budget report when Dan came into his office.

"I got a call from Arlington," Dan said. "They went over every square inch of the property and the recorder is not there. Do you think his wife may know something about it?"

"We won't know if we don't ask," Dave responded, "I'll give her a call."

"Okay, let me know," Dan said as he left Dave's office.

Dave picked up the phone and dialed.

"Aunt Dar," he said when she answered, "It's Dave, how are you today?"

"I'm good, Sweetie, how are you?" she answered.

"I have a question for you," Dave said. "We have been looking for Uncle Will's tape recorder but haven't been able to find it. Would you know anything about where it might be?"

"That blasted thing," she said, "I hated when he would pull that out in the middle of a conversation and talk into it. It was like that was more important than anything else, more important than me."

The line was quiet for a moment, and finally she said, "My God, I miss him." The emotion came through the phone. Then she said, "Sorry, no I have no idea where it might be. He always had it on him, or close by."

"Okay," Dave said, "I had to ask."

"I'm okay, Sweetie," she said, "you find who did that."

They talked for a while longer about other things. She was calm and unemotional when they said good bye. Dave related the lack of information to Dan and went back to his budget work. The next thing he knew, the clock said it was almost five. He picked up the phone and dialed a number he had memorized.

"Jan Thomas," the voice said in his ear.

"Ms. Thomas, this is Dave Harbinger," he said.

"Dave," she said, "call me Jan. I thought you might call."

"I was wondering if you may be free for dinner tonight, Jan," Dave said.

"Yes I am," she answered without hesitation. "I can leave now, how about the Olive Garden in twenty minutes? Or, am I being too forward?"

"Not at all," Dave said, "I like your attitude, I may use lights and siren to get there."

"See you in a few minutes," she said, signing off.

Dave jumped up from his desk and headed for the door. He couldn't remember when he had been so excited. It really seemed like she was as interested in him as he was in her, he wasn't sure why, but he also didn't care.

He didn't use the lights and siren, but he did get there before she did. The hostess asked if he wanted to be taken to a table to wait he declined. He preferred to wait in the lobby for her to come in. In less than five minutes she did. She smiled brightly as she walked in the door. As he walked close behind her on the way to the table, he smelled a slight hint of perfume. It was exquisite.

"I had an extremely busy day, and wasn't able to get lunch," she explained over the menu after they had ordered their drinks. "I'm starving, so when you called I was not about to beat around the bush. Hope you don't mind."

"Not at all," Dave hoped he wasn't noticeably panting, "I find it refreshing, as a matter of fact, I find you refreshing."

"Thanks, how was your day?"

"You mean other than my wife divorcing me?" he asked.

"Yes, other than that?"

"Hectic, but now it's really looking up." He looked into her eyes, grayish green in color and wonderfully intense. The waitress came back with their drinks and took their order.

"So, Jan?" he asked.

"You are wondering why I have not been married and don't even have a boyfriend?" she said looking into his eyes.

He nodded.

"The law," she said. "It's been my whole life since undergrad school. I devoted all my time and energy to learning it and practicing it to the best of my ability. I always billed the most hours, took the toughest cases and spent every waking hour working. I never wanted anything else. I saw relationships going on around me and failing because of the stress and requirements of the job and didn't need that. So, I rejected any and all advances and devoted myself to my work. Now I am a partner in the one of the highest regarded firms in the state, am financially set for life, have met my goals and am alone. It's all good except for the alone part, so I'm thinking of doing something about that."

Dave sat quietly and listened. She seemed to want to lay everything out on the table and he was certainly not going to object.

"When we met, I liked you instantly," she continued, "you seemed sincere and well grounded. You are well known and liked in the community and your ex didn't seem to think you were a really bad guy. You are handsome and financially stable and I thought you may be fun to be around. You are definitely not the full of himself type that most attorneys are, so I thought why not see what you are really like?"

She paused and looked at him with a look that seemed to say, your turn.

"Well," he started, and the waitress interrupted by showing up with their salads.

"I guess I always thought Joyce and I would be back together at some point. But when she asked for the divorce I realized that there was really never a chance of that happening. I would have been for it, but as I think back I'm not sure she ever felt about me the way I felt about her. I think I may have been the right guy for her from the status and position standpoint only. I'm not sure she was ever physically attracted to me as I was to her. I'm ready to move on and find someone that wants to be with me as much as I want to be with them."

"I guess we have opened up to each other," Jan said. "Wouldn't you say?"

"If we have a future, it's safe to say we started it openly," he said.

She laughed, "I think we can say that. Tell me about your sons. You have two, right?"

"Yes, Dave Jr, we call him D and Chris," Dave said, "D is heading back to school at ASU as we speak and Chris begins his senior year at Springfield High next week. D is on a baseball scholarship but I don't think Chris has the sports passion enough to be scholarship material. I'm not even sure he knows he wants to do yet. What about your family, brothers sisters, parents and so forth?"

"I'm from Cincinnati where my dad is an attorney. I went to Ohio State for my undergrad in political science and law school at William and Mary. I have an older sister who lives in Atlanta where her husband is a utility engineer. They have three kids that I don't get to see nearly enough. Mom never worked and is always complaining because I haven't married and work too much."

The conversation went on over dinner and dessert. They were having a great time and as they were beginning to feel pressured to vacate the table, Dave asked if she would like to see his farm?

"Sure," she said, "I'll follow you home, if that's what you're asking, but only for a short time. I have court in the morning."

She was driving a new Corvette, of which Dave highly approved. She followed his unmarked squad out to his farm.

"This is my pride and joy," Dave said, as he opened the door to the car collection. "It's not really all mine, I have joint ownership of most of them with my brother and sister."

"Wow," Jan said, "I had no idea, this if fabulous. I love cars."

He watched closely as she moved from one classic to another. She even knew what most of them were, which impressed Dave a great deal. She had to ask some of the specific years but he had no doubt that she knew what she was looking at.

"Two big block '67s," she exclaimed, looking at the row of five Corvettes in the collection. "And a Superbird. Is it a hemi?"

"No, it's a 440 six pack," Dave explained, "but the Cuda is a hemi."

"440 six pack four speed," she said looking into the lemon twist yellow Superbird's interior. "And the Cuda is a four speed too." She said as she looked over the vitamin c orange Cuda. "These are great, I love them all."

"Let's go for a ride," he said, "which one do you want to take out?"

"Really," her smile was a mile wide. "The Superbird," she said without hesitation.

"Let me pull it out, and then you can drive," he said.

"No, way," she said excitedly and the mile wide smile got bigger.

As they accelerated away from the farm he was impressed with her ability to handle the car. The clutch was a heavy one and took some force to push in, but it didn't seem to be an issue for her at all. She shifted the big four forty through the gears like she had been doing it all of her life. Joyce never had any interest in any of the cars, as a matter of fact she even resented them.

"I can't believe this," Dave thought to himself as he watched her beaming behind the wheel and down shifting for a stop sign. "I can't believe this is happening."

They went all the way into town. When they got back it was almost nine.

"I really have to go," she said after he put the car back in the row where it belonged. "Thanks for dinner, the drive and the wonderful time."

"I can't remember when I've enjoyed being with anyone more," he said.

He took her hand and pulled her close and kissed her gently on the mouth. They parted for a moment then moved back together a kissed passionately.

"Can I see you again?" he asked, as they finally broke apart.

"I guess we'll see, won't we?" she said flirtingly as she got into her Corvette.

He watched her drive away thinking something had just started that he would not be able to control. But then again, why would he want to control the feelings he was having now. Something he hadn't felt in a long time, and he liked it. Liked it a lot.

Chapter 12

There was only a week until the election. No progress had been made in the investigation of the death of Sheriff Will, they were still looking for the idea or clue that would help tie the drug gang to the crime. Bob, Dan and Dave had come to the conclusion that the drug guys were the most logical perps of the crime. But, conclusive evidence still alluded them. The latest transcript of Sheriff Will's notes was on Dave's desk when he got into his office. He began to read. Not far into the document he came across: "DEA likes the idea of road blocks, said today that they will let me know when they have credible information of a possible shipment." The date on the note was about two weeks before the drug bust at the roadblock. Dave read on. In a couple of more pages he came across another related note: "DEA says they lost a probable shipment at the boarder yesterday that they think may be for our boys, may be here tonight." The date was the same day that Dave's roadblock stopped the van with drugs.

Dave was feeling encouraged that maybe the notes would lead to helpful information. He read on and in a few more pages came across what he thought may be meaningful: "DEA conducted another raid on the farm, found nothing, thinks tipped off again, Williams County says no, DEA asked for help." *What kind of help*, Dave thought. He read on but nothing else was noted before the transcript ran out.

At staff meeting that morning everyone had seen the same DEA related notes that Dave had.

Cheryl said, "I'm processing as fast as I can but I have to keep up with my other duties as well."

There was some discussion about having someone else do the transcribing but the general consensus was it was too important and Cheryl was the best at understanding the Sheriff's mumbling. They decided to have another clerk pick up some of Cheryl's other work so she would have more time to devote to the transcribing. About twenty of the thirty five tapes were done.

"Cheryl," Bob asked, "did the DEA ever call Will here in the office?"

"Not that I'm aware of," she answered. "They could have called in direct or on his cell, or maybe home line."

"So we have no idea who at DEA he was talking with," Bob said to the room. "Dan, can you follow up to see if we can determine what he was doing for them while we wait for additional info from the transcriptions."

"I'll make some calls," Dan said.

With the election coming up, Bob and Dave were in the process of swapping duties. They expected the transfer of power to be smooth. Everyone seemed comfortable with the idea that Dave was about to become the boss, except for Dave. It was still a bit of a foreign idea to him, but he was going to have to get used to it.

Dave and Jan had been seeing each other regularly, as in about every day. They had lunch together whenever their schedules allowed and had dinner together almost every night. They often went out to dinner but Jan had taken an interest in cooking for Dave at her house whenever she had time. The relationship was going great guns, they were both having a great time together. Jan told Dave she was even beginning to get some flack at work because she was not always on top of things as much as was normally expected of her.

"I finally have a life outside of that place," she said to Dave one day at lunch, "and I don't think they like it. But I do, and I'm not going back to the way it was. They will just have to deal with it."

That particular evening was the cruise night at Cliff's. They had gotten into the routine of going every week. Chris, Jan and Dave were now the three cars cruising to Cliff's together. They decided to do a Pontiac night so Chris was driving the 1967 GTO, Jan in the 1964 Gran Prix and Dave in the 1965 Catalina 2+2 Convertible.

As the three of them sat down with their meals to eat, Chris said, "Dad, can I move back in with you?"

"Why," Dave asked, "what's up?"

"It's like I'm living alone," he said. "Mom is never there anymore. She goes out every night with Randy and hardly ever gets home before after midnight. I'm up and gone in the morning before she's up. I can go a full week sometimes without seeing her. She leaves me money on the kitchen table and sometimes a note but that's about it."

"Of course, I don't have a problem with it Chris," Dave said, "you are welcome to live with me, but let me talk with your mom first."

"Great, can you do it soon? I don't like living alone."

"I'll call her at work tomorrow."

"Thanks," Chris said.

Dave looked at Jan, she slowly nodded her understanding and continued eating her burger.

After Chris had left and Dave and Jan were alone back at Dave's house she said, "Dave, I've been thinking of leaving the firm, and what Chris said tonight has convinced me to do it."

"What does Chris have to do with your firm?" Dave was confused.

"It's Randy," Jan said. "He used me to get to your ex-wife and now he is keeping her away from your son by keeping her out all night. I have never really respected him as a man, but I just don't think I can work for him anymore. He is a womanizing heel."

"What are you going to do," Dave asked. "Do you have another job lined up?"

"Don't need one," Jan said. "My share of the partnership is payable to me in three equal installments the first coming due within thirty days of my departure and an equal sum on the anniversary of that date for the next two years. I own my condo free and clear, have no debt and spend very little except on clothes and food, oh, and that campaign contribution to some guy running for sheriff. I will miss the car. It was leased by the firm. Maybe I'll buy one."

"I'm curious now. You don't have to answer, but what do you think your share of the firm is worth?" Dave asked.

"The accountants will have to figure that out," she said. "But I would guess it to be in the range of about three million."

"Woo," Dave gasped. "Guess you can take your time looking for a job!"

"Taxes will take a bite out," she said. "But the accountants will give me advice on that. I am restricted by agreement to not join an existing firm, but I have the option to start my own."

"Well, I'm on your side no matter what."

"I thought you would be," she smiled.

The next morning after getting into work, Dave called his sister's pediatrician office where Joyce was a nurse. He asked for her and waited for her to come to the phone.

"What do you want?" she said sharply.

"Chris asked to move in with me," he answered calmly.

"When did he do that?"

"Last night, at the cruise night."

"He hasn't said anything to me about wanting to move out."

"When was the last time you talked with him?" Dave asked.

She was quiet for a moment and then said, "I don't see that is any of your business, I'll talk with him." She hung up the phone.

Dave was sitting thinking about the phone call when Dan came into his office and sat down in a visitor chair.

"I talked with a guy at DEA. He says the investigation of the Williams County drug gang has been handed off to him in just the last few weeks. He is still getting up to speed on things. The former guy who Will was working with has gone under cover and is not available," Dan said. "He says the last note in the file says, quote: Sheriff Lewis may have important information, needs a few days to confirm. End quote. The note was dated the Thursday before the Sheriff was killed."

"Have you told Bob?" Dave asked.

"He's at a Kiwanis' breakfast meeting."

"Did the guy know what Lewis was doing for them?"

"He asked me to give him some time to go through the file," Dan said. "Said he would call me back."

"Sounds like Will was on to something. Maybe the next transcript from Cheryl will tell us more."

"She's working on that," Dan said as he left Dave's office.

It was harvest time. Dave and Chris had started picking corn last weekend, putting in two full ten hour days. Monday and Tuesday nights they had worked four hours each before taking Wednesday night off for the cruise night at Cliff's. They had maybe six hours of picking left to finish up the harvest.

On his way home from work that evening Dave grabbed a couple of meals to go at a fast food place. Thirty minutes later he was pulling into one of the fields in the grain hauler. Chris was already at it, picking corn in the green and yellow John Deere combine, having come to the farm straight from school. Chris maneuvered the combine up beside the truck and swung the boom over the trailer. The trailer already had about a half load from work the other evening. He started the unloading of the corn from the combine into the truck and climbed down.

"Is the machine functioning okay?" Dave asked as they began to eat the burgers and fries.

"Sure," Chris answered. "No issues, so far."

"Did you talk with your mom today?"

"Yeah, and is she pissed." Chris said, "she says I shouldn't have asked you until I talked with her. She says I can't move in with you because she has custody of me. Is that right, Dad, can she force me to stay there?"

"Chris, you are eighteen. Our divorce did not address custody because both of you guys are of age. I have no idea what she is talking about," Dave said. "Maybe you should talk with Jan to get her legal opinion."

They continued to talk while they ate. After finishing the food and the combine was empty they got back to work.

It normally took a little over thirty hours to get the corn in. Dave could do it in a hard week end if he needed to, but he preferred to take his time if the weather allowed. He didn't like to over work the equipment and taking time allowed for better inspection, greasing and fixing issues as they occurred. When both boys were here the three of them could trade off tasks and allow for longer breaks. With only two of them it was still feasible with a little more effort. The weather was looking good this year and things seemed to be getting done.

While Chris continued to pick, Dave pulled the truck out of the field and headed to the grain elevator. The truck would hold about a thousand bushels but only had about eight hundred on it now. Since the bin in the combine would hold four hundred bushels, he normally took less than a full truck load to the elevator. The elevator trip only took about forty minutes. Dave could be there and back before Chris was ready to unload again. *If nothing breaks we could finish up this evening,* Dave thought as he shifted the Kenworth through the gears to get up to speed.

Chapter 13

Election Day came like any other day. Dave went to the polls and voted for people he knew and some he didn't. He did find it rather strange when he got to the box on the ballot that said County Sheriff and saw his name with a box next to it. He left it blank and moved on, I'll let the people decide that one he thought.

As he walked out of the polling place he was struck with a strange feeling of being alone. He didn't really understand why. Was it that what he had just observed had meaning that should be shared? When he got to his car, before he started the engine, he dialed Jan's number on his cell.

"Hi," she said cheerfully as she answered.

"Hi, yourself," he said. "Where are you?"

"I'm in the car headed to the office," she said, "would you like to meet for coffee somewhere?"

"I would like that very much," he said, "exactly why I was calling, as a matter of fact."

"Denny's on Seventh?"

"I'll be there in ten."

"I'll buy, Sheriff, bye," she signed off.

He pulled into the parking lot and parked next to her Corvette. She was waiting in a booth just inside the door and smiled as he walked in. He slipped in the booth beside her and stole a quick kiss.

"It's been a long time," he said.

"What, since last night?" she said.

"Yes, a long time, and a lot has happened since I saw you last."

"Okay, like what?"

"I went into a polling place and saw my name on a ballot for Sheriff," he said shyly.

"Hmm," she said. "So did I. How did that make you feel?"

"Now you sound like a shrink," he said. "But, it somehow made me feel alone. More alone than I've felt for years. That's why I called you. I wanted to see you, I don't feel alone when I'm with you."

She didn't say a word. She took his hand and squeezed gently. She looked into his eyes and said softly, "Me too."

He felt a bond with her that he had never felt with anyone before. They sat silent in the booth at Denny's drinking coffee just looking at each other. They knew conversation was not necessary. This was a time for being and they were.

After enjoying Jan's company for about thirty minutes, Dave headed to the station. He was a few minutes late for the staff meeting and walked into the meeting rather sheepishly.

Bob looked at him frowned and said, "What's this? You think you can come in late? Next thing we know you'll be in charge." He was struggling to keep the frown, as were the others. In a few seconds it was more than they could take, they all started laughing. Congratulations were passed around and plans for the vote results celebration discussed.

When things had calmed down and it was time to get to work, Dan took the floor.

"I have something to report," Dan said, "on a hunch I fed the license numbers that we know are drug gang members into the State Police data base. I found that a black Mercedes registered to the drug farm was stopped for speeding on the interstate at the eighty seven mile marker south bound at one thirty seven on Sunday morning of the weekend the sheriff was killed. That puts it about fifteen miles south of the Gifford exit. The driver was issued a warning for eleven miles over and released."

The room was silent while everyone processed what they had just heard.

"Driver's name?" Dave asked. "Any passengers?"

"Driver was Alfonso Ramirez, address in rural Williams County, two passengers no names." Dan said.

"Do you think that we should go pay Mr. Ramirez a visit?" Bob asked, "Maybe find out where he was on that evening?"

"Yes, but not quite yet," Dan said. "I'd like to see what else I can turn up about the gang around the same time frame. DEA should be getting back to me soon. Let's wait to see if they have any thing or some idea of other questions we should ask when we visit with Alfonso."

"Agreed," Bob said. "Sound good to you, Dave?"

"Yeah," Dave said. "Do we know who the DEA has been working with at the State Police?"

"Good idea," Dan said. "I'll find out."

That evening there was an election returns party at the downtown Hilton. Dave and Jan were with Jim and other party officials in a conference room separate from the main ballroom where all of the speeches and other activities would be held. Since Dave was running unopposed there was really no drama about his race, but others were watching returns closely.

At nine o'clock the party chairman directed Dave to the microphone. He thanked all of his supporters and the voters for electing him to the position of sheriff of Lincoln County. He promised to do his best to serve and protect the citizens and fulfill the duties of the office. There was a considerable amount of cheering, clapping and back slapping. Then it was on to other races and other winners or losers. Dave and Jan left as soon as they could slip out gracefully.

"That's all part of the politics involved with elective office, I guess," Dave said as they pulled out of the parking lot. "It all seems so foreign to me. I don't feel special enough to garner that kind of attention. I just want to do the job that I think I can be good at."

"That's what makes you special," Jan said, "most people who run for elective office want the office because it makes them feel special. Not because they are. As a matter of fact, most elected officials are no different at all, far from it, but they want to feel like they are so they run for office. If they are not elected it's proof to them that they are just like every one else, but if they are elected they feel the people have made them special."

"Well, I got elected and I still don't feel *special*." Dave said.

"Oh, but you are." She reached across the car, rubbed his shoulder and said, "you are becoming the most *special* person in the world, to me."

"Just becoming?"

"Keep trying."

"I will," he smiled.

The next evening the County Board certified the election results for the sheriff race and installed Dave into his new position. He was now authorized to put the three stars on his shirt collar that signified the highest officer in the department. The only other person in the department he had ever seen wear that insignia was Uncle Will. Now as he put them on, he became even more dedicated to finding out what happened to Sheriff Will Lewis.

Dave and Bob had transferred offices after hours the night before, so
when Dave walked into the department the morning after being
installed sheriff, he immediately called his staff into his office.

"People," he said, "it is my intent to find out what happened to Sheriff
Lewis. Bob, you have been acting Sheriff and I want you to continue
with the same duties so I can concentrate all my attention to the
investigation. Dan, you have other cases you have to pay attention to
so I want you to give me everything you have on the Sheriff Lewis
case, I am taking the lead. You are not out of it, I will need your
assistance, but I have it now. In short, I do not intend to run this office
until this case is solved. Running the office is up to you guys. Any
questions?"

Cheryl spoke up. "So any of the normal daily activity I have been
handing to Bob, will still go to him?"

"Yes," Dave said. "Bob, you may want to assign a temporary Major.
I'm okay with that if you do."

"I'll see how it goes," Bob said.

"Okay, that's it for everyone except Dan," Dave said. "I need him to
stick around."

Everyone else left, Dave closed the office door and sat back down at
his desk across form Dan.

"I think I'll start with a visit to Williams County," Dave said, "talk with
the Sheriff down there and see if I can establish a dialogue. What do
you think?"

"Couldn't hurt," Dan said, "I'm not sure how much of the problem
between Sheriff Lewis and Sheriff Alexander was related to the payoff
accusation or just a dislike for each other. You are a likeable guy,
Dave, maybe it will work better for you."

"I don't know about that," Dave said. "But it would be helpful if we
can work with them on this. Any word on who DEA was working with
at the State Police?"

"Yes, Captain Josh Trubaldi is heading the drug task force that had been working with DEA. I talked with him briefly. He knew that Sheriff Lewis was helping DEA but did not know exactly what he was doing for them."

"Let's set up a meeting with everyone so that we can make sure we are all on the same page," Dave suggested, "DEA, State, Williams County and Arlington County."

"Ok, I'll see if I can get everyone here one day next week," Dan said.

"Good, thanks. That's it for now."

When Dan had gone, Dave picked up the phone and called Williams County Sheriff's Department and asked for Sheriff Alexander.

"Congratulations, Sheriff Harbinger," the sheriff said as he answered.

"Thanks, Sheriff Alexander."

"Call me Rob," Sheriff Alexander said.

"Okay, thanks Rob, and I'm Dave."

"I'd like to come down and meet with you if you have a few minutes this afternoon?" Dave asked.

"Well, let me see," Rob said and after a moment pause continued. "Yes, I have time around three this afternoon if that works for you."

"Three is fine," Dave said, "see you then."

Dave pushed down the hook button and dialed again.

"Jan Thomas," the voice he had hoped to hear said.
"This is the Sheriff," Dave said in a command voice, "I need for you to meet me for lunch."

"Yes, sir," she responded. "Reporting as ordered, sir, where?"

"O'Malley's, I need to drive down to Jackson for a meeting this afternoon so leaving from there would work fine."

"Sounds good, see you there at noon," she said.

After they were served a few hours later, Dave asked, "So when do you plan to tell them?"

"I should be finished with my current case in about two weeks," she said. "That's what I've been waiting for. I will be at a point when I can walk out without complications if they want me to, or we can negotiate a date from that point forward. I really don't care which, but by waiting till then it will make either an option."

"Are you feeling okay with the idea?" he asked. "You've put a lot into that firm."

"And they have gotten a lot out of me," she said, rather defensively. "They have billed clients for every hour and I am the one who put in the hour. I owe them nothing."

"They paid you well."

"No doubt about that, but they made money. We're even, I think."

"Good. I wanted to make sure you were okay with your decision."

"Thanks, dad," she frowned and then smiled. "By the way, Chris called me this morning."

"What's the latest in the never ending saga of the move in with dad battle?" he asked.

"It is that," she said. "She told him that she could get a restraining order against you if he tried to move in with you. That you were exerting undue pressure on him and being around you could be detrimental to his health."

"Where is she getting these ideas?" he thought out loud.

"I hear Randy in this," she said. "I told Chris that if he wants to move in with you, I see no reason that he can't. Filing and getting a judge to agree are two completely different things. I also told him that I was on his side and would help in any way that I can."

"Am I going to get a bill for all of this?"

"Maybe not a bill, but you'll pay," she said.

Chapter 14

It was about thirty miles from Springfield to Jackson, the county seat of Williams County. Dave drove the back roads leisurely enjoying the country drive in the cool weather of late fall.

At three p.m., Dave walked into the Williams County Sheriff's Department, Robert Alexander, Sheriff. A hefty brunette showed straight into the sheriff's office. As he walked in, Sheriff Alexander stood and walked around his desk. They shook hands.

"Congratulations, again," Sheriff Alexander said as they shook. "It's a pleasure to meet you. I'm glad you could come by."

"Thanks, Rob. It's nice of you to give me a few minutes of your time on such short notice."

"No problem," Rob said, as he motioned to a pair of chairs around a small conference table. "Glad to do it." They sat down on either side of the table.

"I know you and my predecessor had a strained relationship. I hope we can have a better one."

"Yes, Lewis and I were not the best of friends," Rob answered. "He and I may have been too much alike. Are you like me, or are you a nice guy?"

"Nice enough. But I know a bunch of crooks who wouldn't say that about me."

Rob smiled and said, "You can't be nice to those guys or you won't last long in this business. How long you been in the department up there?"

"Eighteen years and counting," Dave answered. "I know there was animosity between you and Sheriff Lewis about his contention that payoffs were protecting the drug gang that operates down on your CR 18. Was there anything besides that between you?"

"No, not really," Rob said. "That's the lot of it. He thought we were taking bribes and we are not. Plain and simple, but he wouldn't let it go. I don't know how those guys are getting information but it's not from us. I run a tight ship here and I know more about what goes on in Williams County than Lewis did. It was down right mean of him to insist otherwise. I think he just had a mean streak pointed at us. Still, as much as I dislike that man, it is a damn shame that he's gone. And to go that way confuses me. He surely knew he wouldn't be around that much longer anyway."

"We think he was murdered."

"Really," Rob looked thoughtful. "Well that makes more sense. Any ideas?"

"As a matter of fact that's why I wanted to talk with you so soon," Dave said. "We think it's possible the drug gang may have been involved."

"Hmm," was Rob's response. "Any hard evidence?"

"No," Dave said. "Just suspicion and a speeding traffic stop of gang members in the vicinity during the time frame of the murder. We know that they were upset at the attention Sheriff Lewis was giving them. Suspecting they want him out of the picture and being in the area at the time makes them likely suspects."

"Well, Dave, without hard evidence it will be tough to prove."

"Yes it will. I'm hoping that you and I can work together to get something on those guys."

"Sounds like you have the same vendetta as Lewis against the drug gang," Rob said.

"I don't like drugs and what they do to the people that get hooked on them. It's our duty to stop the drug trade anyway we can. That drug gang is part of a larger organization that is preying on too may lives in this country. They need to be stopped and I intend to do what I can. I won't go easy on them and if I find they were responsible for the death of Sheriff Lewis, I won't rest until they are put away for what they have done. So, are we in this together?" Dave asked.

"I don't know what we can do," Rob said. "But we can talk about it."

"Speaking of talking, we are planning to have a meeting sometime next week in our office of all agencies concerned with the drug gang," Dave explained. "We're asking DEA, the State boys and Arlington County to participate. Do you think you could come up as well? Not sure exactly when yet, my lead investigator is setting up."

"Let me know when, and I'll see if I can make it."

Dave left and headed back toward Springfield. As he drove he played back the interaction he had just had and tried to determine if Sheriff Alexander was being straight with him. Were Uncle Will's suspicions founded in something real, or did he just have a mean streak pointed at Williams County? Either of those options gave him an uncomfortable feeling. Or was it the chili dogs he had for lunch giving him the burning stomach?

When Dave got home from work that evening Chris' car was parked in front. He went in and found Chris in the family room watching television.

"Hey, Dad," Chris said as Dave walked in.

"Good to see you, son, what's the latest on the move?"

"Mom still doesn't want me to, but I'm doing it. Can I use the pickup tomorrow after school? A couple of the guys are going to help move my stuff."

"Of course you can use the truck but do you think you should if your mom is so set against it?"

"I talked with Jan," Chris said, "she doesn't seem to think there is anything mom can do to stop me. And, Jan says she will be in my corner if mom tries anything, legal wise."

"Yeah, Jan mentioned that you had called. Chris, it's up to you," Dave said, "and I'll support your decision. I'm just trying to figure why your mom is so against it."

"Oh, I think I know," Chris offered. "That guy Randy likes that she has a kid at home so she won't try to move in with him. If I'm not around she's afraid he'll dump her for someone with family ties."

"Where in the world did you get an idea like that?"

"I overheard her talking to some friend on the phone."

"So you think by moving in here it will cause her to get dumped?"

"Maybe, but the reason I want to move in here is because you actually live here and are home," he said. "Mom isn't."

"Okay, whatever, you know where to find the keys to the truck," Dave said, "do you want to take the truck tonight or come back tomorrow to get it?"

"I think I'll just take it tonight, if that's okay?"

"Sure, see you tomorrow."

The next morning Dan stopped into Dave's office to let him know that the all agencies meeting was set for next Tuesday at ten a.m. Dave made a note in his calendar.

"Is everyone coming?" Dave asked.

"No confirmation yet from Sheriff Alexander, but everyone else is in," Dan answered.

"I think he'll be here, if my read is right,"

The next batch of transcripts was on Dave's desk. He sat down to read. "Corey game at four on Tuesday, should call Doctor Simalaski" was an entry in the notes from Uncle Will. Corey was Megan and John's seventeen year old son and Will's grandson. He was playing summer baseball with the Jackson Tigers and Will liked to go watch anytime he could. Dave checked the date. It was about two weeks before Will was killed.

The next entry got Dave's attention. It read: Juan leaves home ten thirty. There was no date or time note on that one, but judging from the previous note about Corey's ball game Dave thought it must be later the same day, which would make it ten thirty p.m. or the next morning at ten thirty a.m. *He was staking out the drug farm,* Dave thought, *but for what reason.*

Dave kept reading. After a few more pages there was a note that read: "35CS4648." *A license number* Dave thought. He looked at the time, seven forty, and the date. He checked the calendar on his desk; it was a Tuesday. Backtracking to the note on Corey's ballgame it appeared to be the same Tuesday. If Uncle Will was at Corey's ballgame he was most likely in Jackson when he noted the license number. Dave turned to his computer and ran the number. It came up as registered to the drug farm. He made notes on what he had just found and put them in the file. His note said: noted a gang member license number after being at Corey's game and the date and time.

That evening after he and Chris had Dinty Moore Beef Stew for supper, Dave went over to the farm. Temperatures would soon be falling with each passing day. It was the time of year that he prepared the cars for winter. There were a few cars he would keep in driving shape for the winter but most he would winterize. His winterizing process was to drain the fuel, blow out the fuel lines and put battery tenders on the cars before covering them each with the custom car cover. He didn't mind the time it took to winterize a collection this large. The time spent now meant the cars would be up and running quicker and easier in the spring. It was unusually warm for the time of year so Dave had left the door to the garage open. He was pumping the gas out of the tank of the 1949 Hudson Hornet when he heard a car in the drive and a car door. Shortly Bobby Hernandez came in the garage door.

"You da big man now," Bobby said as he held out his hand.

"I guess," Dave said as they shook, "what you doing out this way?"

"Had ta come by an say hey to da man, dude."

"I appreciate it."

"Theys somethin else, bro," Bobby hesitated. "Word is yous gonna come down on us."

"Where'd you hear that?"

"Don't matter, bro, words out, an the homies know," Bobby said. "Thought ya should know they know. Keep ya guard up, huh. Aint tellin, caint tell ya nutin, bro, but thought ya should know."

Dave nodded and said, "I hear you, bro, thanks."

They slapped hands, hugged briefly and Bobby left.

Dave went back to his work. He still had about twelve cars to winterize. He connected the six volt battery tender to the restored Hudson and pulled the car cover on. He thought to himself, "how would Bobby's gang know?" The answer seemed obvious. He would have to handle Sheriff Alexander carefully.

Dave asked Dan into his office the next morning.

"I'd like to talk with the DEA and State Police on a conference call before the meeting on Tuesday. Can you set it up?"

"I don't think it should be a problem. Let me get on it."

"Thanks," Dave said. Dan left his office.

He picked up the phone and dialed the Arlington County Sheriff's Department number.

"Sheriff Allen."

"Sheriff, this is Dave Harbinger. "How are you today?"

"I'm fine, thanks, and congratulations," Sam said.

"Thanks, I understand you are coming down to our meeting next week," Dave said. "Do you plan to bring anyone with you?"

"Yes, Pete Jacobs is coming with me," Sam answered. "I think you met him a couple of times."

"Yes, I know Pete. The reason for my call is that I have reason to believe that we may not want to provide too much detail about the crime scene in the meeting next week. I am not a liberty to say why, but would appreciate your indulgence."

"Of course," Sam said. "What in particular do you wanting to keep under wraps?"

"As far as I know, nothing has been said about where the weapon was found," Dave offered, "I would like to keep it that way for now."

"No problem," Sam said, "I'll tell Pete, we will be vague."

"Good. I think it may help the investigation down the road."

"Are you still thinking the drug gang?" Sam asked.

"They are still number one on the suspect list down here. Anything new turn up on your end?"

"No, nothing," Sam said. "See you on Tuesday." He signed off.

Cheryl came into Dave's office a few minutes later. "Dan has the conference call set up on the speaker phone in the conference room."

"Thanks," he said as he got up and headed down the hall.

"Here's the Sheriff now," Dan said into the speaker phone as Dave walked into the room. "Sheriff, on the phone are DEA Agent George Hoffman and Captain Josh Trubaldi of the State Police."

"Hello, Sheriff Harbinger," two voices on the speaker phone said almost simultaneously.

"This is George Hoffman," said a voice. "Congratulation on your election."

"Yes, congratulations," said the other voice.

"Thanks, guys," Dave said. "Let's get right to it, the reason I wanted to talk with you before our meeting next week is to get a feel from you two about your relationships with the Williams County Sheriff or his department."

The phone line was quiet for a few seconds.

"Sheriff Lewis apparently had concerns about payoffs, my file says," George said. "But Jim Watson, who preceded me, was not able to confirm that there were any. What the file shows is that the farm has been suspected of drug activity for several years now, but no evidence has been found after four warranted searches. As a matter of fact the only evidence gained to date is from the road block activity by Lincoln County."

"We have had no abnormal interaction with Williams County," added Josh.

"George," Dave asked. "Was each of the four searches assisted by Williams County?"

"Hold on," George answered. After several seconds he added. "Yes, Williams County Sheriff's officers and State Police assisted in each search."

"Does your file indicate how much notice was given before each search?" Dave asked.

"No. But it would normally be the day before, or at the very least several hours."

"Okay," Dave said, "gentlemen let me bring you up to speed. The meeting next week is about the murder of Sheriff Lewis. The drug gang is a prime suspect. I've invited Sheriff Alexander to the meeting because the farm is in his county. They have jurisdiction and should be a part of any action. Former Sheriff Lewis thought that corruption exists in the Williams County department but I don't believe he had evidence. At the same time, not having evidence doesn't mean there isn't corruption there. So let's keep that in mind."

"Understood," said George.

"Got it," replied Josh.

"Thanks for your time," Dave signed off.

Dan hung up the conference phone. "You think Sheriff Will was right, don't you?" he asked Dave.

"I can't say for sure, but he may have been," Dave said, "one thing seems sure, the drug gang is getting information from somewhere. So the less information we let out, the more secure our investigation remains. And, the better our chances of causing someone to slip up and tell something they have no way of knowing."

"Unless they are the perp," Dan said.

"Exactly," Dave said, "I talked with Arlington and asked that they not reveal where the shotgun was found. Only we know that. The report has not been released, and there is no way of anyone but us and the Arlington County guys knowing that. I don't know if it will make a difference, but I want to keep that to ourselves."

"Good idea," Dan said, "I'll make sure everyone that has seen the report is in the loop."

"Good," Dave said.

Dave went back to his office and began to read the latest of the transcribed reports. This particular one was older in time than the last few. Dave saw several notes that seemed to indicate the sheriff was tailing or at least watching someone. There were several different license plates noted and when run through the system they all came back as gang members, or to Juan himself. Most of the notes didn't seem to say anything of interest, trips to the store, out to eat, to a movie, and things like that. He looked back in his notes, the only one he still wondered about was the license number after Cory's ballgame.

At just after five that evening Cheryl stuck her head around his office door and said, "Have a great weekend Sheriff."

"It's only Thursday, Cheryl," he said. She smiled, waved and disappeared.

Chapter 15

When Dave got home from work that evening Jan's Corvette was in his driveway. When he walked into the kitchen she was sitting at the table smiling.

"Hi," she said as she got up and kissed him passionately.

When the kiss broke he started to speak but she put a finger to his lips and said. "No, just listen and do what you are told. Go change into comfortable traveling clothes, pack a bag for a weekend in the sun, no gun."

"But," he started to say then changed his mind. "Cheryl knew you were planning this."

"Had to clear your schedule for tomorrow," she said, "I'm treating myself to a weekend getaway to celebrate my resignation, and what kind of getaway would it be without you with me. So get packing mister, we don't have a lot of time."

"You going to tell me where?"

"Nope," was all she said.

Fifteen minutes later they were in her car and on the way with her at the wheel. Dave was a bit confused when she turned the opposite way from the nearest commercial airport which was about an hour away. He was thinking a weekend getaway in the sun must mean an airplane.

His confusion continued when she pulled into the Springfield Municipal airport, since there was no commercial service from there. She didn't say a word, as she wheeled the Vette through a gate marked authorized vehicles only, around and into a hanger. She shut the car off and got out, so he did too. After grabbing their bags she motioned to a private jet parked just outside the hanger with the boarding ladder down. She walked toward it with Dave in tow.

"Who's plane?" he asked.

"Ours," she said. "Chartered."

The pilot was Doug and the copilot was Jeremy. They informed them that they expected a smooth flight and an ETA of about four and one half hours to Key West. Dave and Jan got comfortable in the large leather seats. She was smiling from ear to ear and so was he.

When they had reached cruising altitude, Jeremy came back from the cockpit and showed them where the snacks and drinks were located in the Cessna Citation X aircraft. They reclined the seats and relaxed for the trip.

"So what's with the chartered plane?" Dave asked.

"I did it," she said. "Next week is my last week with the firm. I was thinking of taking some time off and maybe a vacation somewhere, but knew you wouldn't be able to go so soon after the new job. I surely didn't want to go away without you, so I decided to make it several short trips, a week end here a week end there, you know, whatever. That led me to looking into airline reservations and the nightmare of getting somewhere with adequate time to spend relaxing. In about every case, the travel time would take up almost as much time as being there. This works great, it's a bit more expensive, but I think it is going to be a lot of fun."

"Did you finish the project you were working on early? I thought it would be next week before you were done?" Dave asked.

"No, it will be done next week," she said. "But I asked the account for a value report and when it came in, I just couldn't wait."

"Good report?" he asked.

She smiled, looked around the plane then back at him and said. "The three million I was thinking, seems the firm has done far better than I thought. My share is over seven million."

"Let's have a drink," he said.

The airport on Key West was only about two miles east along A1A from the Waldorf where Jan had reserved a room for the week end. It only took them a few minutes in the rental car that had been waiting for them on the tarmac, one of the neat features traveling on a private jet can provide. They said good bye and thank you to pilot Doug as Jeremy was loading their bags into the car. Doug confirmed that the plane would be back to pick them up on Sunday afternoon. *What a way to travel thought Dave.*

It was only about eleven when they got checked into the hotel and up into their room.

"Amazing," Dave said. "Only about six hours ago I was walking out of my office with no idea I would be here now. You say it's your vacation, but somehow I feel like I'm the one getting the treat. You are fabulous. I guess that's why I love you."

"I think you're fabulous, too. We're going to have a great weekend."

The next morning found them sitting together on the second floor balcony of their room wondering why they lived where it got cold. It was before ten in the morning and already seventy degrees in mid-November. They had eaten breakfast and were drinking coffee enjoying the weather and the company. Below them was a white sand beach and the blue green of the ocean.

"What shall we do today?" Dave asked.

"Not much more than we are right now," Jan said. "I may want to see how cold that water is and spend some time laying on the beach. I'd like to have lunch at some touristy place and dinner at some other touristy place. But, most of all, I want to be with you every minute."

"I'm up for all of that. Have I told you lately that I love you?"

"Not since you found out how rich I am," she said.

"Being rich doesn't mean I love you less, necessarily."

"Well, I'm glad," she said, "I love you, too."

They spent the day having fun in the sun. On the beach, walking the shops and being tourists was the order of the day. They had the coconut crusted shrimp platter in a bar that was supposed to be the hang out of Hemingway for lunch. Dinner was a fabulous blacken prime rib and lobster at a pricey restaurant on a boardwalk.

The next day was more of the same, a leisurely day in the sun. Jan had the plane scheduled for a four o'clock departure which should get them back to Springfield by about eight thirty. After a lunch of the most tender scallops ever eaten they were on the beach enjoying the sun.

"Jan," Dave turned to her, "what are you going to do after next week?"

"I'm still working on that. I'm trying hard not to rush into anything. I have always had my life planned out in advance, right down to the last detail. Now I don't have a plan and I find it both exciting and unsettling."

"You'll be fine," he said. "You're the most together person I have ever met. You will be great at anything you decide to do."

"What do you think I should do?"

"What are the options?" he asked.

"Start my own firm, be a sole proprietor, join a legal aid group and do pro-bono, or be a bum and do nothing," she answered.

"You really want me to tell you what you should do?"

"Yes, I really want you to tell me what I should do," she said.

"You should marry me."

Her head jerked around toward him. She looked at him for a moment, a tear came to her eye, "Yes, I should," she said and kissed him.

They stared at each other for a long time.

"Wow," she said. "You have a way of changing the subject. I have to admit I have wondered when you were going to ask, but I wasn't expecting it now."

"So you had already decided to say yes, when I got around to asking," he observed.

"Of course. I have never been happier in my entire life than I've been since I met you. Even though it hasn't really been that long, you've become the main focus of my life. To tell the truth, I never thought I would trust anyone to be in such control of me. So, yes, and I will also say if you didn't ask soon, I would've asked you."

"I think you should plan our next weekend getaway for Las Vegas," Dave said, "we can get married there."

"Nope," she said, "marrying me is going to be long drawn out and expensive. It could take a year of planning, a girl can't just jump into something like marriage without proper celebration. Yes, that's it, my next full time job will be planning my wedding. That's much better than starting a law firm. Oh boy, I love you."

"Aw, well," Dave stammered. "Okay, whatever you want. But a year?"

"Got cha," she laughed. "I'm kidding. I do want a ceremony, if you don't mind. Nothing elaborate, just a nice church wedding where my mom can be mother of the bride, and I can walk up an aisle with you standing up front watching. That's what I would like. Would that be okay?"

"Of course," Dave said, "but now that you've said yes, I don't think I can wait a year."

"Maybe a month, two at the most," she smiled.

Later, as they headed for the airport to take their private jet back to Springfield, their relationship had changed as they both expected it eventually would. And they were both comfortable with the change.

Dave looked out the plane window at the patchwork of landscape far below. He wondered if he had been as happy when Joyce agreed to marry him. He didn't think he had been but that was a long time ago. *It goes back to the old adage, if I knew then what I know now,* he thought. *But what do I know now that I didn't know then* he asked himself? *I guess I know more what is important about a relationship now than I did then,* he thought. *Or maybe I'm able to better recognize that for a relationship to truly work it takes an attitude of giving to the other than taking.*

He looked across the aisle at Jan. *Naw, that's all bull shit,* he thought to himself, *she the most beautiful woman in the world, she's intelligent, she has a perfect personality, she has a perfect body, she likes me, and she is rich. Who wouldn't be happy?*

Chapter 16

Dave brought doughnuts for the Tuesday morning meeting. Dan brought doughnuts for the Tuesday morning meeting. Bob brought doughnuts for the Tuesday morning meeting.

"We need to coordinate better," Dave said as he put the third dozen down on table next to the coffee pot.

"Let's see how many are left over," Dan said. "We are all cops, you know."

Sheriff Allen and Pete from Arlington County were the first visitors to arrive. Closely following them was Josh Trubaldi and Paul Adams from the State Police. All four had coffee and doughnuts, plural on the doughnuts as in more than one. Sheriff Alexander from Williams poured coffee for himself when he came in but passed on the doughnuts. George Hoffman from DEA was the last to arrive. He got coffee, he carried what was left of one of the boxes of doughnuts over to the conference table with him.

After every one was introduced and some general chit chat Dave began the meeting.

"The reason we're here today is to talk about the murder of Sheriff Lewis," Dave said. "The initial opinion of the investigators was suicide. Further developments have proven that analysis to be flawed. We now believe with reasonable certainty that it was indeed murder. Arlington County is in agreement with this assessment. The prime suspects at this point are the members of the drug gang that operate out of a farm in Williams County. I felt it to be important that we meet together as a group to share information and discuss possible courses of action to help determine if the gang members were the culprits and how we can prove it if so. With that introduction, I will now turn it over to George Hoffman of DEA."

"Thank you, Sheriff," George began. "DEA has a full plate to say the least. Therefore, the Williams County operation has not been getting a high level of attention. We dedicate our manpower to the areas that have the highest probability of producing results. We have been aware of what is going on there for some time, but our efforts so far have not produced the results required to justify a higher level of effort. Therefore, our efforts have not been extensive.

Here's what we know. The farm is owned by an offshore company which is suspected to be under the control of one Antonio Carlos Martinez, a Mexican drug lord. The farm is operated by Juan Martinez, who is thought to be Antonio's nephew, but this is not confirmed. The farm is run as a legitimate corn and soybean operation. There are about ten to fifteen farm workers at any given time, all of whom seem to have Mexican heritage. We believe the farm is being used regularly as a distribution facility for the Martinez to disperse drugs around the mid-west and east coast. To date we have executed four warranted searches of the farm when we had reason to believe drugs were present. No illegal substances were found in any of those searches. Drugs we suspect to be heading to the farm, have been found during routine traffic stops in the vicinity but we have had no proof of their destination or direct connection to the farm operation."

"Thanks, George," Dave said, "Josh, what does the State Police have to add?"

"The State Police has had no direct involvement in the investigation of this gang or the stated facility other than as support to the DEA during the warranted searches," said Capt. Trubaldi.

"Okay, thanks Josh, Sheriff Alexander?" Dave asked.

"The Williams County Sheriff's Department has participated with DEA in the afore mentioned warranted searches," Rob said. "We have also kept a close watch on the supposed drug farm, by way of stake outs on many occasions, following and monitoring the activities of suspected members of the organization, and investigation of banking activities. Although we have uncovered some unusual activity, nothing has been uncovered of an illegal nature."

"What sort of unusual activity?" Dave asked.

"They have an unusual way of paying bills," Rob answered. "They pay mostly in cash. For example, the electric bill is paid at the electric company office every month in person and in cash. When they go grocery shopping they pay in cash. When property taxes are due they pay in person and in cash. They buy gas with cash. Any expenses billed to the farm are payed in cash. Payments are made in person by one of their people. As far as we can tell they pay cash for everything, we have not observed any member using a credit card or paying by check. As I said, unusual but not illegal."

"How do you know this?" Dave asked.

"From tailing a member of the gang on several occasions while he made the payment rounds," Rob said. "Then we asked around and got confirmation from everyone who has dealings with them in the county.

"Was it the same member each time?"

"Yes, seems to be a monthly routine," Rob said.

"Okay, thanks Rob, Sheriff Allen?"

Sheriff Allen nodded at Pete Jacobs.

"Okay," Pete said, "What we know is that Sheriff Lewis was killed in his lake house in Arlington County sometime between early evening on Saturday and ten a.m. on Monday the last weekend in July. The ME believes the actual time of death to be between noon and midnight on Saturday. The weapon suspected was a twelve gauge shotgun found near the body. There was no sign of a struggle and we suspect the sheriff may have been asleep as the assailant approached. The doors were unlocked and there was no evidence of forced entry. All finger prints lifted at the scene have been identified as people who had reason to be there. None of the identified finger prints, other than the Sheriff, were in the cabin that week end as far as we know. There was no other unusual physical evidence found at the scene."

"Are you sure it was murder?" Capt. Trubaldi asked.

"Yes," answered Pete. "No doubt, but we are not yet ready to make the details public, I hope you understand."

"Leaving something for the killer to tell you, huh?" Trubaldi said.

"Something like that," Pete answered.

"Now," Dave said, "Here's what we have to add. Sheriff Lewis was the one who implemented the routine traffic stops which allowed for the confiscation of the drugs that were suspected to be heading for the drug farm. He accomplished this by means of safety check road blocks on the direct route from the interstate to the drug farm. Two shipments were confiscated before they realized what was going on and they blamed Sheriff Lewis for the disruption in the flow and profit lost. In order to avoid the road blocks they were required to reroute the shipments costing them time, money and exposure. We suspect they wanted Sheriff Lewis out of the way so that they could resume the direct transport route without fear of additional road blocks. On the weekend of Sheriff Lewis' death at approximately 1:30 on Sunday morning one of the vehicles leased by the drug farm was stopped by State Police traveling south on the interstate about thirty miles south of his cabin. The driver, one Alfonso Ramirez, was issued a warning for eleven miles over the speed limit. There were two unidentified passengers in the car. Thus we have motive and gang members in the vicinity at the time of the crime. What we do not have is proof they were at the cabin and committed the crime."

"Alfonso Ramirez is definitely one of the gang," Sheriff Alexander said. "We have reason to believe that he is near the top of the organization. He has often been seen entering or leaving the home of the gang leader."

"Does anyone have any idea where we go from here?" Dave asked.

The room was quiet as they all thought about the issue at hand.

"We have no probable cause to even ask questions," Rob said. "I could haul Ramirez in on some petty stop sign roll through or something, but they would have their lawyer there before the squad was in park. We couldn't get a thing."

"What about their lawyer," Dave said, "do they always use the same one?"

"Yes, and he's a good one," Rob said. "He from one of the firms up in Springfield. He must have a big retainer because he is always Johnny-on –the-spot when any of them is involved in anything."

"Got a name?"

"Yeah, I think it's Sherwood."

"Randy Sherwood?"

"Could be," Rob said thoughtfully. "Don't know that I've heard a first name. You know him?"

"Yes, I do."

"George," Dave asked. "You got anything?"

"Not really," George said. "We can feed any info we get from the Antonio Martinez side of things but I don't see DEA being very helpful in the murder investigation. Of course if we can help we will be glad to, within manpower limits."

"Josh," Dave asked. "Got anything?"

"Sorry, Dave," Josh said. "I think we need more to concretely tie it together. Although I can see where you are and how you got there. I don't see enough to get to an indictment, or even and arrest warrant. It's going to take more than we have and I don't see where it will, or even may, come from."

Dave looked at Dan and exhaled deeply. Dan took the hint.

"I'm not so sure," Dan said. "What we have before us is a puzzle that no one has seen all of the pieces until now. I think we each need to take some time to process what we know, and have known for some time, along with what we have learned new here today. There may be something that has changed or been enhanced is a way that may not be obvious until we have had time to digest it. I suggest we sit on it for the rest of the week and see if something comes up. Let's all plan to contact Dave on Monday with an idea or two each that we think is a reasonable next step."

"I think that is an excellent idea, Dan," spoke up Sheriff Rob. "I agree."

"I also agree," added Josh.

Everyone was in agreement with Dan's directive. The meeting broke up and they headed their separate ways. Bob picked up the empty donut boxes on his way out of the conference room.

Dan and Bob came into Dave's office and sat after the meeting.

"What do you think?" Dave asked.

"Sheriff Alexander seemed interested in helping," Dan observed. "He offered information that we didn't know."

"But that doesn't mean much," Bob said. "I still don't trust him. He could be on the phone right now letting them know what we talked about. Will was not one to jump to conclusions and if he thought Rob was on the take, to me that says there is something there."

"I'm thinking we may want to get more information on the bill paying in cash of the gang," Dave said. "Maybe if they are paying the Sheriff off they are doing it in cash on a monthly basis as well. If Will was tailing the guy making the payoff maybe he saw something that got him killed."

"Are you thinking we set up our own surveillance in Williams County without their knowledge?" Dan asked.

"I think that's what Will was doing," Dave said. "But I'm not suggesting the Lincoln County Sheriff's Department should set up in

Williams County. But, if three private citizens begin to watch a certain farm on their own time, unofficially, there may be some information to be gained."

"I think I might give some thought to how three private citizens may go about doing something like that in an organized manner," Dan said.

"I think that's a good idea," Bob said.

"Let's talk after you have had some time to think about it," Dave said. "I think the gang gets their cars from that luxury import dealer, Delagoto Motors, out by the interstate here in Springfield, I'll take a run out there and talk with them. I wonder if they pay cash there."

Dave always liked car dealerships, so going into a high end car dealership seemed to some degree like playing hooky from work, but someone needed to do it. As he walked into the showroom a dark blue seven series BMW caught his eye. He had to look it over. As he was doing just that a salesman asked if he needed help or would like a test drive?

"No test drive. I would like to see the manager," he said. "Official business."

The salesman nodded and disappeared through a doorway at the rear of the showroom. A few seconds later the salesman opened the door he had gone through, held it open and motioned for Dave to follow him. He took Dave to a large office in the rear. As Dave entered, a fifties something man in a bright white shirt and yellow tie got up from his desk and extended his hand.

"I'm Winston Delagoto. How can I help you?" he said.

"I'm Sheriff Harbinger," Dave said. "I'd like to ask you some questions about a customer."

"I'll help all I can. Please have a seat," Delagoto said as he sat back down.

"There is a farming operation just across the county line into Williams County on their CR 18 that has purchased several cars from your dealership," Dave said. "Do you know who I am talking about?"

"Yes, of course," Delagoto said. "The Martinez Agricultural Corporation. But they don't buy the cars. They are all leased."

"Leased," Dave said. "Do they lease through you or some leasing agency?"

"They lease directly from us," he answered. "All are three year leases."

"Do they pay on a monthly basis?" Dave asked.

"Oh, yes, and they are always quite prompt with payment," he said. "Very good customers."

"What day of the month is the payment due?" Dave asked.

"I believe they pay on the fifteenth," said Delagoto.

"Do they make the monthly payments in person in cash?" Dave asked.

Delagoto hesitated before answering, but said. "Yes, they do."

"How many cars do are they currently leasing from you?"

"I think about fifteen, if memory serves."

"About how much per car per month?" asked Dave.

"These are all high end cars," Delagoto said. "They lease on average for about eight hundred and fifty dollars."

"If my math is right, that's near nine thousand dollars per month," Dave said.

"I think they are paying us more like eleven thousand per month," Delagoto said. "There are a couple of high priced cars in there."

"In cash?" Dave asked.

"Yes, sir," Delagoto said.

"What denomination of currency?" asked Dave.

"Hundred dollar bills banded together with one hundred in a bundle," he answered. "Sheriff it's not illegal to pay in cash."

"No it's not," Dave said. "Did you ever ask why they pay in cash?"

"Not our business," Delagoto said, "maybe you should ask them."

Dave thanked him for his time and left. As he pulled out of the lot, he wondered why a business would not flag such large cash payments to the authorities. Could they continue to take in that much money without thinking of the possibility of money laundering or some criminal activity?

When Dave got back to his office, he dialed his phone.

"Sheriff Harbinger," Jim Keller answered. "What can I do for you?"

"Official business today, Jim," Dave said. "Does Delagoto Motors bank with you?"

"Yes they do. Winston is an old friend and good contributor as well I might add," Jim answered.

"Can you tell me if they often make large cash deposits?" Dave asked.

"I can't say without a warrant, Sheriff," he said, "but we've never had to inform the feds of a large cash deposit from any of our customers, if that helps."

"What size cash deposit requires you to inform the feds?" Dave asked.

"Over ten thousand in a month," Jim said.

"Okay, thanks, Jim," Dave said and signed off.

Chapter 17

After work that night Dave and Jan had a date to visit a local jewelry store. There was the task of selecting the perfect ring for the perfect ring finger. Dave was planning to agree with anything she wanted and help her make her decision by voicing only his agreement with what she wanted. He wondered how well that would work.

The store they selected was in the middle of downtown Springfield. It had been in the same location as long as Dave could remember. It had always been there. The owner was a grey haired man, named James, who had worked the store when his dad had owned it. It was a local business with a long history in the city. *A good place to shop,* thought Dave.

"Price range?" James asked Dave.

"Let's say under twenty thousand," Dave said.

"No," Jan cut in, "I would not be comfortable wearing something on my finger that cost more than a Buick. I want it to be beautiful but I don't want to feel devastated if I should lose it. I appreciate you wanting to give me something like that, but I don't want it. Five thousand or less is great for me."

So the process began with a nod from James and shrug from Dave. The final turned out to be a very nice two carat oval shaped diamond solitaire with a matching wedding band that would encircle it with smaller stones. The total cost rang up at just over thirteen thousand eight hundred. Higher that she had intended, but Jan was pleased and so was Dave.

Jan had agreed to the shopping trip because she just couldn't wait to pick out the rings, but she had a tremendously busy week ahead of her and begged Dave to let the evening end there.

"Learned something today you may find interesting," Dave said as he drove her home.

"Do tell."

"Seems your friend Randy Sherwood is the number one counsel for drug farm guys."

"No. Where'd you hear that?" she asked puzzled.

"Sheriff Alexander from Williams County says Randy is there before the cruiser cools off anytime one of them is brought in."

"I've never seen any billing records for something like that."

"Could he be billing some corporate account, or under some other name?"

"I don't know what it would be. Sounds like he is doing something the other partners don't know about. At least this one, anyway. But it doesn't matter, I'm out of there," she said. "I need to be sure I have met all of my obligations to the best of my ability. I only have three days to make sure and get it done. I think I'll make it, but I need to be sure. I'll see you Friday night, and I will be free."

"Okay," Dave said as they kissed good night at her front door, "get 'em tiger."

They had told Chris about the engagement when they arrived home from Key West on Sunday night. Then a phone call to D in Arizona brought both boys into the loop. D and Chris were both very happy for their dad, although Dave sensed they did felt a bit of a loss from the realization that mom and dad would not be getting back together. D asked for as much notice as possible so that he could make sure to be able to make it home for the wedding.

Jan had called her mom and dad Sunday night as well. Shock may best describe her mother's initial response, but soon followed all of the motherly questions about her soon to be son-in-law. Yes, mom and dad would be at the wedding no matter when it was scheduled.

As Dave was pulling into his driveway his cell phone rang. *Joyce* the caller ID said.

"Hello," Dave said.

"Dave, it's Joyce," she said. "Chris told me you are marrying my attorney."

"She hasn't been your attorney since our divorce was final."

"Kind of young for you isn't she?" Joyce said sarcastically.

"No. I think she's perfect for me. Besides our age difference is less than ten years."

"Ten years is a lot. You should have more decency. Think of your sons, for God's sake."

"Think of my sons? Wait a minute," Dave said sharply. "You had a boyfriend while we were still married who is, what, thirty years older and you have the gaul to tell me to think of my sons. I…"

The line clicked off as she hung up on him.

"That went well," he said out loud sitting in his car in the garage.

The next day Dan, Bob and Dave plotted out a plan to see if they could find out who the drug guys were paying off, if anyone. From Sheriff Will's notes Dave thought Will was picking up the currier by waiting in a roadside rest spot on the state highway just a few hundred feet from the county road near the farm. It appeared that the currier left the farm, or maybe Juan's house, in the mid-afternoon on delivery days. Their plan was that they would use civilian cars and communicate by way of hand held radio on a tactical channel. They knew the car leases were paid on the fifteenth and Will's notes seem to indicate that to be the bill paying day for all the operation. They suspected there would be different people paying the Jackson bills than the one in Springfield. They would put the plan into effect on the fifteenth, which was about two weeks away.

Jan had asked Dave to help her carry stuff out of her office on Friday night. So, at four forty-five he walked down the hall toward her office. She was in her doorway talking with a tall very well dressed older man standing in the hallway, as Dave approached.

As he got near them Jan turned to him and said, "Dave, I would like you to meet Randy Sherwood. Randy this is Sheriff Harbinger."

"Hello, Dave," Randy said, extending his hand. "Nice to finally meet you."

"You too," Dave said shaking hands. "I've heard so much about you."

"Yes, I bet you have." Turning back to Jan, Randy said, "well good bye Jan, don't be a stranger." Randy turned and walked away. Jan gave Dave a quick kiss and pulled him into her office. On the desk and on the floor were boxes, about ten of them.

"You see why I wanted you to bring the pickup," she said looking at the boxes.

"It's no big deal. Just a few boxes."

"Wait till you lift some of them. I got this to help," she said pointing at a hand truck along the wall.

"We'll be out of here in no time," Dave said. He picked up the first box and set it down on the hand truck. "Are you done here? Can we go now?"

"All done and ready to go."

Dave was able to get four boxes on the hand truck per trip, so in about ten minutes all of the boxes were out of her office and loaded into his pickup parked in a loading zone at the back of the building. He walked with her and she introduced him as she said good bye to a few people. The last order of business for her was to hand a set of keys to a man she introduced as the office manager. Then out the back door they went. They climbed into the truck and kissed. The kiss may have lasted for half an hour. Dave wasn't sure, but he loved every minute of it. They were in no hurry.

"Where do you want to go for dinner?" he asked when their lips finally parted.

"It's a special occasion," she said. "Where do we go on special occasions?"

"Olive Garden," he said. "Where we had our first date."

"You are such a romantic. I love you."

"Shall we drop the boxes off first?" he asked.

"Yeah, let's do that," she said. "Get the work done before we get into the evening."

"How do you feel?" Dave asked as he drove.

"That's a good question," she answered. "I have been so busy all this week getting everything done and making sure that I hadn't missed anything that I haven't had a single second to think. Right now I just feel an unbelievable amount of relief that this week is over. I'm sure over the next couple of hours things will begin to sink in. But right now the two things on my mind are the week is over and I'm finally with you."

"Me too," he said. "I have missed you. It's been almost a whole three days."

"I'm kind of surprised either one of us survived," she said.

"Me too."

"Any new developments in the case?" she asked.

"Not really. We've decided to run some surveillance on the drug gang to see if we can find out what Will discovered that maybe got him killed. I'm not confident about it, but at least we're doing something."

"You don't think stopping the road blocks was enough motivation for the killing?" she asked.

"I don't know, maybe. I think there was something else going on. I just don't know if it was related or not, but I want to find out. But enough about work, tonight is a celebration of the new Jan. Let's get to it."

They went to dinner and a movie. The entire evening was spent without another single conversation about work of any kind. It was all about them and their future together. There was some wedding planning, but only about the possible date and size of the guest list. The rest they would deal with later. Tonight was just them and they kept it that way. It was a time for romance, touching, kissing and being together. They enjoyed it immensely.

Dave sat in a booth at Cliff's at just before 9 on Monday night. A Sheriff's car pulled into the lot and Sergeant Brian Rodriguez got out and walked inside. He slipped into the booth across from Dave. Brian ordered coffee and Dave ordered a strawberry shake.

"Got your note," Brian said. "What's up?"

"Brian, do you think Bobby would lie to us?"

"Wouldn't put it past him, if he thought he needed to. You still thinking his gang may have been involved in Will's death?"

"Still working that angle, yes. But don't you think Bobby would just not answer a question he didn't want to answer, rather than lie?" Dave asked.

"Maybe," Brian said thoughtfully. "But I guess I really don't know. He's in with a bad crowd and knows they are bad. And as much as I hate to admit it, that has to make him bad too. You know he's kin and I would like to think that means something to him. But I don't know."

"Yeah," Dave said. They sat quietly for a few moments. Dave sucked on the straw of his shake and Brian sipped coffee.

"He came to see me after you asked him to, you know?" Dave said.

"No, I didn't," Brian said. "But I figured he had. He apparently didn't give you the answers you were expecting."

"Yes, as a matter of fact he answered exactly how I expected," Dave said. "I'm just wondering if I got the truth, or if the answers I got were lies. And, I'm wondering if there is more to ask?"

"I have no idea."

"Yeah, I understand," Dave said. "Could you ask Bobby about a guy by the name of Alfonso Ramirez? See what he will tell you about him."

"Okay," Brian said as he wrote the name down in his note book, "I'll give him a call right now." He took out his cell phone and pulled up his call list. He punched the call button and put the phone to his ear.

"Hey, Bobby, it's Brian," he said into the phone after a few seconds. "Can you talk?"

He listened then said, "Good. Say bro, I wonder what you can tell me about a guy by the name of Alfonso Ramirez, do you know him?"

He listened for several seconds before saying, "No, the name just came up and Dave was wondering if he might be one of your guys."

More listening, then he said, "Okay, thanks, appreciate it, see ya."

He hung up and said to Dave, "he says they don't come any worse, a real bad dude. Came up from Mexico about a year ago and has been the main muscle since he got here. He says he is real tight with Juan."

"Thanks," Dave said.

"Who is he?" Brian asked.

"He was in the area of the cabin the night Will died," Dave said. "We don't know any more than that."

"I guess I'd better get back on the street," Brian said.

"Okay, thanks," Dave said. "Coffee's on me."

Chapter 18

The first thing in the morning on the fifteenth of the month Dave, Dan and Bob pulled out of the parking lot heading for Williams County. They were each in their own personal vehicle and each had a hand held radio. Dave was in the farm pickup truck, a five year old GMC half ton. Dan was in his wife's year old Toyota Camry and Bob was in his Buick Lacrosse. All three vehicles were somewhat non-descript and would blend in well.

After about thirty minutes they were in position. Dan was sitting in the roadside rest area that Will had used. Bob was about five miles up the state highway off to the north on a county road. Dave was situated near the Jackson city limit. The plan was that Dan would follow the suspect when he came onto the highway. As they approached Bob's position Dan would drop back and let Bob fall in behind. Dave would pick up the tail as he entered the city. From there on they would blend into city traffic and keep the tail up as needed. They settled in and waited.

Dave had the morning paper with him. He read the entire paper and completed the Sudoku puzzle. He was working on the crossword, more for something to do than an expectation of getting it done, when he heard Dan say on the radio. "Black Mercedes heading east into town, plate ending in 487. Driver and one passenger."

Dave looked at his watch, 9:48 a.m. About five minutes later he heard Bob say, "Got him. Still heading into town."

In less than ten minutes Dave saw a black Mercedes heading toward him. He pulled out of the gas station and convenience store lot where he had been sitting. He fell in behind the Mercedes with plate ending in 487. They were in a highly commercial part of the city of Jackson. Traffic was moderate but there was no issues keeping the Mercedes in sight without being obvious. Only about a quarter mile after Dave began the tail, the Mercedes turned into a large parking lot on the edge of a strip mall. Dave drove on by and Dan, who had been several cars behind Dave, pulled into the lot behind the Mercedes.

Dave entered the strip mall from the other end and was heading back in the other direction when the radio spoke to him in Dan's voice. "They parked and both subjects are heading into the supermarket at the west end. The driver is in a red golf shirt and the passenger is in a blue button up."

"I've got them too," Bob's voice came back.

"Okay," Dave said, "looks like we wait again."

He found a parking spot where he could see the exit door of the super market far across the strip mall. Dan and Bob also took up spots a good distance from each other. After about forty minutes, the two suspects came out of the store pushing a fully loaded shopping cart. As they approached the Mercedes the trunk popped open and they loaded their groceries into the trunk. They got into the car and drove toward the parking lot exit. Dan fell in behind them as Dave and Bob held back. The Mercedes turned west back toward the farm.

"Appears to not be our guy," Dave said into the radio. "You guys follow them back to make sure, I'm going to stop in at talk with the Sheriff."

"10-4," was the response back from the radio.

Dave drove to the sheriff's department. He found Sheriff Alexander in his office.

"Rob, I was in town on another matter and thought I would stop by," Dave said after they had talked about general stuff for a while. "I have some information you may find helpful."

"Oh," Sheriff Alexander asked. "What kind of information?"

"I talked with the car dealership in Springfield where the drug farm gets their cars," he said. "They lease the cars and pay the monthly lease payments in cash."

"That follows the pattern," Rob said.

"They pay in one hundred dollar bills, bundled," Dave continued. "A thousand per bundle. The lease payment is eleven thousand per month."

"That's a lot of cash," Rob said.

"Makes me think the warranted searches should have turned up a stash of cash," Dave said. Wouldn't you think?"

"I'll bet our old buddy Juan keeps the money at his place," Rob said thoughtfully.

"There has never been a search of his place?" Dave asked.

"No," Rob said. "We have never believed he'd have the drugs at his place. They do the repackaging in one of the barns at the farm, we think."

"Just thinking he may have a lot of cash at his house is not much to get a warrant," Dave said.

"Unless we thought there were drugs there too," Rob agreed.

"Well I thought you should know what we found," Dave said. "I need to run."

"Okay," Rob said. "Thanks for stopping by."

As Dave walked to his car he noted the clock on the bank sign down the street said it was 12:10. He pulled out of the lot, but instead of heading north back toward Springfield he went toward the south side of Jackson and the home of Sheriff Will and Aunt Dar's daughter Megan.

Megan and Major John Barker of the Williams County Sheriff's Department lived in a very nice neighborhood on the south side of

Jackson. Their home was about ten years old and Dave guessed it to be about three thousand square feet. It had a nice lawn and an end loaded three car garage. Megan did not work, so Dave expected she would be home in the middle of the day. He parked the pickup on the driveway, walked up to the front door and pushed the button on the door frame. The sound of Big Ben chimes could be heard from inside the house. Several seconds later the door opened.

"Uncle Dave," said the tall young man with the athletic build.

"Hi, Corey. Is your mom home."

"Come on in," Corey said as he pushed the door open and stepped back. "She's home, but is not feeling well today. I've got some coffee made, why don't you come in and have a cup. I'll see if she feels like coming down."

Dave followed Corey into the kitchen. Dave sat on a bar stool at the island with the cup of coffee Corey had poured him. Corey went upstairs. After several minutes Corey came back into the kitchen.

"She's sorry to make you wait but is glad you stopped by. She needs a few minutes before she can come down."

"No problem. I was in town on business and thought I would stop by. I should have called. Sorry about your grandfather."

"Thanks. It was a shock," Corey said. "He came to my ballgame the week before. My car was on the fritz and mom asked him to bring me home. She had something going that afternoon."

"Oh, so he brought you home after the game," Dave said.

"Yeah, and he stayed for dinner. It was a great time," Corey said.

"I know how much he enjoyed watching you play ball. He always talked about your games afterward."

"Yeah. Hhe was planning to go to my away game that Saturday with dad and I. But he canceled out. I wish he had gone with us." Corey got quiet, before smiling widely. "Oh, congratulations Sheriff."

"Thanks," Dave said. "What are you up to these days?"

"School and sports is mostly it, I came home for lunch today," Corey said looking down at his watch. "Oh, damn, I've got to run. Mom will be down in a few."

He grabbed a jacket off a hook by a door and went out. Dave heard a garage door opener whine and soon heard a car start and back out of the garage. He heard the door opener do its thing again. In the opposite direction he assumed, and then there was quiet. He drank some more coffee.

In a few minutes Megan came into the kitchen looking like she didn't feel well at all. She looked very much like a younger version of her mother. Her hair was darker and she was a bit taller but other than that they looked strikingly similar. She was wearing a light blue pullover and dark blue slacks. She had on Nike cross trainers with no socks. Even though her blue eyes were glassy, she was still quite attractive.

"Dave," she said. "It's so good to see you. Congratulations "

"Thanks," Dave said. "Sorry to impose, but I was in town and thought I'd take the opportunity to stop by before heading back up to Springfield. You look like you feel bad."

"Oh, it's just the flu, I think. I actually feel a little better now that the drugs have had time to do their job."

"How are you getting along, otherwise?"

"I'm fine," she said. "Dad was here the week before it happened, and we had some time to talk. We had not been getting on very well, but we were able to clear some things up. I was feeling better after that. Mom told me you think he was murdered. I'm not sure how to deal with that. Do you have any idea who?"

"No, we're working some leads but nothing concrete,"

"What kind of leads, what does that mean?"

"I can't really go into detail," Dave said. "We think we may know who was involved and are working right now to try and prove it."

"Have you arrested someone?"

"No, we're not that far along."

"Have you brought anyone in for questioning?" she persisted.

"No, we're looking at the suspects," Dave said.

"Suspects," she said thoughtfully. "So more than one guy."

"We don't know," Dave said. "Has John said anything about what Sheriff Alexander had told him?"

"No, John doesn't talk about his work with me," she said.

"Well, I really need to run. I wanted to stop by and see how you were doing. Hope you feel better soon."

"Thanks for stopping by," she said as they hugged briefly at the front door.

Dave drove back to Springfield with a sense that he had learned something, but he didn't know what it was. Watching some farm workers get groceries didn't seem to be earth shaking out front, but maybe there was something to be learned that would be clear later. Or was it that Will and Megan had worked something out. He didn't know what. It just felt like there was something in this trip, somewhere.

When Dave got back to his office another transcribed report lay on his desk. He picked it up and started reading. This particular tape was older than the previous ones. As he read through it he realized that there was going to be no information related to the current investigation. He read the entire report carefully anyway, just to be sure. When he finished he walked out to Cheryl's desk.

"That was the last tape, huh?" he said as more statement than question.

"Yes," she said. The way I figure it there is only one more tape missing. Chronologically the tapes cover the entire six month period before he was killed except for the last two days. I'm thinking he put a new tape in the recorder on Thursday night or Friday of the weekend he was killed. That tape is probably still in the machine, where ever it is."

"Yep, I think you're right," Dave said. "I would certainly like to find it."

Dave asked Dan and Bob into his office. He closed the door when they came in.

"Did we learn anything?" Dave asked.

"We learned where they shop for groceries," Dan said. "At least some of the time."

"The car was one we already had on our list," Bob said. "They went right back to the farm. So, I don't think we learned squat."

"If they only make the payoffs once a month and it's always on the fifteenth, we've lost a whole month," Dave said frustrated. "What else do we have that we could work on?"

"Just that Alfonso character," Dan said. "We could put some pressure on him, see if we can get him to make a mistake or crack, or something."

"I don't think he'll give us anything," Dave said thoughtfully. "I think he is probably a tough character that won't crack. But maybe he'll give us something without knowing he has. Let's go out tomorrow and talk with him."

"You going to tell Williams County?" Bob asked.

"Yes, I am," Dave said. "I don't want to make Rob think I don't trust him."

"Do you, trust him that is?" Dan asked.

"No," Dave said. "I don't think I do, but let's keep that in here."

Dan and Bob nodded as they got up and left Dave's office. Dave picked up the phone and dialed Williams County.

"Hey, Dave," Rob answered. "What's up?"

"Rob, we're thinking about going out to the drug farm tomorrow to talk with Alfonso Ramirez. Would you have a problem with that?"

"Of course not, Dave," Rob said. "What you want to talk with him about."

"Just to see if he'll give us a reason he was in the area of the cabin when the Sheriff was killed," Dave said. "See if we can stir things a bit to get a reaction that might lead us somewhere."

"I see," Rob said. "Would you like me to go along?"

"You are welcome to, if you like," Dave said. "But not necessary I wouldn't think."

"To tell you the truth, I wouldn't mind getting my face in front of those guys," Rob said. "Let them know we're working together, you know."

"Okay with me," Dave said. "Do you want to meet us at the county line at nine in the morning?"

"Sure thing. See you then," Rob said and hung up.

The next morning at just before nine, Dave, Dan and Bob approached the county line in Dave's unmarked black Dodge Charger. Although the car was unmarked and had regular license plates on it, any observant person would recognize it as a police car. It had blue and red lights in the grill, the back window, in the side rear windows and at the top of the windshield. There were also antennae on the rear quarter panel and in the middle of the trunk lid.

At the county line they saw a similar brown Charger coming toward them. Dave stopped in the center of the road and hit the power window switch. There was no other traffic on the road. Rob pulled up next to them with his window down as well.

"What're we doing?" Rob asked.

"Just pulling up to the front door and asking to talk with him," Dave said.

"Okay, I'm right behind you."

Dave moved ahead, Rob pulled off onto the right side shoulder, did a three point turn and dropped in behind Dave's squad. They drove the quarter mile or so to the farm and pulled up the long lane to the main building. At one point that building had been the farm house, but it had been added onto so many times that it now looked more like a commercial or industrial building. It faced east and had a large parking area on the south side. There were six luxury cars in the lot all facing north toward the building. Dave stopped his car facing west immediately behind the last three cars, blocking them in. Rob stopped behind Dave which effectively blocked all six of the cars. Dan checked the license number he had in his note book from the State Police traffic stop. He pointed at the car with the same number.

"He's here," Dan said.

The four uniformed officers exited the vehicles and walked up to what they assessed to be the main entrance. There was a doorbell, Dave rang it.

Chapter 19

After about a minute the door opened. Standing in the middle of the doorway was a huge dark haired man who appeared to be in his late twenties. He was about six foot five and maybe three hundred pounds. He had a dark complexion and wore a baggy Chicago Bulls shirt and gym shorts. He didn't say a word. He stared down at the four officers.

"We'd like to talk with Alfonso Ramirez, please," Dave said.

The big guy did not change in anyway, no change in facial expression, no body language, no head nod, nothing. He gave no recognition that he had heard what Dave had said. He closed the door.

"What was that about?" Bob asked. "Is he getting him, does he speak English?"

"I don't know," Dave said. "Let's give it a couple of minutes, see what happens."

They stood on the porch by the door and waited. After about a minute the door opened again, this time by a smaller dark haired man. He was about five foot nine inches tall, maybe one seventy pounds and had a scar on his left cheek. He was wearing a white short sleeved golf shirt, jeans and cowboy boots.

"What?" he said with less of an accent than Dave was expecting.

"Are you Alfonso Ramirez?"

"Why?" was the response.

"We are following up on a traffic stop on the interstate a few months ago. You were issued a warning for speeding by the State Police," Dave gave the date and time.

"So?" he questioned.

"Why were you there at that time of night?" Dave asked.

"None of your business," he said bluntly.

"Look, you can answer our questions here of we can take you in for questioning."

"On what charge?" was the reply.

"Don't need a charge, non-cooperation with law officers in performance of their duties is enough to run you in," Dave said.

He didn't say anything for a minute, then nodded.

"Was picking my cousin up from the airport," he said.

"You are Alfonso Ramirez?" Dave asked.

"Yes."

"Where was your cousin coming from and what time did the flight get in?" Dave asked.

"Dallas, don't remember the time."

"Your cousin was in the car with you?"

"Yeah."

"What is your cousin's name?" Dave asked.

"Pablo."

"Pablo Ramirez?"

"Yeah."

"Anyone else in the car?"

"My brother, Tony," Alfonso said. "What's this all about?"

"Just routine. Thanks for your cooperation," Dave said. They headed back to the cars.

"What do you think?" Rob asked.

"We'll see if his story checks out," Dave said. "It's something to look into."

"Yeah, I guess," Rob said. "Well, let me know what you find out, or if you need anything from me."

"Okay, thanks," Dave said and they got in their cars and headed back in opposite directions.

"I can check with the airlines to see when flights from Dallas came in that night, and if Pablo Ramirez was on it," Dan said as they pulled away. "He seemed to be giving it to us straight."

"Yeah," Dave said, "seemed to be. But at the same time how would we know if he wasn't? Let's run those names through DEA, see if they have anything on them. We may as well ask other agencies too."

"Good idea," Dan said. "I'll get on that, too."

Dave and Jan had planned to go out at lunch that day to do a little car shopping. She picked Dave up at his office at noon. She had been driving the farm pickup since turning the Corvette back into the firm.

As they pulled away from the station with Jan still at the wheel, Dave asked where they were going.

"Remember that dark blue BMW you told me about," Jan said. "I think we should go look at it."

"I thought you wanted another Corvette," Dave said.

"Hey, I'm getting married. I need to think more of a family car."

"Oh," Dave said. Well, that's a nice car, but it's awfully expensive."

"I know," Jan said. "And just because I can spend that kind of money doesn't mean I should. But looking doesn't hurt."

Soon they pulled into Delagoto Motors. The blue BMW was still in the showroom. Jan sat in it and took in the black leather interior and the feel of the luxury inside. Of course the salesman was right with them.

"Would you like a test drive," the salesman, Steve, asked. "We have another one that you can drive with about the same equipment as this one. It will save us from taking this one out of the showroom."

"Okay, let's do that," Jan said.

After the test drive Jan told the salesman that she and Dave would talk it over. He took her contact information so that he could continue to "be available to answer any questions."

They went to a burger joint for lunch. With burgers, fries and drinks on the table in front of them they got into serious discussion.

"So, what do you think of that car?" Dave asked.

"I love it. It has near the performance I'm used to in a luxury package. That is a very fine machine."

"Yes, it is," Dave said. "But more money than anyone should spend on a car that wouldn't look right in my collection."

"Give it about fifty years and it would fit perfectly in the collection," Jan said.

"True, except we don't have any foreign cars," Dave said. "All American."

"Maybe it's time to change that."

"Are you seriously considering buying that car?"

"No," Jan said, "I'm considering leasing it. I have decided to set up a small firm or a solo practice to keep up my law license. I'll take cases that make sense to me. I'll need some expenses to offset my income. A car lease is a direct write off and a higher end car actually works out cheaper in the long run due to the residual value of the car."

"What kind of cases?" Dave asked.

"Well, things like your divorce, for example," she answered. "Dealing with family issues and things that help people. I really don't want to be in criminal or the high dollar corporate contract stuff I've spent most of my time doing. I want to be a family law specialist now."

"I think that sounds great," Dave said. "Have you begun the process of sitting up your new firm?"

"As a matter of fact I have," she said. "I filed the incorporation papers with the state this morning. You are looking at the President of the Harbinger Law Office, P.C."

"Wow, I like the name of your firm," Dave said.

"Technically, it's not my firm, yet," Jan said. "Jan Harbinger doesn't exist yet. She is the owner. If you don't marry me the Harbinger Law Office will never be legally able to take a client."

"So you don't plan to take any clients until after the wedding," Dave said.

"Right, between now and then, I'm just a bum. Doing nothing for the good of society."

"Well, I guess I should get to marrying you," Dave smiled.

"What are you doing on the thirteenth of next month?"

"I think that must be the day I'm marrying you," he said.

"Good answer," she smiled brightly.

After they finished their lunch she drove Dave back to the station.

"If you're okay with it, I think I'll go back and lease that car," Jan said as he was getting out of the pickup.

"I'm good with it," Dave said. "Will it be in the name of the new firm?"

"Yep," she said. "When I set up the corporation I made Jan Thomas a signatory as well as Jan Harbinger, so it's all legal."

"Okay, have fun," Dave said.

"I'll meet you at your house after work," Jan said. "We can go out to dinner and we may need to go get this truck off of Delagoto's lot."

"Whatever, you gorgeous hunk of woman," Dave said as he kissed her and got out.

He watched her drive away, once again in complete amazement at how lucky he was.

As Dave walked into the station, Dan was standing by Cheryl's desk. He followed Dave into his office and shut the door.

"It seems our new friend Pablo Ramirez has a reputation," Dan said.

"Oh, how so?"

"DEA tells me that the authorities in Guadalajara, Mexico have him pegged as a possible hit man and enforcer for the cartel," Dan said. "He is suspected as being the perpetrator of as many as ten cartel assassinations. He came in from Dallas on the evening in question after entering the country via Mexicana Airlines from Guadalajara on a tourist visa. The airline tells me his flight from Dallas arrived at eight twenty seven PM."

"That's about five hours before the traffic stop," Dave thought out loud.

"Right. Let's figure it takes an hour to get out of the airport. Maybe thirty minutes to get to where the State Police pulled them over. The question becomes: where were our three friends during the missing three and a half hours?"

"Yes," Dave said. "But the more important question is: how do we find out where they were and what they were doing?"

Dan left his office and Dave sat thinking. Was there anyway to find out if the three had been in the area of Uncle Will's cabin. It would have been dark, so even if someone had seen their car, there would have been nothing remarkable about it that would have caused someone to notice or remember it. Also since it was dark, any recognition of the occupants would be impossible. The other thing running against the odds was the area around the cabin is so sparsely populated that hardly anyone is ever out around there at that time of night.

Dave dialed his phone.

"Hey, boss, what's up?" the voice on the other end of the line said.

"Got a new development in the case, Brian," Dave said. "I need to talk with Bobby again."

"Okay, want me to ask him to come for a visit?"

"I think we should try to be low key, do you think he may be at your folk's place this weekend?" Dave asked. "Maybe you and I could go meet with him while he is there."

"Don't know, let me check, I'll get right back to you."

Dave hung up the phone and continued to think about a way to tie the three drug gang members to Uncle Will's murder. After about three minutes his phone rang.

"Yeah, Mom says he told her he would be over for Sunday dinner this weekend," Brian said. "Do you want to come for a good meal."

"No, I won't come for dinner. I would like to come by after, what time do you think?"

"I'd say about one thirty. You're not planning to drive the squad, are you?"

"No, got a new ride to show you," Dave said.

"Is it older than me?" Brian asked.

"No. See you Sunday."

When Dave got home that evening there was a dark blue BMW parked in his driveway. When he walked into the kitchen from the garage, Jan was sitting at the kitchen table with an owner's manual.

"It's going to take me some time to get used to this "I Drive" system," she said looking up at him with a smile. "It's sort of like a computer mouse on the console that controls all of the functions of the sound system, heat and air conditioning, navigation, and who knows what else."

"I think you'll be able to figure it out," Dave said as he kissed her. "So, everything go well at the dealership?"

"They were very nice," Jan said. "And helpful with all the details. I got it on a four year lease. The car has a five year warranty that covers just about everything, so we should have no other expense for the entire term of the lease."

"Monthly payment?"

"Too much," Jan said, "but it will be less than I expect to make in my law business. So I don't really care. If I break even I'm fine with it. You want to go for a ride, buy me dinner and pick up a truck?"

"You going to let me drive?" Dave asked.

"Nope, not today, I always heard that you don't have to share the first day you get something," she said as they walked out the door.

They went to dinner at a steak house that Dave liked. He had blackened prime rib and she had a rib eye. After dinner they headed for Delogoto's lot to pick up the truck Jan had left sitting in a visitors parking place out front. True to her word, she drove the BMW, but Dave got to drive the pickup.

Sunday morning Dave picked up Jan and they went to church together. After services they went out to lunch at local owned restaurant where Dave liked the liver and onions. Not one of Jan's favorite meals but she liked their baked perch so all was well. After lunch Dave took Jan home, he left his car there and borrowed the BMW to head over to talk with Bobby.

He got to Brian's folk's at 1:40. Brian's car was on the driveway along with Bobby's BMW. Dave parked on the street in front of the house, walked up and rang the bell. Brian opened the door.

"Come on in," Brian said. "I told mom and dad that you be stopping by."

Dave went inside and spent the next forty minutes visiting with Brian's family. Eventually he asked Brian and Bobby if they would like to see Jan's new car. The three of them went outside. It was chilly so they sat in the new car and talked. Dave and Bobby in the front and Brian in the back.

"Nice car," Brian said. "Like yours, huh Bobby."

"Your chick got this?" Bobby asked Dave. "Better hang onto her."

"We're getting married next month," Dave said to Bobby. "You're invited to the wedding."

"Thanks, bro," Bobby said, "but too dangerous fo me ta be there."

"I understand," Dave said.

"Ya got somethin else come up,huh?" Bobby started the conversation.

"Yes," Dave said, "I didn't want to hang you out with your associates."

"Preciate, that," Bobby said, "what's sup?"

"Tell me about Pablo Ramirez."

"Bad dude," Bobby said, "don't know much, cept he come up here to get way from somethin down south. Hangs with Alfonso and pretty tight with Juan. Bout all I know."

"Is he still here?"

"Yeah, saw em las week," Bobby said.

"He came into town on the night we think Sheriff Will died. We know when his plane got in and that he was near the cabin three hours later. We don't know what he did during that three hours," Dave said.

Bobby looked down at the floor board of the car. He was quiet for several seconds, then inhaled and exhaled deeply.

"Bobby," Dave said slowly. "This could be big. I hate to put you on the spot but I know you thought highly of the sheriff. I don't think you would have wanted anything to happen to him like this. I know what it could mean if your gang finds out you even know me, but I'm not sure I have anywhere else to turn. If you could help, it would mean a lot to Brian and me. We just want to know what happened to Sheriff Will and bring someone to justice. I think you would want that too."

"I didn't have nothin to do with it," Bobby said.

"I never thought you did," Dave said softly.

"Dunno if ma homies did it?" Bobby said. "Dunno I could find out they did. Don't like it, if they did."

Bobby sat silent Dave and Brian waited while he thought things through. He looked at Dave with anger in his eyes, Dave wasn't sure at whom.

"Let ya know," Bobby said and got out of the car.

Brian got out of the car too. Dave sat and watched as Brian caught up with Bobby just before he got to his car. Brian said something, they hugged and Bobby got in his car, backed out of the driveway and drove away.

Chapter 20

Dave drove back to Jan's house, all the way thinking about what Bobby might be getting into. If he pushed too hard the gang may suspect something and take action. The action they would take would most likely mean Bobby would never be seen or heard from again. *He must know that*, Dave thought. If he knows that he will be careful to not raise suspicions. Dave was seriously worried that he may have pushed too hard and put his friend into harms way. He hoped not, but hope was not making him feel any better right now.

"You look worried," Jan said as he walked in the door and kissed her hello.

"I am," he said, then proceeded to tell her all that had happened.

"I see," she said when he had finished. "Are you sure they are the ones who did it?"

"I don't have any other reasonable alternatives," he answered.

"For the sake of argument," she said. "If they didn't do it, would Bobby be in trouble with them?"

"No," Dave answered, "I don't think so, unless he pushed hard enough to raise suspicions."

"Do you think he would push hard enough?" Jan asked.

"No, I don't," Dave answered, "Bobby is looking for conformation that his buddies didn't do it. If he finds out they did, he will high tail it out of there and tell us what he found. I think if he gets the slightest reasonable impression that they didn't, he will drop it and tell me to take a hike."

"Okay, so you have a chance of getting conformation of your belief that they did it, or having a friend think you are a heel." Jan concluded.

"That's about it," Dave said.

"I understand you're worried, but sounds to me like it has a good chance of working out," Jan said, "I think it's a good plan and worth the risk."

"I hope so," Dave sighed.

"Let's watch football, eat summer sausage, cheese and crackers," she said.

"I get the recliner," Dave said.

"Okay, but so do I," she said with a sly grin.

Midway through Monday morning Dan and Bob came into Dave's office, closed the door behind them and sat down.

"We've been talking about the investigation," Dan said. "And neither of us has the foggiest idea of where to go from here."

Bob shook his head as a strange form of agreement.

"If the drug gang did this, they've left us no apparent leads and we have no idea where to look for non-apparent leads."

"Maybe we need to get back up to the scene and knock on some doors and look under some rocks to see what we can come up with," Dave said.

"Couldn't hurt," Dan said.

Bob nodded.

"Dan what's your schedule look like today?" Dave said, "Bob you can hold things down here."

"Give me a few minutes to shuffle a few thing around," Dan said. "Be ready to go in half an hour."

"Good," Dave said, "I'll call Sam Allen and see if we can get an assist."

"Dave Harbinger," Dave said into his phone when Sheriff Sam Allen answered, "Dan Muscovy and I plan to come up there today and look over the crime scene again to see if we can shake something lose. We may also want to knock on some doors and talk to people to see if something comes out. Can you give us some local support?"

"Sure, Dave, hold on a second," was Sam's reply, and the phone went to elevator type music. After a few seconds Sam came back on the line, "Pete Jacobs will meet you at the scene in ninety minuets, does that work?"

"Sure does. Thanks, Sam."

A little over an hour and a half later, Dave and Dan pulled up at Sheriff Will's cabin at the lake, as Dave had always known it. Now it needed a different designation, Dave thought to himself as they pulled up. Pete's Arlington County Sheriff's van was parked in front of the cabin. The cabin looked the same as the last time Dave had been there except that Uncle Will's pickup truck was gone from where it had been parked in front of the garage. They walked up to the door.

"Hi, guys," Pete said as they walked in, he was sitting on the couch watching a day time game show. He turned the TV off.

"Hello, Pete, how have you been?" Dave asked.

"I've been good," Pete answered. "Been busy, but good, you?"

"Would like to get a break on this case," Dave said, "any ideas?"

"Not really," Pete said. "We've not spent too much time on it. Sheriff said you guys seemed to have more to go on than us, so we've been waiting to see what you come up with."

"Yeah, we've been working it pretty hard," Dan said. "But just don't seem to have the evidence to take us any further in our investigation. Dave thought a trip up here may give us some direction, or some idea of a direction."

"Well," Pete said. "We released the scene to the family but asked them to keep it as much the same as possible. They said they have no intention to do anything with the place in the short term so it appears they have touched very little. The truck is gone, and the kitchen has had perishables removed, but that's about it, as far as I can tell."

Dan sat down on the other couch as Pete talked. Dave wandered over to the reloading desk where Sheriff Will had been when he was shot. The desk chair had been righted and put back under the desk where it belonged. Dave pulled it out and sat down. The top of the desk was the same as he remembered from the day of the murder. The shot gun was gone and Dave thought some of the ammunition that had been there was gone, but other than that the same. Dave absent mindedly looked over the desk top attempting to pick up on some detail that might have been missed. He saw the book off to the right that it was suspected he had been reading. He looked at the book, it was turned to page three forty seven. He closed the book and read the title: "Dealing With Addiction At Home." The book was written by Dr. Victor Simalaski.

"Why would Sheriff Lewis be reading about addiction?" Dave asked out loud.

"What?" Dan asked, turning toward Dave.

"This book, on the desk is titled "Dealing With Addiction At Home," Dave answered. "Why do you think he was reading this?"

"Maybe some background on the drug business?" Pete said.

"Maybe," Dave said. "But would you need to know why people do drugs to better catch the guys in the distribution business?"

"I was not aware of any drug use in his family," Dan said. "Were you?"

"No," Dave answered, "but I think I'll ask his wife about it. Maybe she can tell me something I don't know."

"Good idea," Dan said.

"Pete, your report said you talked with the neighboring properties owners, did you do those interviews yourself?" Dave asked.

"Most of them," Pete said. "A few were done by one of my guys."

"Did you reach all of the nearby properties?"

"Yep," Pete said. "Everyone within about a quarter mile."

"Let's go talk with some people in town, and maybe some out toward the interstate," Dave said.

"Okay," Pete said, "but this long after the murder, what are you expecting to learn? Hardly anyone remembers last week end let alone six months ago."

"You are probably right," Dave said, "but I don't know what else to do, and I've got to do something, at least feel like I'm doing something."

"I understand," Pete said, "let's start in town."

They all got into Dave's car and drove into the small town of Grifford. They went to Pop's service station first. Pop was sitting in the window just inside the small office. They got of the car and walked inside.

"Hi, guys," Pop said as they walked in, "you're the officers looking into Will Lewis' death, right?"

"Right," Dave answered, "we talked a few months back. At that time you told us that you had not seen any foreign luxury cars go up toward the Lewis' cabin that day. Do you remember what time you closed up that Saturday?"

"Can't say for sure," Pop scratched his chin. "But I always try to get out of here by six."

"I don't think we asked you when the last time you saw Sheriff Lewis, do you remember?" Dave asked.

"Yeah, I remember," Pop said. "It was that Saturday morning. He stopped in and filled up his truck. He had just got into town, he said. Said he had planned to come up on Friday, but something came up so he waited till Saturday morning to come up."

"Did he often stop in here?" Dan asked.

"Oh, yeah," Pop answered. "Hardly ever went by without stopping to chat for a minute at least. Liked to keep up on what was going on around town and stopped in here to make sure he didn't miss anything."

"He say anything else that you remember?" Dave asked.

"Said he needed some time to himself and planned to just be alone for the week end," Pop said.

"So that was in the morning, and you didn't see him again after that?" Dave asked.

"Nope, never saw him again," Pop answered.

"And you didn't see any luxury cars go up toward the cabin that day?" Dan asked.

"I remember you asking before about foreign luxury cars," he said.

"Yes, just confirming," Dan said.

"Nope," Pop said.

"You open on Sunday?" Pete asked.

"Nope," Pop said.

"Okay, Pop, thanks," Dave said, and they left.

"You know, it might make sense to talk with the gas station out by the interstate," Pete said. "That would be the only gas around after Pop closes. And, maybe they watch as close as he does."

"No reason not to talk with them," Dave said as he headed the car in the direction of the interstate.

Chapter 21

Just before the interstate there were several interstate related
businesses, a couple of fast food places, a cut rate chain motel, and a
Shell gas station. Dave turned the car into the gas station. There were
two cars in the station, both at pumps with owners pumping gas into the
tanks. They got out and went inside. There was no one in the station
except the attendant who appeared to be in his mid to late twenties. He
was tall and had red hair, cut medium length on the top and buzzed on
the sides. His Shell shirt said, "Red" on his right chest.

"Afternoon," Red said as the three of them walked in the door.

Dave introduced himself, Dan and Pete.

"We are investigating a death at a cabin on the lake back in the
summer," Dave began, "and would like to ask a few questions."

"Oh, yeah, Will Lewis?" Red asked.

"Yes," Dave said, "did you know him."

"Knew who he was," Red said, "I've lived here all my life, you get to
know who's around and what goes on."

"Do you always work the same shift?" Dave asked.

"Mostly, straight days for me now, I've got seniority on the other guys,
so I get to pick first," he said.

"So you were on day shift when Will Lewis died?" Dave asked.

"No, that was vacation time. We shift around to a twelve hour schedule when someone goes on vacation," Red said, "I was on the night shift then, seven p.m. to seven a.m."

"Any chance you remember a Hispanic looking guy or guys coming in that Saturday night late, like mid-night or later. They would have been driving a black Mercedes?" Dave asked.

"I remember a guy in a black Mercedes with a nasty scar on his left cheek," Red said. "He came in sometime back in the summer, it stands out to me because he paid for gas with a hundred dollar bill. He peeled it off a roll of hundreds that looked to be eight or ten deep. Maybe I can check the video to see if it was that weekend."

"Video?" asked Dave.

"Yeah, we have cameras on the pump islands we use to catch the drive offs," Red said. "Video is recorded on thumb drives, one will last about a month. We change the drives when they fill up on a rotation basis keeping the newest one on file and replacing it with the oldest. It's almost a year before we get back around to rerecord one. If you know the date, I can go look to see if we have it."

Dave gave him the date of the Saturday night they suspect Uncle Will was killed. Red disappeared through a door behind his counter. The search took several minutes, and additional time because Red needed to come out often to take care of customers who came in the door while he was looking. But, eventually he came out with a small box with the date in question penciled on a label on the front. He opened the box and pulled out a thumb drive and put it under the counter.

"If you guys want to come around here, I can plug this in the player and you can watch the monitor here behind the counter," Red said.

Dave, Dan and Pete walked around behind the counter and saw a small TV monitor down below the counter angled up toward them. Next to the monitor was a small computer like device that had the thumb drive plugged into it. There was a key pad with buttons labeled like a tape recorder. Red hit the play button. There were six cameras that covered the pump islands from different directions. All of the gas pumps were visible. The screen was divided into six boxes with a camera shot in each box.

"The drive covers a long time so we will need to fast forward awhile to get to the right date." Red said as he hit the fast forward key. "These numbers are the date and time." He pointed to the upper left corner of the screen where numbers were tallying up. When the numbers got to twenty four hundred on the date in question he hit the play button and the video appeared.

"There is a motion sensor at each pump. It only records if there is movement by the pumps. The recording is jumpy because it records in one second blips several times a minute. We can slow it down or stop it any where we want." Red explained.

They watched the monitor, Alfonso Ramirez had been stopped fifteen miles south of here at 1:37 on Sunday morning. If he went straight onto the interstate, he should be on the recording somewhere around one fifteen to one twenty. When they got to one ten they all watched closely. When the recording got to one forty they had seen no Mercedes at any of the pumps.

"Can it play backwards?" Dave asked.

"Yep," Red said, "we just hit the play button with the direction set in the reverse direction."

"Let's go back to midnight and run it backwards from there," Dave said.

Red hit the fast rewind button and ran the recording back until the counter said twenty four hundred. Then he hit the play button with the tape direction still in reverse. They watched. The recording was even more very jerky because Red was playing it at a higher speed, but it was not hard to make out vehicles and people stopping and filling up their cars.

"Stop the tape," Dave, Dan and Pete all shouted almost at the same instance.

Red hit the freeze button. On the screen in the lower middle box was a Mercedes with a man pumping gas, Dan checked his note book and confirmed that the license plate matched the plate issued to Alfonso Ramirez. They looked at the time stamp in the corner, it read twenty three zero three, or 11:03 p.m.

"Let's go forward now," Dave said. "Regular speed."

Red hit the buttons and the recording started moving slower than before. They could see more of what was going on. They watched as Alfonso filled his car, went out of camera probably to pay, came back in a couple of minutes later and got into the car. The car sat there for a long time then moved out of the station heading east, away from the interstate and out of the camera frame.

"How can I get a copy of that?" Dave asked.

"No problem," Red said, "I can copy it to a file and email it to you."

"We need to put that thumb drive into evidence," Pete said, "I'll give you a receipt and it will be returned at some point in time, but I can't say when."

"Shouldn't be a problem," Red said. "We won't miss it."

Pete took a written statement from Red detailing all that had happened and confirming the source of the video recording. Red signed the statement and Dave and Dan witnessed it.

Dave, Dan and Pete visited each of the other businesses in that area. None had any information. Those that were normally open in the middle of the night were staffed by people who were not present during the day. Each said they would pass the request for information along to those who would have been present. Pete left his contact information so that he could be contacted.

They drove back into the town and talked with some other people, but no one had any information of value. They drove back out to the cabin so that Pete could pick up his vehicle.

"Thanks for your time, Pete," Dave said.

"No problem, it is officially our case anyway," Pete said. "Glad to help."

"Well," Dan said, "we can now prove that they were in the area, and headed in this direction with plenty of time to do the deed. But, we still can't put them at the scene. We still have work to do, but at least it's something."

"Okay, Pete," Dave said, "we'll keep in touch, thanks again." Dave and Dan headed back to Springfield.

"So, what now?" Dave asked Dan as they got up to speed on the interstate and settled in for the drive. "Do you think we could bring the three drug guys in for questioning, interview them separately and see if their stories check out?"

"If we bring them in, they will probably lawyer up and not answer any questions," Dan said, "that would get us nowhere and let them know that we are on to them. Maybe we can just go out and talk with them individually and see if they will tell us anything."

"The trick to that may be finding them," Dave said. "Alfonso shouldn't be much of a problem because we know his car, but we have nothing on the other two. We may get a line on Alfonso's brother, but I'm thinking Pablo will not be easy to run into. We have no way to trace where he might be at any given time. Do you agree?"

"Yes, it may not be possible to get all three without a warrant," Dan said. "And I don't see us having enough solid evidence right now to get one."

"That's a problem all right," Dave said. "They certainly seem to be good suspects, but we just don't have anything that ties them directly to the scene, let alone to the murder."

"The best way to cover your tracks is to not make any," Dan said. "Appears they didn't make any."

"Maybe not," Dave said. "But at least we have the video of them near the scene. It's something, I'm just not sure if it tells us they did it or if it's just a coincidence."

"I think they did it," Dan said. "But proving it is something entirely different."

They drove on in silence for sometime. Each with his thoughts, attempting to figure out a next move that would provide them with information or evidence to prove what they thought they knew.

"So, the wedding day approaches," Dan finally broke the silence and changed the subject.

"Yes, only a few weeks away," Dave said.

"Are you actively involved in the planning?" Dan asked.

"Not really, Jan has the time and is totally immersed in the whole planning thing," Dave said. "She's like a kid in a candy store, and I just let her go. After all, it's her day. I'm just a participant."

"Maybe, but it wouldn't be much without your participation," Dan chuckled.

"Are you coming?" Dave asked.

"Of course, wouldn't miss it. Julie sent the reply card in the day it arrived," Dan said.

"Good," Dave said.

"Are you taking time off after?" Dan asked.

"Not right away," Dave answered. "Jan will be moving out to my place by the farm that week. She is also trying to get her condo ready to put on the market. Her folks will be in town the week of the wedding and her sister. So with all of that we thought it would be better to stay around here than to tie the knot and take off for parts unknown. We are planning a long weekend in Vegas a few weeks after the wedding."

When Dave got back into his office there was a message that Jim Keller had called and asked for a return call. Dave pick up the phone and dialed.

"Sheriff," Jim's voice said soon after it stopped ringing. "Thanks for returning my call."

"No problem, Jim, what can I do for you?" Dave asked.

"I know you must be busy, so I'll get right to the point," Jim said, "I got a call a little while ago that Judge Andrew Wallisinski had a heart attack and died."

"Oh, no," Dave said, "I'm sorry to hear that, Jim, that's terrible."

"Yes, it is," Jim said, "a real loss to the county. He was a fine man and a brilliant jurist."

"Be sure to give my condolences to his family," Dave said.

"I will, thanks," Jim said. "But as heartless as this may seem, I need to find a suitable replacement for his seat on the bench in a hurry to get them on the March ballot. Which is why I called you, I need a phone number for Jan. I would very much like to talk with her to get input on possible candidates."

"Sure, Jim, I'm sure she would be glad to help in anyway she can," Dave said and he gave Jim her cell number.

"Thanks, Dave," Jim said, "I appreciate your help."

That evening Dave and Jan went to dinner at Red Lobster. Jan had shrimp tortellini and Dave had the popcorn shrimp. While they were eating the conversation turned to the events of the day.

"Jim Keller called me today to get your phone number," Dave said.

"Yes, he called me," Jan said.

"Did you have any recommendations for him about who might be a good replacement for Judge Wallisinski?" Dave asked.

"He told you he wanted to talk with me about my recommendations?" she asked.

"Yes, why, what did he want?" Dave was puzzeled.

"He just asked if I would be interested in running," she said.

"Really. That didn't come up when he and I talked," Dave said.

"Well, that's all he wanted to know," she said.

"And?" he asked.

"I said yes," she smiled and fluttered her eyelids. "How'd you like to be married to a judge?"

Chapter 22

Christmas was on Monday this year. As it approached Dave thought about what it would be like to spend the rest of his Christmases with Jan. It was a prospect that seemed very appealing to him. He realized that he had fallen for her in a way that he never felt was possible. Celebrating Christmas with her, and then the wedding just three weeks later was going to be wonderful. And now, on top of that, they had another election to plan for. But he still dwelled on what could be done to get the evidence needed to bring Sheriff Will's killers to justice. He was aware that a large percentage of cases this old are never solved. But he was not about to let that happen to this one. At least he hoped not.

Dave and Jan were sitting in the family room of his, soon to be their, house. They had spent this particular Saturday afternoon moving furniture, boxes and things from Jan's condo. She wanted to get as much as possible out of the condo. Only leaving furniture and a few paintings that made it look appealing to potential buyers. It would be going on the market on Monday. The bad news was there was normally not a lot of interest in house hunting over the holidays. The good news was inventory of properties on the market was low. Competition for the buyers that were out there was less. Jan's condo was in a very good location, relatively new, priced right and in tip top condition. A fast sale was anticipated.

"What are you thinking about so hard?" Jan asked.

"The case," Dave answered. "It appears the gang did it. But I can't find evidence to prove it. Do you think it would be a good idea to bring the three guys we suspect in and question them?"

"No," Jan said. "If they did it, and you bring them in, they'll most likely call a lawyer who'll instruct them to not answer any questions. You won't get anything out of them. You have no evidence to charge them, so you'll have to let them go. They would walk. And knowing that you are on to them, they'll probably keep right on walking out of the country."

"So you think that as long as they think we don't know, or suspect them, they'll stick around. If they think we're on to them they'll take off."

"I couldn't see them hanging around facing a murder rap," she said.

"I don't know; they're making a bunch of money. That might hold them here," Dave countered. "But, I guess you're right about tipping them off until we have enough to hold them."

Before Dave finished speaking his cell phone rang. He looked at the caller I.D. It was Brian.

"Hey, Buddy. What's up?" Dave said into the phone.

"I just got a call from Bobby. He says we're all wet. His guys had nothing to do with it."

"What did he base that on?" Dave asked.

"He didn't say. But he sounded convinced," Brian said.

"Was he lying?"

"Could be. But I got the feeling you got to him in the car that day. I don't know."

"Okay," Dave said. "I'd like to talk with him. Next time you hear from him see if he'll come see me again?"

"Sure, Sheriff. I expect he'll be at Mom's for Christmas. I'll ask him then." Brian signed off.

"Well," Dave said to Jan. "That was Brian. Bobby says his guys didn't do it."

"That could be why they're still around," Jan said.

"Or he could be lying."

"Yes, there is that," Jan said thoughtfully. "So, what're you going to do, Sheriff?"

"Go out for dinner, think about Christmas and our wedding," he answered.

The Christmas holiday season was busy but enjoyable for Dave. Dave and Jan went to Cincinnati on the Friday before Christmas and came back on Sunday, Christmas eve. Dave got to meet Jan's parents and her sister's family who were also there. On the way back home Jan told him that they all thought he was great. They told her they were pleased.

D was home for the Holidays and was staying at Joyce's. Chris was over there a lot, but the boys also spent a good deal of time with Dave and Jan. D had not spent a lot of time with Jan up till now. So he took the opportunity to get to know her better. He told Dave he liked her a lot. D said he was sad that his mom and Dave were no longer together. But he wanted Dave to be happy and he saw Jan doing that. All in all it was a good Christmas. Dave was satisfied, except for the case that still lingered on: the open item of proving who killed Sheriff Will.

Late on Christmas night, Dave got a text from Brian. *At your place. Around 6 on Wednesday* was all it said. Bobby would meet Dave at the farm.

After getting home from work on Wednesday, Dave changed and headed for the farm. The winter weather was colder than normal with a temperature near the zero mark. Dave turned the heat on in the shop. It wouldn't be up to room temp, but it would be warm enough to work in. He had a tractor that was just about to reach the one hundred hour mark since the last oil change. He walked to the other barn and moved the tractor over into the shop. He started to change oil while he waited on Bobby. He had the oil drained out and was installing the new oil filter when he heard a vehicle pull to a stop outside. A few seconds later Bobby opened the door to the shop area and walked in.

"Hey, bro," Bobby said. "Need some help?"

"Always can use help," Dave answered. "You want to wheel that oil drum over here for me?"

"Sure." Bobby said as he walked over to the side of the shop. He wheeled the 55 gallon drum of oil toward the tractor Dave was working on. "Don't seem too full, they enough in here?"

"Should be," Dave said. "We get about eight oil changes out of a drum. That one's only done six, so I think there's enough."

"How much this thing hold?"

"A little over twenty six quarts."

"How often ya change?" Bobby asked.

"About a hundred hours of operation. Sometimes more if we're working them hard, but never more than one fifty. These engines like to be up to temperature. In the middle of planting or harvest we can go longer because they're up to temperature for long periods of time without cooling off."

Dave put the hose from the pump on the barrel in the oil fill tube of the engine. He set the dial on the flow meter to zero and began pumping oil from the barrel into the engine.

"Brian tells me you're convinced your guys didn't kill Sheriff Will," Dave said as he pumped. "What makes you so sure?"

"Know ma dudes," Bobby said. "Aint no vibes comin down, Homeboys did nothin."

"You didn't ask them, did you?"

"No, man, ain't crazy," Bobby said. "Don't wan no one lookin at me? Jus feel em out, ya know. Ain't feelin no vibes, man, they cool."

"Would you know?"

"Yeah, bro, I'd know," Bobby looked into Dave eyes. "Jus like I'd know if you jivin, man."

The flow meter clicked over six gallons, Dave stopped pumping and checked the dip stick.

"Still a couple of more quarts," he said as he began to pump again. "Bobby, since we last talked, I saw a video of your buddy Alfonso getting gas near the cabin. I watched him drive out of the gas station and head in the direction of the cabin. The time stamp on the video puts it about the time we think the Sheriff was killed. We think Alfonso's brother and his cousin Pablo were in the car with him. When we talked last, I thought they were in the area. Now I know they were. I don't know if they did it, but it sure looks to me like they did. I wanted you to know what I know. Now you do."

"Well, I see why you'd think they did it," Bobby said. "But, don't matter, none. Still no vibes, bro. They'd be vibes, if'n they done it."

Dave stopped pumping and checked the dip stick again, it was full. He put the pump back in the holder on the side of the barrel. As Dave was wiping his hands Bobby rolled the barrel back across the shop to where it had been.

"Thanks for the help," Dave said.

"Any time, bro," Bobby said. "Somethin change'll let ya know."

Bobby left. Dave moved the tractor back to it's spot in the other barn. He continued to think about how convinced Bobby was as he locked up the barn and the shop and headed back home. It didn't make sense to him that Bobby would be so adamant in his belief without knowing. He didn't understand how he could rely so much on feelings and faith in his ability to read people. He also didn't want to believe that Bobby was leading him on or lying to him. He wanted to believe in Bobby, he really did, *but could he?*

Soon after getting into his office on Wednesday morning Dave called Aunt Dar and invited her to lunch. She said she would be delighted and would meet him at the cafe down the street from her condo at noon. She was there when Dave arrived and had taken a table by the window in front of the cafe. Dave sat across from her. After the usual pleasantries and ordering lunch Dave wanted to get to the reason he had asked her to meet him.

"How have you been?" he asked.

"Okay," she said. "How about you?"

"I've been fine, a lot going on over the holidays. And getting ready for the wedding."

"Yes, the wedding, you must be on pins and needles over that."

"I am. But I'm also still working on Uncle Will's case. I was up at the cabin a few weeks ago and noticed that someone had been up there."

"Yes. About a month ago Megan asked about the pickup," she said. "She and John wondered if they might have it to give to Corey. They've been having a lot of trouble with Corey's old car and felt it would be a way to get rid of it. I said it sounded like a good idea to me. The sheriff up there had said it was okay to go in but to let them know if we were going to do anything. So I called and they said it would be okay. John and I went up and he got the truck. I cleaned out the refrigerator and threw out spoiled stuff and the like. It was the first I'd been back up there. I didn't enjoy it. It brought it all back."

Dave thought he saw a tear come to her eye.

"Didn't Megan and Corey go up as well?" Dave asked.

"No. Corey was off doing what ever he does and Megan said she didn't want to go. So just John and I went."

"I noticed a book on the sheriff's desk that I wanted to ask you about," Dave said cautiously. "It was titled "Dealing with Addiction at Home."

Dave paused and waited for a reaction. She was looking down at the table top and didn't look up. He thought he could see her inhale deeply and shudder slightly.

"Yes," she said without looking up. "I had some problems with prescription drugs after my surgery a few years back. It concerned him greatly and he got that book as a way to help. I'm all better now."

She looked up at him slowly, with a tear in her eye.

Chapter 23

The wedding day arrived. The guests in the church were looking at Dave who was standing at the front looking back out at them. He waited for the music to switch to the old favorite, Here Comes the Bride. His brother, Kent, stood next to him in a rented tux. At the back of the church stood, in rented tuxes, stood his ushers D and Chris. Jan's sister, Joy, was her maid of honor. Joy was walking slowly up the long aisle toward them. Dave had not seen Jan since dinner last night and even though it was an early afternoon wedding he was anxious to just see her. Let alone see her in a wedding dress walking up to become his wife. His heart was pounding. He felt like teenager on his first date.

Kent leaned over and whispered in his ear. "As your best man, and your only brother, I feel it my duty to tell you it is now time to run. Or suffer the consequences."

"Thanks for the tip," Dave whispered back as Jan stepped into the doorway at the end of the aisle. "But those consequences look awfully good to me."

She walked up the aisle toward him on the arm of her father. She had on a beautiful white dress that Dave hardly noticed. He was fixated on her beautiful face and the beaming smile so wide he couldn't take his eye off her.

The ceremony was brief, as they had designed it. The reception was also short as receptions go with only about two hours total time. Dave and Jan talked briefly with all of the guests. They fed each other bites of three tiered, vanilla cake decorated with real flowers. They opened some wedding gifts and called themselves married.

By five they were ready to change and get ready to go out for dinner. They headed home. Jan's parents were staying with them and Chris. Dinner was planned at the best steak house in Springfield. They were joined by Dave's brother and sister, Jan' sister and all of their families. It was a great opportunity for the new family to be together for the first time as family. Dave and Jan had a great time. Jan's dad picked the check and after several rounds of doctors and lawyer bickering, finally won the argument.

Jan's parents headed for home on Sunday, as did her sister and Dave's brother. D was going back to school. Chris had volunteered to take D to the airport. This turned into excitement when Jan offered to let him take the BMW. So at two o'clock on Sunday afternoon, Dave and Jan were alone. Relaxing together in what was now their home. He was sitting on the sofa in the family room with her snuggled up against his chest.

"Um, I like this," she said. "This is probably going to sound strange, but until this minute, I don't think I ever really understood what happiness was. I thought I was happy with my career and the success I achieved at such a young age. But now I know I wasn't. I was so wrong to think I was. This is what happiness is and I have you to thank. I love you and am scared to death to think about what may have happened to me if you hadn't come along."

They kissed passionately for a long time.

"I think you may misjudge yourself," he said. "If you hadn't spent those years in that career you may never have gotten to the point where you were ready to be really happy. I think it's all a cumulative process. You finally got to the point that you were ready for this. And, boy, am I glad you were."

They went upstairs and the rest of the afternoon was Dave and Jan time, even when Chris got back from the airport they stayed behind closed doors.

Monday morning Dave was late getting into the office. He knew he was going to get ribbed over it and was not disappointed.

"Up all night, were we?" Cheryl said, as he tried to slip by her into his office.

"No, I got to bed at a reasonable time," Dave said.

"I didn't say anything about what time you got to bed," Cheryl said and laughed.

Later, Dan came into Dave office and sat down.

"Been thinking about how to shake something loose on the case," Dan said. "What would you think about another round of tailing the drug gang members? Maybe split up and follow more than one of them. See if that gets us anything."

"Maybe worth a try," Dave said. "Do you think we could pull it off without getting burned with only one of us per guy?"

"We'll need to be careful," Dan said. "I think we can do it. I think it's worth a try."

"Maybe we could get some help from DEA," Dave thought out loud. "I'll give them a call. When do you think?"

"Tomorrow is the fifteenth," Dan said.

"Okay. You get Bob up to speed. I'll call DEA." Dave turned to his phone and dialed as Dan left.

"George Hoffman," the voice on the phone said.

"George, this is Dave Harbinger. We want to run several tails on Williams County drug farm members tomorrow and are a bit short handed. Any chance you have people available to help out?" Dave asked.

"What are you looking for?"

"We think Sheriff Lewis may have found out something about their payoff racket by tailing a gang member when he made the rounds on the fifteenth of the month. We have notes from him that seemed to indicate that. We tried to run a tail on them some time back but got nothing out of it. We think it was because we could only tail one of them. We want to step it up this month, but I only have three of us."

"You think it always happens on the fifteenth?" George asked.

"Yes. I've talked with the car dealer they lease cars from and he confirms they always pay on the fifteenth. Sheriff Lewis' notes also said that."

"How many people you need?"

"At least three, but six would be great. Plain clothes in civilian vehicles."

"Hold on, let me check my sheets," George said. Dave heard him lay the phone down, a chair creaking and then the noise of typing on a keyboard.

"Looks like I can do three of us, counting me. If that works."

"Great. That will give us three two man teams. That should be enough."

"Where and when?" George asked.

"Here at the Lincoln County Sheriff's office at seven in the morning. Does that work for you guys?"

"I'll make it work," George said. "See you then."

At shortly before seven the next morning when Dave pulled into the parking lot at the station he saw three cars sitting near the door that he didn't recognize. There were three men standing by them, one of which was George Hoffman.

"Good morning, Dave," George said as Dave got out of the pickup.

"Morning, George. Glad you could make it."

George introduced the two agents with him, Jeff and Doug.

"Let's go in and have a cup of coffee while we lay it out for you," Dave said holding the station door open.

They went into the conference room. Cheryl had already made coffee and was bringing in extra cups as they came in. As they were sitting down, Bob and Dan came in. Dan had a box of doughnuts which he put down in the middle of the table. There were introductions all around. As they drank coffee and ate doughnuts, Dave and Dan explained what they thought was about to happen. They divided up into two man teams with Dave, Dan, and Bob taking lead in each team due to their local knowledge. Dave and George were together as team one, Dan and Jeff were team two and Bob and Doug were team three. Dave gave the DEA guys each a hand held radio on the Sheriff Department frequency for communications. They all made sure the radios were switched to the tac three channel. By 7:35 they were on the way to Williams County.

The plan was that Dave would find a stake out location where he could see the drive to the drug farm, and hopefully, to Juan's house as well. When one of the gang left he would radio the car description to the teams. Team two would pick up the first drug guy, team three the second one and Dave and George the third one. They would only follow gang guys that headed toward Jackson. At 8:30 they were in place.

Dave was sitting on a small rise about one quarter mile east of the farm on an adjacent county road. He had binoculars and a telescope. The binoculars gave him a good view of the farm. He could see the entrance to Juan's driveway as well. He was comfortable that they could not see him because he was in a small grove of trees that would conceal the pickup. Also, the sun was behind him, which would add to his cover.

Over the next few hours several cars came into the farm, but none left. Finally at about ten, a black Mercedes came out of the farm and drove the short distance to Juan's drive and turned in there. As the Mercedes waited for the gate to fully open, Dave was able to get the license number with the telescope and jot it down. It was the same car he, Dan and Bob had followed before.

Grocery shopping again, Dave thought to himself, as the car disappeared up the driveway toward the house.

In about ten minutes, the car came back down the driveway and out the gate headed in the direction of Jackson.

"Team two, black Mercedes headed your way," Dave said into the radio. He also gave the license number he had written down on his note pad.

Almost before the Mercedes was out of sight a silver Audi came out of the farm and drove over to the gate. Dave got the telescope and wrote down the license number. As with the Mercedes, the Audi came back down the drive a few minutes later and headed in the direction of Jackson.

"Team three, silver Audi," Dave said into the radio and added the license number.

Dave waited. In about ten minutes a black BMW came out of the farm and repeated the same process. But the BMW turned north out of Juan's drive. Dave watched it go with no other action. Nothing happened for a long time.

"Mercedes at grocery store," he heard Dan's voice say over the radio.

A short time later he heard Bob's voice on the radio, "Audi at the electric utility office."

Over an hour later, a familiar gray BMW came out of the farm drive and went up to Juan's gate. The process was followed again. The telescope license check confirmed what Dave already knew, it was Bobby. As he pulled out of Juan's drive headed for Jackson, Dave keyed the radio, "Team one, gray BMW," and the license number. He put the pickup in gear and headed for the state highway.

George picked up Bobby as he was headed east on the state highway. He fell in behind him three cars back. Dave was to intercept just before the Jackson city limit by turning in from a county road to the north. He had a problem since he was concerned that Bobby may recognize his pickup. Dave pulled off the side of the county road short of the state highway. He was blocked by a farm building from being seen to the west. He waited until he saw Bobby drive by before he moved out. This put him farther behind than he would have liked to be, but gave him additional cover from being recognized.

As they got into Jackson, Bobby was about a full block ahead of Dave. Too far to be an effective tail.

"10-20, George?" Dave said into the radio.

"Parallel to state highway, two blocks north, approaching 27th Street," came the reply.

"Intercept at 25th and state highway?" Dave said.

"10-4"

The light just ahead of him turned yellow and the car ahead hit the brakes. "You could have made that easy," Dave said out loud, frustrated. He had no choice but to stop behind the cautious motorist and watch as Bobby disappeared in the traffic ahead.

"No joy," he said into the radio. He waited to see if George had picked him up.

After a couple of minutes he heard George confirm his fear, "No joy."

"Teams report," Dave said into the radio.

"Team two, subjects heading back in direction of farm," Dan said.

"Team three, subjects made several stops and seem to also be headed back," Bob said.

"Okay, all teams break off and return to station for debrief," Dave said.

Back at the station, they sat down and reviewed what they had learned. The two gang members in the black Mercedes did the grocery shopping. The guy in the silver Audi apparently paid the utility bills since he went to the electric company, the cable tv company, a propane gas supplier and other such places. The gray BMW, which Dave knew as Bobby's but did not share with the others, was lost before they could determine a destination. Since the guys in the Mercedes were observed doing the same function on two separate occasions they would assume that future roles would be the same as well and concentrate their next surveillance strictly on the gray BMW.

Chapter 24

Jan's campaign for elected office was not going to be nearly as easy as Dave's. She had competition in the form of a former associate at Whitman, Wallace and Sherwood. Plus another attorney of whom she thought highly. Jim Keller was confident that she had a good shot and the party was fully behind her. They got yard signs printed up. They printed up and distributed, flyers, and put up posters all over town. Jan Harbinger for Judge was a phrase seen all over Springfield and throughout Lincoln County. She was appearing at all kinds of functions such as rotary club meetings, church socials, women's clubs, park district functions, and on and on. She tried to meet as many people as she could, where ever they were and ask for their vote.

"I don't remember you working this hard to get elected, Sheriff," she said to Dave over lunch one hectic day when she had four events on her schedule.

"I didn't," he said. "Remember, I ran unopposed."

"Oh, yeah. Tell me again, how did you accomplish that?"

"Just lucky, I guess," he smiled.

"Well, this is more effort than I thought it would be."

"Maybe, but you know what," he offered. "I don't see either of your competitors putting in the kind of effort you are."

"Maybe, because they have jobs."

"Gives you the edge," he answered. "Don't you think?"

"I guess," she said. "Got to run, the ladies club meeting starts in half an hour."

Back in the office Dan came in to see Dave.

"I got a call from Pete up in Arlington County," Dan began. "He was just checking in to see if we were working on leads. I told him about our efforts with the drug gang. He says they are about to move the file into the inactive category. Apparently the prosecutor's office up there is trying to show some process improvement by reducing the number of active files or something. I told him I didn't think you want the file to be transferred. He says he can keep it open if he can put something new in the file. Got any ideas?"

"He didn't think our efforts with the drug gang were enough?" Dave asked.

"No. I kind of agree. We are tailing them to see if we can find out who at Williams County they are paying off. That really isn't a direct factor in the Sheriff Lewis case, unless we can tie that to a motive. Maybe we can, but it still remains to be seen."

"Okay, what do you think we can do to keep it open?" Dave asked.

"If we show some new investigation, that would do it," Dan said thinking out loud. "If we change the investigation away from the gang, and move it in another direction, that would do it."

"I see," Dave said. "And what direction would we go?"

"Well, most investigations start with the family."

"Oh," Dave said. "And the book he was reading would give us that direction. Even if we still think the gang is our number one."

"Keeps it open," Dan said.

"Okay, do it."

"I'll call Pete and tell him we have shifted our investigation to focus on Doris Lewis," Dan said.

Friday night was a home basketball game for the Springfield Tigers. Dave and Jan were there in the stands early, armed with Jan Harbinger for Judge flyers and buttons. They had taken seats along the first aisle a couple of rows up for maximum exposure to the incoming fans. Dave suspected that it didn't hurt Jan's campaign in this crowd that one of the starting guards for Springfield High was also named Harbinger. After a few minutes, Joyce came in the door. She walked in front of them, followed closely by Randy Sherwood. Dave was sure she saw them, but she walked right on by without a glance. Randy looked at Jan, quickly looked away and kept walking after Joyce.

"That was a bit strange," Jan said. "I can understand Joyce's reaction, but I would have thought Randy would have at least pretended to be gracious."

The game was more exciting than had been expected. Springfield came in as the underdog to the previous year's champions, who only lost two starters from last year. Springfield won by four points but it was a hard fought duel. Chris played a good game, scoring eight points on three field goals and two foul shots. But his real forte was his defense. He held his opponent, an all state guard, to below his average in scoring. Dave was really proud of how well Chris played, but even more of the effort he put into the entire game. He had always told his sons that ability was not as important as putting in the effort to achieve.

"Okay, Dad," Jan chastised him. "If you don't settle down you won't be able to ever wear a hat again."

"It shows?"

"Yes, but it's okay. He played well, and you should be proud."

After the game they were in the lobby of the gym about to head out the door when someone called Jan's name. They turned around and Jim Keller was hurrying toward them.

"Glad I caught you two," he said as he got near them. "I just got off the phone and we need to talk. Have you got a few minutes?"

"Sure, Jim," Jan said. "What's up?"

"Not here," he said. "Can you come over to my house?"

"Sure, Jim," Dave said, as Jim's wife, Sally, came up behind him.

Sally said hello to Jan and Dave.

"They are coming over for a few minutes, dear," Jim said to Sally. "Something has come up."

"Something is always coming up," Sally said, still smiling. "That's fine, we'll see you in a few minutes."

Jim and Sally headed off. Dave and Jan got their car and headed to Jim and Sally's house. The garage door was open and Jim was standing in the doorway when they pulled into the driveway. They all went in together through the garage. Jim showed them into his study which was in the front of the house opposite the formal living room. Dave and Jan sat together on a small sofa and Jim sat in an overstuffed chair across from them.

"I got some troubling news," Jim started. "I'm not at liberty to say how I know this, but the source is credible and I believe it to be true."

He paused as if trying to compose himself.

"We have reason to believe an attempt will be made to rig the election to favor one of your opponents. It has been reported that votes are being bought against you," he said. "Apparently a lot of money is being spent to see to it that you are not elected."

"Why?" Jan asked. "What have I done?"

"I don't think it is what you've done as much as someone wanting to make sure someone else is the new judge," Jim said. "The ramifications of this are huge, it may also point to corruption in the past as well. I'm flabbergasted at the possible implications of this scandal."

Jan and Dave looked at Jim in disbelief.

"I thought you should know what's going on," Jim continued. "I understand the State Attorney General's office may be investigating, so this might blow up in a hurry. It may also involve the FBI, I don't know. But something is going on."

"Wow," Dave said. "I haven't heard a thing about this."

"If there is corruption in the county, it stands to reason that no county official would be brought in on it, Sheriff," Jim said. "As I say, I can't tell you how I know. Let's keep it between us. I'm not sure how it will come out, or even if. But I didn't want you to be blindsided."

"Well, thanks for that," Jan said. "What should I do?"

"Nothing," Jim said. "It doesn't really involve you, other than that someone is trying to steal votes from you. You are fully in the right and should keep doing just what you are doing. I don't think they can succeed now, but you never know how deep the corruption runs."

"Do we know which of the other two candidates they are for?" Dave asked.

"I don't know if it is known or not," Jim said. "I only know it's against Jan. Maybe either of the other two are acceptable to them, I don't know."

"Great," Jan said. "I'm not only putting more into it than I thought I'd need to, now I find out big money is against me."

"Ain't politics grand?" Dave smiled.

In the car on the way home Jan was quiet. Dave let her be for a while but then thought maybe she needed to talk through what she was thinking.

"Let's talk about it," he said.

"Yeah, I guess we should."

"What are you thinking?"

"I'm thinking I should pull out of the race," she said.

"I thought so. And if you do?"

"That's the rub, isn't it? If I pull out and Jim is right that either of the other two are acceptable to whomever is trying to buy the election then the corruption continues."

"Uh huh," Dave said.

"So, now I can't quit. I have to stay in the race and more importantly I have to get elected," she said defiantly. "I don't have a choice. I have to win this election. It's a matter of what's right and wrong and I need to make sure it's right."

"I thought you'd see it my way," Dave said smugly.

"You know, Sheriff, a judge is more powerful than a peace officer," she said.

"Yeah, but I get to carry a gun," he said.

Monday morning when he had a few minutes to spare Dave thought he would follow up on something that came to mind after the talk with Jim on Friday night. He went into records and looked up the resolution of the arrest he made of the guy in the van headed for the drug farm. The records showed the driver of the van had been released on bond after his arraignment on drug trafficking charges. He was to appear for trial but did not. A warrant had been issued but the bond had not been revoked. The case was continued and had yet to be rescheduled for trial. The judge in the case was the late Judge Andrew Willisinski.

As Dave was sitting contemplating what he had just read, his phone rang.

"Dave Harbinger."

"Pete Jacobs," was the response. "Got some information you might find interesting."

"Oh," Dave said. "I'm listening."

"With the change in direction for the investigation I asked a few more questions," Pete said. "I stopped by Pop's station and asked about Doris Lewis. Pop said she has a pink Cadillac. He said she was at the cabin sometime before Christmas, on a Saturday maybe the first or second week in December. My records show she called on November seventeenth and asked if it was okay to get the pickup. Pop says he saw Sheriff Lewis' pickup go back by about an hour later with a man driving. He says Mrs. Lewis went back toward the interstate about an hour after that."

"Not news to me," Dave said. "The pickup was gone when we were up there last. Mrs. Lewis told me the last time I talked with her that she and her son-in-law went up to get it."

"Yes," Pete continued. "But, I also asked Pop when he had last seen her pink Cadillac. He said it was the Saturday Sheriff Lewis was killed."

"What?" Dave gasped. "He didn't tell us that."

"Says we didn't ask," Pete said. "He said he remembers the car going by sometime late afternoon, before he closed. Didn't see it again. He was sure about the date because he remembers wondering about the car when he heard about the Sheriff."

"Would have been nice to know at the time," Dave said frustrated.

"One thing about Pop," Pete said. "He doesn't miss much, and I think his memory is good, but I'm not sure he puts thing together very well."

"Maybe so," Dave said. "But geez, this is important stuff."

"I understand," Pete said. "Don't come down on Pop. He's trying to help. I'm just not sure he's all there."

"Well," Dave said. "I guess we need to talk with Mrs. Lewis again."

"Do you want us to come down. Or do you think it best for you to handle it?" Pete asked.

"I think it may be best for me to talk with her alone, for now at least."

"Okay," Pete said. "Just keep in mind that my state's attorney is going to be on me about this development."

"Understood. Give me a couple of days."

"You got it," Pete said and hung up.

Chapter 25

Dave was reaching for the phone to call Aunt Dar when Cheryl's head came around his door frame.

"Someone here to see you, Sheriff," was all she said and disappeared.

The doorway was now filled by two men in uniform. They came in as Dave stood to greet them. Both were State Police, one Dave knew and one he didn't.

"Sorry to barge in, Sheriff," Josh Trubaldi said. "This is Colonel Paul Adams. Do you mind if we shut the door?"

Josh shut the office door while Dave and Colonel Adams shook hands.

"Not at all," Dave said. "Good to meet you Colonel."

"Call me Paul," Adams said.

"Have a seat," Dave said, gesturing to the chairs in front of his desk as they all sat. "Call me Dave, what can I do for you?"

"Dave, we are here on a very sensitive issue," Paul began. "We asked around headquarters and found out that you've been working with Josh recently on a drug matter. I talked with Josh and he said he thought you to be a straight up guy. Since you have only been in office for a few months we decided to gamble that you are not part of what brings us down here."

He hesitated, looked at Josh, then back at Dave.

"I have to ask that the information I share will be kept in the strictest confidence," Paul continued. "No one is to know of this conversation. Agreed?"

"Agreed," Dave said.

"Good," Paul continued. "I'm in command of the State Police Investigation Division. We've been asked by the State Attorney General to investigate suspected corruption in Lincoln and Williams Counties at the judicial and county board levels. Our investigation will include the County Board Chairmen, the County Clerks and the head of Elections in each county. We have been apprised of possible corruption of several judges. Our investigation stems from reported payoffs and bribes flowing to these individuals from a Mexican drug cartel. Although we have no indication that anyone in your department or the Williams County Sheriff's Department is involved, we do have suspicions. We are bringing you into our confidence because of our knowledge of your predecessor's suspicions. We are interested in any evidence you may have, either obtained from your predecessor or directly by you, which may assist with our investigation."

"I'll help all I can," Dave said. "Sheriff Lewis did have concerns about the Williams County Department, but I don't think he had any idea that it went any further than that. He thought there was information being funneled to the drug gang about raids and such, but I think that was as far as he thought it went. Here's what I know."

Dave took the two State Police officers through all of the information he had in a step by step process. The only information he did not share was the relationship he and Brian had with Bobby. He felt it was somewhat of a gamble on his part. He figured it would probably come out at some point and he would have to explain why he had not shared it. But at the same time he was worried that the consequences of the drug gang suspecting Bobby were far greater. His risk was less than the risk on Bobby if they suspected he was feeding information to Dave.

"There is one other thing I need to mention," Dave said as the meeting was coming to a close. "My wife is running for judge."

"We're aware of that, Dave," Paul said. "And we hope she wins the election."

"I would like your permission to share this conversation with her," Dave said.

"Of course," Paul said. "We fully vetted her before we came down here, just like we did you."

"So, what is the next step?" Dave asked.

"I like the idea of putting the tail on the suspected payoff guy," Paul said. "Let's do that next month. We'll fill the city of Jackson with plainclothes. He won't shake the tail this time. Until then we're going to be checking some bank accounts to see what that tells us. We think we know most of them. It's just a matter of proving the ones we have, and finding who else is out there. We'll be in touch."

They left. Dave picked up his phone and dialed Aunt Dar.

"Hello," she said after a couple of rings.

"Aunt Dar, it's Dave. Are you going to be home for a while? I'd like to come over and talk."

"Sure. I'm here, come on over."

Dave drove over to her house. The pink Cadillac was sitting on the driveway in front of the garage. As he walked by he noticed a flowered hat on the seat. *Aunt Dar always liked to wear hats,* he thought. He went up to the door and rang the bell. She opened the door and invited him in. She had on a casual outfit that fit her perfectly. Her hair was like she had just walked out of a salon and her makeup was perfect. Dave marveled at how she always seemed ready to go out on the town.

"Aunt Dar," Dave said as they sat on the living room sofa. "When was the last time you were up at the cabin before you and John went to get the pickup?"

"Well, let me think," she said thoughtfully. "I think it was the summer before, I went up with Megan's family. We went swimming and boating on the lake. I think it was August."

"August the year before Uncle Will died?"

"Yes. It could have been July, but I know it was in the middle of the summer," she said.

"Aunt Dar, listen to me," Dave took her hand and looked in her eyes. "You are saying you weren't up at the cabin on the weekend that Uncle Will died."

"Of course not, Dave. Why would you suggest such a thing?" Dar asked.

"Because we have an eye witness that says they saw you in Garnett on that Saturday afternoon," Dave said, still looking into her eyes.

"That's preposterous. Why would I have been up there then?" she said. "They must be lying. I was here in town all that weekend. They couldn't have seen me."

Dave saw nothing in her eyes that would indicate she was not being truthful.

"Do you know Pop at the gas station up there?" Dave asked.

"Of course, a nice old gentleman he is too," she said.

"Pop says he saw your Cadillac turn up toward the cabin late that afternoon," Dave said.

"Well, he…" she started to say. Dave saw what he thought was recognition in her eyes. She looked quickly away from him. She got up from the sofa and walked to the other side of the room. She looked back at him, tears were in her eyes.

"I think you'd better go," she said and walked over and opened the front door.

"Aunt Dar," Dave pleaded. "You have to tell me what happened."

"Go," she said.

"If you push me away I will have no choice but to turn this over to the Arlington County Sheriff. Please tell me!"

"Get out," she said, sternly.

He did. He walked to his car wondering what had just happened. Had she had some sort of mental block about being at the cabin? Had he forced her to remember that she was there and that the whole episode had come crashing back into her mind? Had she killed Uncle Will? He started his car and drove straight home. It was just after noon, but he had had all he could take in one day.

When he walked in the door Jan was sitting at the kitchen table writing thank you cards. She looked at him, dropped her pen and ran to him.

"What happened?"

"Let's go sit down."

He told her the whole story of his morning, starting with his visit with Aunt Dar and working backwards. She listened intently, holding his hand in one hand and gently rubbing his shoulder with the other. She didn't say a word until he was finished.

"Have I had a day, or what?" he concluded.

"This job is certainly not worth what they're paying you," she said. "No wonder there's so much corruption. People are just trying to break even."

"That's not funny," he said.

"It's a little funny," she said.

"Okay," he said. "A little."

She kissed him and they hugged for a long time while he calmed down in her arms. "So, let's deal with one thing at a time," she said. "Do you think Dar killed him?"

"No. It makes no sense. She seemed relieved when I told her he had been murdered. It was like she felt responsible for the suicide and murder relieved that stress. If she had done it, she wouldn't have welcomed the murder call. That should have been depressing to her."

"Okay," Jan said. "If she didn't do it why would she deny being up there?"

"I don't know," Dave said.

"Maybe she got up there, found him murdered by the drug gang and went into shock," Jan suggested.

"No," Dave said. "The timing is all wrong. The drug guys were up there around midnight or so. She was seen in the late afternoon."

"Maybe the drug guys killed him on the way to the airport in the afternoon."

"If they did, we have even less to put them there."

"Okay, say Dar was there, asleep in the bedroom at midnight and the drug guys came in killed Will. Dar saw him and went into shock," Jan offered.

"The beds were all made. I wouldn't think she would make the bed before getting out of Dodge," he said.

"I've got nothing else."

"Yeah, me either," Dave said. "Want to talk about the payoff stuff now?"

"Not really," Jan said. "I think I'm depressed enough for one day."

"Me too," Dave said. "Let's go to bed."

"In the middle of the day? What will the neighbors think?"

"They're cows," Dave said. "They'll get over it."

"That could change the day from being an utter disaster," she said as she ran up the stairs with him right behind her.

Chapter 26

"Missed you yesterday afternoon," Cheryl said as Dave got into his office the next morning.

"Sorry. I should have called in. Tough day," Dave said.

"Messages are on your desk," she said. "Nothing that couldn't wait."

"Okay. Could you ask Dan and Bob to come in, please?"

A few minutes later Dan was already in Dave's office when Bob came in. Dave motioned for him to shut the door as he came in. Bob shut the door and sat down next to Dan.

"New development in the case," Dave began. "Sheriff Will's wife was seen heading for the cabin late in the afternoon on that Saturday."

Dan looked shocked. Bob looked confused.

"Pop, the gas station guy up there, said he saw her pass his station and head in the direction of the cabin sometime before he closed at six that night. When I confronted her with this information she denied it and then asked me to leave. Wouldn't talk with me anymore."

"Have you told Pete?" Dan asked.

"Not yet. I wanted to run it by you guys first," Dave said. "Any comments?"

198 • R.I.P. Sheriff Will

"Can't think why she would deny being there, if she didn't do it," Dan said.

"Are we sure of the identification?" Bob asked.

"Reasonably, there aren't that many pink Cadillacs. Even fewer that would be in Garnett on a Saturday afternoon," Dave said.

"There is that," Bob agreed.

"I think the Arlington County boys are going to want to talk with her," Dan offered.

"Yep, I think you're right," Dave said. "I guess I'd better give them a call."

Dave dialed the phone as Dan and Bob were leaving his office.

"Pete Jacobs," the voice on the line said.

"Pete, Dave Harbinger, I talked with Mrs. Lewis. She denied she was up there at first, but when I told her Pop saw the car that afternoon she clammed up and asked me to leave."

"Okay," Pete said. "I'll let the state's attorney know and see what they want to do."

He signed off. Dave felt a churning in his stomach. He knew he had no choice in reporting what he had learned but it just didn't feel right.

The rest of the day was spent on routine activity in the office. Dave was relieved to be doing less stressful things that helped him get back into more of a normal attitude. But although it was lessened, the stress of the case was still there.

Two days later just after he got into the office his phone rang.

"Sheriff, this is Paul Adams with the State Police," the voice on the phone said.

"Hello, Paul. What can I do for you?"

"I'm calling to inquire about a gentleman by the name of Jim Keller," Paul said.

"Yes," Dave said. "I know Jim, he is president of a local bank and political party chairman."

"How well do you know him?" Paul asked.

"Fairly well, I guess."

"In your opinion can he be trusted?"

"Yes, I think so. He told my wife and I that there may be a concern for voter fraud in her election," Dave said. "He said he had an undisclosed source who had provided him with the information."

"When was that?" Paul asked.

"Last Friday night."

"Okay, so you think he's straight up?" Paul said.

"Yes. Can you tell me why you are asking?"

"Several of the suspects we are investigating have accounts at his bank," Paul said. "We would like to exercise warranted searches of those accounts but do not want the word out that we are looking. It is imperative that we can trust the banker."

"I see, yes. I think you can trust him," Dave said.

"Good. Also, are you known in his bank?" Paul asked.

"Yes."

"Would it seem unusual to anyone in the bank if you stopped in to see him in his office?" Paul asked.

"Not at all. I've been in to see Jim quite often," Dave said. "His secretary knows me."

"Good, then could you assist with the searches?"

"Of course," Dave said.

"Is this afternoon okay?" Paul asked.

"Yes."

"Okay, I'll be in your office about two."

Paul signed off.

Jan was going to be in town so they planned to meet for lunch. She was already there when Dave walked in the restaurant. He gave her a quick kiss and sat opposite her in the booth.

"So what brings you her today young lady?" he smiled.

"A handsome young man in a uniform," she batted her eyes.

"Been doing some shopping?" he asked.

"Yes, and getting my hair done this afternoon. With all the money I'm spending on clothes it only makes sense to spend some on the body they are going on."

"I'm not sure it's needed," he said, "but whatever you want."

"You're so sweet. What's going on at the office today?"

"Going to look into some corruption this afternoon," he said.

"Oh, got names?"

"Paul is coming down and we're going to check out some people," he said.

"Wow," she said, "that's exciting."

"Maybe, but I'm not sure I really want to know who."

"Yeah," she said. "There is that. But it's best to get it out and done. Your job is to uphold the law and protect the law abiding citizens that elected you."

"I know," he said. "But life seemed so much easier when I was just a patrol officer and a farmer."

"You didn't have me then," she said.

"Good point. Life was easier then, but so much better now," he said.

She smiled.

At a little before two that afternoon Paul Adams came into Dave's office. He was wearing a green golf shirt under a leather jacket. No uniform or other outward indication of his State Police affiliation. He was carrying a leather document pouch about the size of a legal pad. He and Dave headed for Jim's bank.

As they walked toward Jim's office, Dave nodded at Helen and gestured toward Jim's door. Helen smiled and waved Dave on in. Paul followed Dave onto Jim's office. Dave shut the door after they were both in. Jim stood with a curious look on his face.

"Jim," Dave said. "This is Colonel Paul Adams with the State Police."

Jim and Paul shook hands. Paul showed Jim his badge as Dave continued. "He's here on official business of a highly confidential nature."

"Mr. Keller," Paul said, as he pulled a document out of the leather pouch and handed it to Jim. "I have here a document subpoena requesting information about each and every bank account held by the named individuals and their spouses with the express intent to assess whether or not there are repeated cash deposits in excess of five hundred dollars into any of the accounts. If there are such deposits this subpoena provides for the identification of such by date and amount over the period of the last two calendar years and this year to date. I would like for you personally to provide me with the information requested without the knowledge of any of your staff or other bank personnel."

"Oh," Jim said. "Okay, let me see."

He sat down at his desk and began reading the document that Paul had handed him. After a couple of minutes he looked up at them.

"Everything seems to be in order," Jim said. "I can access the records right here on my desk top computer. I can also print anything you need here in my office so that confidentiality can be maintained. Would you like to start at the top of the list and just go down in order?"

"Yes, that would be fine," Paul said.

Jim typed on his keyboard and studied his computer screen. Dave could not see the screen, nor could he see the names on the paper Jim had on the desk in front of him. They waited while Jim apparently looked through bank account records.

"Here's something on the first name," Jim said. "This account shows cash deposits in the range of seven thousand dollars on a monthly basis. Amounts seem to be between sixty five hundred and seven thousand. Dates are in the middle of every month between the fifteenth and the nineteenth. It goes all the way back for two years. I can read them off if you want?"

Paul took out a pen and a legal pad and wrote down the dates and amounts as Jim read them. The process was repeated four more times as Jim called up the accounts of each of the names on the list. All had repeated cash deposits in excess of five hundred. The lowest amount was three thousand and the highest was eight thousand.

"All right, Mr. Keller," Paul said. "We appreciate your assistance."

"You're welcome."

Dave and Paul left Jim's bank and headed back to the station.

"We have the county board chair, the head of elections and three judges. One of the judges is recently deceased," Paul said as they sat at a stop light.

"Is that enough for arrests?" Dave asked.

"No," Paul said. "We need some indication where the cash came from. As of now it is purely circumstantial. We need some means to be able to tie the cash in those accounts to bribes paid. Progress, but not there yet."

"So we shift to the suspected source of the cash," Dave said.

"Right. You have already done some of that. Now we pick up where you left off and get to the bottom of it."

"You know, we didn't come into Lincoln County with our surveillance," Dave said. "We were just looking in Williams. Guess we didn't have our scope wide enough."

"Yeah, but now we have an idea of where to look," Paul said. "Speaking of Williams County, I'm doing similar checks down there as well. We should have a pretty good idea how far this goes by the end of the week."

As he walked back to his office after finishing up with Paul, Cheryl stopped him.

"Sheriff Allen called and said it was urgent that you get back with him as soon as you returned," she said.

Dave went straight into his office and called Arlington County.

"Dave, the case is solved," Sam Allen said. "Pete and I went to the DA with the information you gave him about Mrs. Lewis. The DA wanted to jump right on it so we all piled into a car and headed down there this morning to interview her. Pretty much as soon as we were in her door she confessed. We brought her back up here and she is being processed as we speak. Her attorney is coming up from Springfield and hasn't arrived yet. We expect a bond hearing in the morning."

Dave was listening to what Sam was saying, but wasn't sure he was hearing what was being said.

204 • R.I.P. Sheriff Will

"Are you kidding? I don't believe it."

"Not kidding, Dave," Sam said. "She seemed like she had resigned to the idea when we showed up at her door. She says it was accidental that she really didn't mean to pull the trigger."

"Do you think the DA is going to go for murder, or maybe involuntary man slaughter?" Dave asked.

"I don't know. She wanted to wait for her attorney before giving us the written confession. I think the DA will want to see that before he makes a determination."

"Okay, Sam," Dave said. "If it makes any difference at this point, I would be in favor of bonding her out. She would not be a flight risk, in my opinion."

"Good to know," Sam said, "I'll tell the DA. I'll give you a call when I have more information."

"Okay, thanks, Sam."

Dave slowly lowered the handset back to it's cradle. He stared at the phone. It just sat there like phones do without disputing what he had just heard.

Chapter 27

Once again on the fifteenth of the month they prepared to tail the drug guys. There was a slight difference this month because the force was much larger and the scope of the surveillances was broader. Dave was once again posted at his surveillance location in the small grove of trees where he could observe both driveways. But unlike the other occasions, he would not be doing any of the tailing. There was an adequate number of units for that so his job today was to identify who was to be tailed. Along with Bob, Dan and the three DEA guys there were four state police officers in the mix today. One of the State Police guys was Josh Trubaldi. The prime targets were the gray BMW, Bobby, and the black BMW that had headed into Lincoln County. Dave was also going to continue to observe longer to see if there were other vehicles they should be concerned with.

Because of their local knowledge Bob and Dan were given lead responsibility for two four man teams. Bob's team would go north to Springfield and Dan's team would go east into Jackson. George Hoffman from DEA would lay back. If there should be a need for a third surveillance he would take lead. One unit from each of the other two teams would be diverted to George's team. Each unit was a civilian looking vehicle. The cars were the team members personal car, a confiscated or undercover vehicle from the respective organization.

The chase vehicles were spread out in both directions to provide adequate coverage. Their numbers gave them the ability to assure the subjects did not elude the surveillance. As the morning progressed, things developed as they had in the past. The black BMW was followed into Springfield and the gray BMW was followed into Jackson. There was also a blue Porsche SUV they had not seen before, which came out of Juan's driveway directly rather than from the farm. It headed toward Jackson. George took up the Porsche chase. A couple of the units broke off from the other tails to pick it up as it came into the city. They successfully followed all three cars for their entire routes, then the team met back at the station to go over what they had learned. It was almost four in the afternoon when they were all back at the station. Colonel Paul Adams had not been one of the team members, but he had driven down in the afternoon and was waiting in the conference room for the reports.

"We followed the black BMW," Bob began as he gave the license number and a brief description of the driver. "He first stopped at Delagoto Motors. He entered the building carrying a brown shopping bag with rope style handles. He was in the building for seven minutes. When he came out he still had the bag, but it appeared to be empty or at least much lighter. He then drove to the west post office branch in the twenty two thousand block of West Main Street. He entered the building carrying the same, or very similar, bag with similar weight to when he entered the car dealership. He returned to his car after a little over a minute with the bag empty. He returned to the farm with no other stops."

Bob's report was confirmed by the other members of his team.

"We followed the gray BMW," Dan said as he gave the license number and a description that fit Bobby. "He went to the main post office in Jackson with a bag similar to what Bob described. Full when he went in and empty coming back out 3 minutes later. He returned to the farm with no other stops."

Dan's team confirmed his report.

"We formed a third team when the Porsche was reported headed for Jackson," George reported with license number and description. "The driver was alone in the vehicle. He went to a high end restaurant in Jackson. He entered at about eleven fifty and came back out at one twenty seven. During the time he was there, a total of fifty six other individuals entered either alone or in groups of two to three. No group larger than three entered together. We took photos of all the patrons, going in and out, with a long lens from down the street. When the subject left, we followed him back to the residence."

George's team confirmed his report.

"Okay," Paul said. "Sounds like we need to put someone into the post offices next month to see if we can find out what is in those bags and what they are doing with them. My guess is they are mailing the cash. Let's find out to whom. Based on the description, the driver of the Porsche appears to be Juan himself. We will take a look at the pictures to see if any of our suspects went in after he did."

"If the person he was meeting got there before him and left after we won't have a photo of them," Dave said.

"Yes, that's true," Paul said. "But if he was meeting someone with a regular job, it stands to reason that they would not get there before twelve. So I think the odds are in our favor. I'll talk with the post master and get one of our people in each post office next month. Dave and George, I'll send copies of my reports to you."

"Sounds good," Dave said.

The meeting broke up and Dave went back to his office. There was a message from Sam Allen in Arlington County that Mrs. Lewis had been released on bond. The preliminary hearing would be held week after next. The note said that Mrs. Lewis had confessed to an accidental shooting but it looked like the prosecutor was going for second degree murder.

Dave thought about Aunt Dar and the interactions he had had with her since Uncle Will was killed. Something was bothering him. He needed more information. He picked up the phone.

"Sam Allen," the voice on the phone said.

"Sam, it's Dave Harbinger. Could you send me a copy of Mrs. Lewis' full confession?"

"Sure, Dave, something on your mind?"

"I'm not sure. Just a feeling, maybe nothing," Dave answered.

"Do you want to see all that she had to say, or just the formal confession?"

"I guess I'd like to see everything, if it's not too much trouble," Dave said.

"No trouble at all, glad to do it. If there is something we are missing we need to know. I'll put it together in the morning and get it on the wire to you."

"Thanks, Sam."

When Dave got home that evening, Jan had dinner ready. She had never really been into cooking and domestic stuff. But found she not only didn't mind it, but actually enjoyed some of it. Dish washing and general cleaning she could do without but cooking was turning out to be more fun than she had anticipated. Tonight she had made a beef stroganoff from scratch. She told Dave she didn't think it was bad at all.

Dave and Chris both went at it like they hadn't eaten in a year. Dave went on and on about how good it was. He and Chris both had three helpings. After dinner and a quick clean up, Chris excused himself to go hang with some friends at the local pizza place.

"You just ate, you can't be hungry," Dave told him.

"It's not about the food, dad. Cortney is going to be there," Chris answered.

"Cortney?" Dave asked.

"Yeah, she's a fox. And I think she likes me," Chris said as he was heading out the door, "I know I like her."

"Jim Keller called today," Jan said after they settled into their favorite sofa and got comfortable.

"Oh, what's the latest?"

"He says the state board of elections will be sending people down to monitor the election," she answered. "They're going to monitor Lincoln and Williams counties. Jim says it looks like we'll have a fair election after all."

"That's good," Dave said. "It looks like the investigation into the pay offs will last well past the election. We found out today that the drug gang takes bags of something into the post offices. It may be that they're sending the cash payoffs through the mail. We're going to have people in the post offices next month to see what they're mailing and where it's going."

"Won't you need court approval for that?" Jan asked.

"I suppose so," Dave said. "But the state police and the attorney general are handling it so that's up to them. I'll get the report on what they find next month and we'll see where we go from there. But back to the election. It's coming up Tuesday after next. Are you ready?"

"I've got a full plate over this week end and next with a smattering of stuff next week. The party is having the returns watching shindig at the Hilton. I told Jim we would be there," she said.

"And, if you are elected it's pretty much the same as with me. The county board certifies the results and you're sworn in to fill the remainder of Judge Wallisinski's term," he said.

"Yep, in just over two weeks, I'll be Judge Harbinger or back to being a bum," she smiled.

"But my bum," Dave said. He hesitated for a second and asked. "Question, aren't bums supposed to be penniless?"

"Bum - a tramp; a vagrant; a person who avoids work and sponges on others; loafer;" she read from her google search. "But nothing about being poor or penniless. I kind of like the sponges on others thing. Can I sponge on you for a while?"

"Of course. Sponge away for as long as you like," he said. "I know it's going to be worth it to me."

She stuck her tongue out at him and jabbed him in the ribs. That started the wrestling match that ended up with him pinning her down to the sofa before picking her up and carrying her up to the bed room. She didn't fight that part with very much effort.

Two weeks later two important things happened in Dave's life. One was an election in Lincoln County and one was a preliminary hearing in Arlington County. The election was on Tuesday and the hearing was on Thursday.

Dave and Jan voted in the morning on election day and tried not to think about it the rest of the day. Of course neither of them could help but wonder what was going on in all of those election booths around the county. In particular was the involvement of the state watch dogs enough to assure a fair election. Jan was on pins and needles all day and Dave wasn't much better. He found he could not concentrate on even the easiest task. Finally at about two in the afternoon he gave up and told Cheryl he would be out the rest of the day and headed home.

"How you doing?" he said to Jan as he walked in the house.

"How do you think?" she said. "I'm a nervous wreck. You know it's strange. I don't need the job, but the way I feel you'd think my life was depending on it."

"Me too," Dave said. "I'm more nervous than when I was running."

"Wait a minute," she glared playfully. "You ran unopposed, you wimp."

"Oh, yeah, there was that," he said sheepishly. "But it was still an election."

"You're not helping much, but some," she said. "I'm glad you came home."

"You want to go for a drive?" Dave said. "I can have the Superbird ready in about fifteen minutes if you help."

"Do you want to take it out this early in the year?"

"Special occasion. Besides the roads are clear and dry. Why not?"

"You're on," she smiled widely. "Let's get to it."

"Okay, Judge," he said.

"Wasn't that a GTO?"

"Yep, we may need to get one."

They grabbed jackets and headed for the farm. Once there, Dave pulled the cover off the orange Plymouth that he knew was her favorite in the collection. She helped fold the cover and put it in one of the designated storage slots for car covers. Dave dumped a pint of octane boost into the tank and poured in about two gallons of fuel. He opened the hood, removed the battery tender and checked the oil. He took the air cleaner off the triple carbs and sprayed a shot of starting fluid in each. He nodded at Jan and she hit the starter. The starter whined in that high pitch that sixty and seventy vintage Chrysler products all had. Dave hit another shot of starting fluid and the engine barked to life. It died almost immediately. They repeated the process to get the fuel pumped up to the engine from the tank, the second time it barked to life it kept running. Jan's smile beamed. Dave replaced the air cleaner and shut the hood. He replaced the clips in the little holes in the hood pins sticking up through the hood. He went around the car checking the air pressure in each tire with a pocket gauge. When he was satisfied the car was ready to go he walked around to the passenger side and climbed in. Jan hit the door opener and put the car in first gear. She let the clutch out slowly with only a small amount of throttle. Dave was impressed with her ability to handle such a heavy clutch and high horse power. As they drove out of the building she hit the opener to close the overhead door. It was still cold but clear. Temperatures had been in the high thirties all week. Spring was coming but still a few unpredictable weeks away.

They drove straight to a gas station to fill the fuel tank. For the next hour they drove the country roads. No particular direction or plan. Jan did the driving and Dave could tell it was true therapy for her. She was having a great time and although he knew the stress was still there it was masked in relaxation for now.

"Let's head over to Cliff's for a burger," he said as they stopped at a cross road.

"Sounds like a great idea," she said as she checked for traffic in both directions. Seeing none, she put her right foot to the floor and dumped the clutch. The rear tires objected violently. The orange rocket sucked gas through all six barrels causing the big four forty to send more pound feet of torque to the rear axle than the tires could hold. Two dark black stripes were left across the intersection as the tachometer told Jan it was time to grab the pistol grip and jerk second. She did just that with only a slight hesitation off the gas and continued the tire burning launch. Just after banging into third she backed off and let the car coast back down to a more reasonable rpm and speed.

"Does that make you feel better?" Dave asked.

"Almost as good as sex with you," she said.

They had burgers, fries, and milk shakes at Cliff's.

"Your turn to drive," Jan said as they walked across the parking lot to the winged super car.

"Had your fill?" Dave asked.

"Never," she said. "But you need some fun, too. And besides, I feel like being able to just sit and watch my man for a while."

"Your man doesn't object," he said getting behind the wheel.

By the time they had gotten back to the farm, put the car away and headed home it was past six. They were supposed to be at the rally by seven, but neither of them wanted to be there that early. They figured it would be ten or later before the results were in enough to determine a winner and they had little interest in sitting around all that time. They showered, dressed, and finally were headed out the door at seven thirty.

The party was in the main ballroom. There was a smaller conference room set aside for the candidates and party officials. Jan and Dave walked into the conference room at just after eight. Jim Keller made a bee line toward them when he saw them.

"It looks like it's all over, Judge," he said to Jan. "The polling places that have reported in are showing you by nearly sixty percent over the other two. Only seven of the twenty two polling places have reported, but the percentages have been almost identical in all seven and those are not from areas we expected you to be strong. There is absolutely no reason to expect a significant change with future reports."

"Okay," Jan said. "But seven out of twenty-two is not significant. What if no one voted for me in the other fifteen districts?"

"Take my word for it. I've been through this many times. I can't remember such high numbers for any candidate in any race where there were three people running. You'll see."

Jan was squeezing Dave's hand so tight that it almost hurt. She had a look of excitement that she was obviously trying to suppress. He put an arm around her waist, pulled her toward him and whispered into her ear.

"I think you are going to look mighty sexy in that black robe," he said. "Will you be naked underneath?"

"You pervert," she whispered back. "You'll just have to take it off me sometime and see."

They took up a spot at a small round table where they could see the large screen in the corner where results were being posted. After about ten minutes another district reported in and they saw Jan's name next to a figure which read fifty-seven percent.

"Well, only fourteen more to go," Dave said. "You know, this is kind of fun. I'm not sure why we didn't want to come here tonight."

Jan just beamed.

Over the next two hours another eight more districts reported in with similar results. Jan was called to a phone by one of the campaign workers. It was one of her opponents declaring her the winner and congratulating her on her campaign. A few minutes later the other opponent called with the same message. Jan was asked to go out to the ballroom and thank her supporters.

Her speech was full of gratitude to all of the party staff and workers who helped. She spoke for about ten minutes trying to make sure she didn't miss anyone. She had a note card which held the most significant names. Number one on the list was Sheriff Dave Harbinger, but she didn't read that one. After she finished, she showed him the note card and said she didn't think the thanks she had in mind for him should come from a podium.

On Thursday of that week Dave drove up to Arlington County to sit in on the preliminary hearing of Mrs. Doris Lewis. When he walked into the court room he saw Aunt Dar seated at a table in the front of the room with a forties something gentleman he didn't recognize but assumed to be her attorney. Sheriff Allen was also in the front of the court room near the prosecutor's table, talking. When Sam saw Dave come in, he waved and moved in his direction. The met in the aisle about half way.

"The DA is not going to accept the man slaughter but go for a second degree charge. I think the defense is going to take it to jury trial," he said as they sat down in the gallery seats.

"Yeah," Dave said. "I would think you're right."

"Did you see anything in the files I sent down?" Sam asked.

"Sort of," Dave said. "I noticed she didn't say where she left the gun. It seemed she was vague about that every time she was asked."

"Yep, we noticed that too," Sam said. "Every time we asked, she avoided a direct answer. There was never any statement about putting it in the vise."

"Makes me think she didn't know it was in the vise," Dave said.

"I understand that and agree, but why would she confess? We didn't force her into a confession. We didn't even begin questioning her before she did. I know what your concerns are, Dave, I just don't see what else to do."

"Isn't the prosecutor concerned about a jury thinking she didn't do it when they learn she didn't say anything about putting the gun in the vise?" Dave asked.

"He says he can convince the jury that her saying she left the gun near where she fired it includes in the vise since the vise was near where she fired the gun," Sam said.

"Sounds weak to me," Dave said.

"I suspect the prosecutor may want to see how the trial gets going. If he thinks he is going to be in trouble he can always cut to manslaughter plea bargain and close the case," Sam suggested.

"But that doesn't solve it if she didn't do it," Dave said. "I want to get the guy and I'm not convinced she did. I just don't know why she'd confess."

"I think we need more to go down that road, Dave," Sam said. "Your hunch may be right, but we need evidence."

"I'm working on it," Dave said. "Keep me up to speed on thing up here."

"Sure will," Sam said.

The court came into session and Dave sat with Sam and watched. The judge called the case and asked the prosecutor what charge he was bringing against Mrs. Lewis. The response, as Sam had predicted, was murder in the second degree. The judge turned to the defendant table and asked if they wanted a jury trial, to which they answered in the affirmative. The judge looked down at the bench in front of him and suggested a date for trial of June 7. Both parties agreed with the date and the session was concluded.

Dave sat where he was as the court room began to empty. Aunt Dar came up the aisle toward where he was, she looked at him. Then turned away and walked right by him out the door.

Chapter 28

Jan was invited to the County Board meeting on Tuesday evening. The board was expected to review and certify the election results. If all was in order, Jan would be sworn in as the newest judge in Lincoln County. It had also not escaped the attention of most people in the county that she would also be the youngest. Dave suggested that it had not escaped the attention of the entire male population of the county that she would also be the most attractive. "A downright Hot Sexy Judge," he had said. He had also made some comment about how the crime rate would surely go up because so many guys would want to get hauled into her court room just to look at her.

They sat in the gallery as the board went through the agenda. When they got to the election item, the motion was moved and seconded to accept the recommendation to certify the results. The motion passed with no discussion. Jan and Dave were then invited up to the front. Dave held the Bible while she took the oath of office and became Judge Jan Harbinger.

It was the middle of the month again. Dave and his guys were not directly involved in the drug gang surveillance this month, but they were anxious to learn what information was gained. The state post master had allowed the placement of surveillance officers in the post offices to see what the drug guys were mailing and, if possible without touching the mail, to who. The fifteenth fell in the middle of the week this month, on Wednesday, so there was no reason to expect the need for more than one day of surveillance.

Dave's phone rang on Thursday morning just after nine.

"Hello, Dave, it's Josh Trubaldi," the voice said. "The colonel asked me to give you a call and update you on what we learned yesterday."

"Good," Dave said. "What did we learn?"

"We learned that the bags they carried into the post offices had small fixed rate shipping boxes in them," Josh said. "There were five boxes in the Jackson post office and seven in Springfield. Each of the boxes appeared to be addressed to Occupant and a post office box. Our agents watched as the boxes were placed into individual post office boxes in the same post office. The only exception was that three of the Springfield parcels went into the same box. We learned that each of the boxes have been rented by an offshore company. We're making arrangements now to get access to the video cameras that cover the post office box area. Hopefully we'll be able to see who picks up the packages."

"How big are the boxes?" Dave asked.

"I'd say the size of the box your bank checks come in the mail," Josh answered.

"I wouldn't think the packages will stay in the box very long," Dave said. "If it's pay off money they get it into their bank accounts pretty quick."

"Our thoughts as well," Josh said. "We should have pictures soon. I'll let you know."

Josh signed off.

Dave got Bob and Dan together in Dan's office to let them know what had been learned. They all felt like progress was being made and they were getting somewhere on the investigation. Dave also told them about what he had learned from Sam when he was up in Arlington for Aunt Dar's hearing. They did not feel as confident with that investigation. They were in agreement that it didn't feel right and they were not convinced Mrs. Lewis' confession was the whole story.

"It's just the way investigative work goes," Dan said. "Sometimes you get lucky, sometimes you don't. Good investigation just gets you to where luck can decide whether you score or not."

"Maybe," Dave said. "But we still need to keep the investigation going to find out who killed Sheriff Will. I don't think she did. But if she did, I want to be convinced. If I'm right and she didn't, I want to find out who did."

"We're with you, Sheriff," Dan said. Then he paused. "Are you going to talk to her?"

"Yes. At least I'm going to try," Dave said. "I'll only be convinced if she tells me she put the gun in the vise. I don't think she knows were the gun was which means she wasn't there. I don't know if she'll talk to me, but if she will that's what I want to hear her say."

"And if she doesn't say it, we still have a case to solve," Dan said.

"I'm afraid so," Dave answered.

Dave was looking over his budget sheets the next morning to see if there was going to be enough on hand to keep the county safe, when his phone rang.

"Dave Harbinger."

"Paul Adams, Dave," the state police colonel said. "We have pickups on all except for two of the boxes. We have good photos of every one. So far we only recognize two of the subjects, the County Board Chairman of Williams and a judge there in Lincoln County. Several of the subjects were women, so we suspect wives or maybe administrative assistants. I'm sending you the photos of the people in Lincoln County to see if you recognize anyone."

"Ok, Paul. I'll take a look. If I don't recognize them maybe someone of my staff will. I'll show them around."

"Okay, let me know who you know," Paul said.

"What's the next step?"

"We are making progress, but we still don't have evidence against the big guy, Juan Martinez," Paul said. "Although the state's main interest is to clean up the corruption at the county level, DEA really wants Martinez. We don't have real proof that the cash came from Martinez. Yes, the car came from his house, but we have no evidence that he put it in the boxes or even ordered them to be sent."

"Maybe we can get one of subjects to finger him?" Dave suggested.

"Maybe, but I don't think DEA will want to rely on that," Paul said. "Right now we are going to work on getting positive IDs on everyone who picked up a box. Then we try to tie them to our subjects. Once that is all done we get with DEA and form a plan."

"So we don't want to move on any of the suspects until we know the big picture plan."

"That's about it," Paul said. "I think we're still a few months away from any resolution."

"Okay, keep me informed," Dave said.

"Will do," Paul said. "Oh, and by the way, congratulations to your wife."

"Thanks," Dave signed off.

Dave left his office and drove over to Aunt Dar's condo. He parked on the street and walked slowly up to the door. He rang the bell and waited.

"Hi, Davey. Come on in," she said as she opened the door wide.

"I wanted to come by and talk a bit, if you don't mind?" he said.

"Of course," she said as they sat in the living room. He on a stuffed chair and her on the sofa. "I do need to apologize to you for how I've treated you of late. I've been rude and there is no call for it."

"No, no, no need," Dave said. "I understand."

"Well, just the same, I'm sorry," she said. "So, what do you want to talk about?"

"To be blunt, I don't think you killed Uncle Will. And I wish you would tell me why you confessed," he said.

"Of course I did," she said. "I didn't mean to, but I did. Why do you think I didn't?"

"Because you have not said what you did with the gun after you shot him," Dave told her. "The location of the gun has not been disclosed. Only the investigative team and the killer know where it was found. If you can tell me, then I'll believe you and will help with the manslaughter aspect all I can. If you can't tell me, I have no choice but to continue to look for the killer, and convince the court that you didn't do it."

"Oh, Davey, that preposterous," she said. "Why would I say I did it if I didn't? You need to just accept it. There's nothing else to say or do."

"Aunt Dar," Dave said. "All you have to do is tell me where the gun was when you left the cabin. That ends it and we can move on."

"You know where the gun was," she said. "You were there. It was right there where I left it. You saw where it was, I don't have to tell you."

"Where?" Dave asked again.

"Right there, near where they found him," she said.

"Not good enough, tell me exactly."

She paused, he thought she was going to say she didn't know. But instead she said, "Where are my manners? Do you want some coffee?"

"No, no coffee, I'm fine, You really don't know, do you?"

"I'm going to put the pot on anyway," she said, getting up and heading for the kitchen. "I always like to have a pot at the ready."

Dave was convinced she was not going to prove that she didn't do it by confirming that she didn't know where the gun was found. He saw no reason to push harder. She was apparently also not going to tell him why she continued with the deception. He followed her into the kitchen and they chatted about normal things for a while. After about thirty minutes he left and went back to his office.

At home that evening after dinner Jan started talking about what it was like to be a judge. She had picked up the staff of the former judge so she was the only newbie. Her administrative assistant was a seasoned veteran, in her fifties, who had been there almost thirty years. She had two other office staff for filing, scheduling and word processing and two law clerks to help with the legal stuff.

"I've been getting up to speed on the case load," she said. "It's pretty heavy but I don't think it to be unmanageable. Most of the stuff is pretty routine on my part, divorce proceedings, child custody, adoptions, property disputes, and stuff like that. I only have two criminal cases right now, one is a breaking, entering and theft and the other is a robbery. It seems that most of the case load has been handled by other judges over the past few months."

"So what do you think?" Dave asked.

"I think I liked being a bum," she said. "How did I let you talk me into getting a job and going to work every day?"

"I don't recall my input being that forceful," he said. "As a matter of fact, I only remember being asked how I would feel about you being a judge."

"Well, you didn't try to stop me, wimp. You could have stopped me. You know, I value your input. I would have listened. It's all your fault." She said and looked at him with a big smile.

"So you are saying you think you are going to like it," he said.

"Yeah," she said. "I think that's what I'm saying."

Chapter 29

The state police sent Dave the photos taken in the post office box of the people who opened the boxes with the drug gang packages. He looked at the pictures of the five people. One he recognized as a Lincoln County judge. One he thought may be the wife of the county board chairman. The other three he did not know. Two were women, one younger and one middle aged. The third was a young man, or maybe a boy.

"High school age," Dave thought. "I need to show this to Chris and see if he knows him."

He asked Dan and Bob to come into his office. When they were there, he showed them the pictures. They both confirmed the judge without hesitation. Dan also thought Dave was right about the chairman's wife, he thought her name was Alice or maybe Allie. Neither knew who the two woman were or the boy.

Cheryl was more help. "I think that's Nicole Martin," she said. "She works in the board of elections office." She pointed to the younger of the woman.

"Really," Dave asked. "Are you sure?"

"Pretty sure," Cheryl said. "We went through a computer training course together last fall. She seemed nice."

"You don't know the other woman or the boy?" he asked.

"No, those kids all look alike to me," she said and went back to her work.

Dave showed the photo to Chris when they were all sitting at the table after dinner.

"Chris I'm going to show you a picture to see if you know someone. This is a very sensitive matter that I can't discuss with you. I need to ask that you not tell anyone about this, can you agree to that?"

"Sure, Dad," Chris said. "I can keep a secret."

"Okay, do you know this guy?" he asked showing him the picture.

"Yeah," Chris said looking at the photo. "That's Eric Quincy."

"As in Judge Edward Quincy?"

"I think that might be his grandfather," Chris said.

Dave looked at Jan. She frowned and looked at the picture of the high school boy.

"I just don't understand it," she said. "What's so important that you would throw away a career like that."

"It may be that that's how he got the career," Dave offered.

Jan leafed through the other pictures.

"Oh, my God," she said, as she got to the middle aged woman they had not yet identified.

"Do you know her?" Dave asked.

"Know her? That's Randy's secretary."

In the picture she was carrying three boxes. Since Chris was in the room, they didn't discuss any more about the pictures at that time.

Later, when Dave and Jan were alone, he asked, "You never saw any billings for work for the drug farm or any of their people?"

"No, and I was privy to all of the billings and client lists," she said. "I'm wondering if the reason I miscalculated the value of the firm so badly was because there were other receivables that didn't make the billing lists."

"Is that possible?" he asked. "That sounds like two sets of books. Or something going on off the books."

"Not necessarily two sets, but there could be earnings posted over and above client billings," she said. "It would normally be things like interest on deposits or sale of property, things like that. Any income would have to show up somewhere or an audit would be like fireworks."

"So the firm could be taking in money outside of the normal billing structure," he said. "Why wouldn't they just leave it off completely?"

"Because all of the books have to be open to the audits," she said. "Including the partners' personal accounts. If significant funds show up unaccounted for, red flags go up and auditors start digging."

"Money laundering?" he asked.

"Maybe, but more probably just retainers and fees from a client or clients that they don't want to identify," she said.

The next day he called Paul Adams.

"We have positive ID on the five pictures you sent me," he said and then explained who each were.

"Good," Paul said. "That means we only have one left to identify. A woman picked up one of the boxes in Jackson that nobody knows so far."

"I don't think I can help there," Dave said. "I don't know very many people in Jackson."

"Yeah, didn't expect you would," Paul said. "We'll keep working on that one."

"Are we ready to talk about where we are taking all this," Dave asked.

"I guess so. I'll talk with DEA. Maybe tomorrow morning, can we meet there in your conference room?"

"Sure, just let me know what time," Dave said.

"I will, and I'll bring the doughnuts," Paul signed off.

At nine the next morning the group assembled in the conference room to discuss what they knew and determine a course of action moving forward. Present in the meeting along with Dave, Dan and Bob was Colonel Paul Adams and Josh Trubaldi of the State Police and George Hoffman from DEA. Cheryl had prepared the coffee and Paul had brought Crispy Crème Donuts. The doughnut eating was delaying the start of the meeting to some degree but no one was complaining.

Paul Adams began the meeting with a final chew and a swig of coffee. He started with a discussion of all the information they had obtained from the various actions taken so far. He concluded his remarks by stating, "The only open item is the one PO box key holder in Jackson."

As he said that he dropped a photo in the center of the conference room table. It was Megan (Lewis) Barker carrying a small box.

"That's Sheriff Lewis' daughter!" Dave gasped.

The entire room looked at him, it got quiet. Dan looked at the photograph and nodded.

"No doubt about it," Dan said.

"Her husband is Major John Barker, Williams County Sheriff's Department," Dave said.

"Well, I guess you do know someone in Williams County, Dave," Paul said.

"Guess I do," Dave said.

"Okay," Paul turned to George from DEA. "Now that we know all of the recipients, or at least who picked up the boxes. Can we go after them or do you want to try to get it pinned on Martinez? We don't have him directly involved."

"Let me run it by my team," George said. "But my gut tells me we should clean up this mess even if we can't get Juan. Anyway, maybe if we pull them all in we can get someone to finger him."

"So you're alright with turning this over to the Attorney General?" Paul asked.

"I will confirm, but I think we are," George said.

"Dave, do you see any reason we should not move forward?" Paul asked.

"No, we have no ongoing investigations that would be affected, do we Dan?"

"No," Dan said.

"Okay," Paul said. "After confirmation from George I'll pass this investigation along to the AG. My guess is he will want us to pick up the subjects when they clean out the boxes next month. I'll let you all know."

Later after they had all left Dan came into Dave's office and sat in one of the visitor chairs.

"What do you make of that?" Dan asked.

"Looks like John Barker is dirty," Dave said. "Sheriff Will's own son-in-law taking bribes."

"Do you think Will knew?" Dan asked.

"No," Dave said. "At least he hadn't known for long if he knew. What did Pop say about Will wanting to be by himself? Like maybe he was going to have to do something hard."

"Like turning in his son in law?" Dan asked.

"Yeah. Like that."

"Maybe Doris knew he was going to do it and went up there to stop him," Dan suggested.

"Maybe," Dave said. "And if that was her reason, she wouldn't want anyone to know."

"Yeah," Dan said. "But that still doesn't explain not knowing about the gun."

"No, it doesn't."

Again, Dave found himself driving to Aunt Dar's house. This time Dan was with him. They parked in front of the condo and rang the bell. Doris Lewis answered the door looking as she always did, like she was about to go out to dinner.

"Sorry to barge in," Dave said. "Do you mind if we talk?"

"No, Davey, I don't mind," she said. "Hello, Dan. This is really bothering you isn't it? You know, Davey, you need to just let it go. I'll be fine."

"Aunt Dar," Dave began. "I want to know the truth. Yes, I'm concerned about you, but I feel an obligation to Uncle Will to make sure justice is done. You understand that, don't you?"

"You're just like him in a lot of ways, Davey," she said as they went into the kitchen. She poured coffee for all of them and they sat at the kitchen table. "That's exactly what he would have said. But sometimes people are more important than the law."

"The law is to protect people," Dave said. "If we don't have the law our society will crumble. It is not only important to uphold the law, it's imperative. And that's what I intend to do."

"Is that why you came here?" she asked. "To uphold the law?"

"I'm sorry. That was a little harsh. We came here because we have learned something and want to ask you about it."

"Okay," she said defensively.

Dave position himself so that he could look into her eyes as he spoke. Dan was positioned a little to her left and across the table. He could also see her eyes.

"How did you learn that your son-in-law was accepting bribes?" he asked.

Dave saw her eyes open wide for an instant then settle back down and look worried.

"John is a fine man, an excellent husband and father. He is as honest as the day is long. He would never take a bribe for anything," she said defiantly. "For God's sake, he's a police officer in fine standing."

"You didn't know he was being paid off?" Dave asked.

"No, of course not. Because he's not," she said. "I don't know where you got such a hair brained idea, but it isn't true."

"Okay," Dave said. "Well thanks for the coffee. Sorry to take up your time. We need to go."

Dave and Dan left.

"She didn't know," Dan said. "Did she?"

"No, I don't think she did. That look in her eyes when I told her was complete surprise."

"Yeah, my read too," Dan said. "So what does that tell us?"

"Tell us that if Uncle Will knew he didn't tell her," Dave said.

"Which means our idea of her killing him over that is all wet," Dan said.

"It would seem," Dave said.

They drove on back to the station in silence. Each man trying to put pieces together to complete the puzzle without knowing if they had all the pieces. Or if they were right side up.

Chapter 30

"So, you know John Barker is dirty. You know the drug gang was paying him off, probably to inform them of raids. John is married to Will's daughter. You know that Dar has confessed to accidentally killing Will, and you have her in the location near the time of the killing. You also have drug gang members in the area at the time of the killing, one of whom is a suspected assassin. You know that Will was tracking gang members, but you are not sure why. You know Will suspected Sheriff Alexander of being dirty. What you don't know is what happened," Jan said.

"That's pretty much it," Dave said. They were home in the family room after dinner. Chris was out somewhere with friends. "I think Will was wrong about Sheriff Alexander being dirty. He was right about someone in that department, but it was John not the Sheriff."

"That couldn't have made Will very happy to find out his son-in-law was the leak," Jan said.

"Right, but it is still only speculation that Will knew. We have nothing concrete to base that on."

"You really don't think Dar did it?"

"No, I really don't," Dave said. "And I don't think she knew about John."

"You really don't have a motive, do you?" Jan said.

"No, I don't," Dave said. "We have a confession from someone with no motive."

"I don't know Dar, but from what I've heard people don't think she did it," Jan said.

"Who have you heard from?" Dave asked.

"At the salon, mostly," Jan said. "They talk about everything and I listen."

"That's it!" Dave said with a degree of excitement. "You really are a genius."

"Huh?" Jan asked quizzically.

"The salon," Dave said. "I need to talk with her hair dresser. Who else would know everything about her?"

"Oh, do you know which salon she goes to?" Jan asked.

"No clue, but I'm going to find out," Dave said.

The next morning Dave started calling salons near Aunt Dar's house to find out where she got her hair done. It took him twelve calls before the clerk told him that she was in there every Saturday. He took a ride over there.

"Hi, is this a raid?" The young girl behind a desk in the front of the salon asked when he walked in.

"No, why? Is there illegal activity going on here?" he asked.

"Some of the hair that comes in should be," she said. "But we fix it so that it's all nice and legal before they leave."

"Good to know," Dave said. "I'm here to talk with the person that does Doris Lewis' hair. Are they here now?"

"That would be Nora and, yes, she's here." She got up and headed to the back of the salon and through a closed door. After several seconds she came back out and walked back to her desk.

"She's on break, but will be out in a couple of minutes," she said. Dave sat down on a plastic chair by the door. In a little while a tall thin woman came out the door in the back and walked up to him. She held out her hand as he got up.

"I'm Nora," the woman said. "You want to talk about Doris Lewis' hair?"

"I'm Sheriff Harbinger," Dave said taking her hand. "I don't really want to talk about her hair as much as about her." They sat down on the plastic chairs.

"Well, Sheriff, I think you probably know her much better than I do."

"Call me Dave. She talked about me."

"Oh yes," she said. "She thinks the world of you. Said you remind her so much of Will. She says you are as close to a son as they had."

"I appreciate that. Do you see her often?"

"Every Saturday, one o'clock appointment. She says she always likes to be ready for a Saturday night on the town. Never misses, even in the snow or rain. Always walks the three blocks from her home. Says it is her only exercise of the week."

"Do you keep records of past appointments?"

"Sort of, we have an appointment sheet on our computer. We don't erase appointments unless they are canceled."

"Can you check a date for me to confirm Doris was here?" Dave asked as he quoted the date of the Saturday Will was killed.

"Sure." She got up and walked across to the desk where the girl was still sitting. She motioned for the girl to stay seated and moved the computer mouse around while looking at the screen. "Yes, she came in at twelve fifty six and was finished at three twelve."

"So precise," Dave said. "Do you really keep it that close."

"Yes, our receptionist is required to log the coming and going of all of the customers so that we can accurately schedule appointments. It also gives the owner a sense of how much we are goofing off."

"I'm sure you never goof off," Dave smiled. "So tell me, has she talked about her legal problems?"

"Not really. She told me she finally had to confess to what happened and that she would be on trial but that's about it. I try not to press on such things."

"Did she talk at all about the sheriff's death when it happened?" Dave asked.

"Oh, yes. She came in the following Saturday, I remember because I was surprised that she would keep that appointment. She said she felt she needed to try to keep her routine. It really did upset her, I could tell. She talked about how much she was going to miss him and how her life was going to change, you know stuff like that."

"Do you remember what you thought when you first heard about the Sheriff's death?"

"I thought she would be devastated," she said.

"Do you remember any thoughts about her mood that last time you saw her before the death, like was she preoccupied or seemed worried or anything like that?" he asked.

"No, just the opposite. I remember thinking how happy and comfortable she seemed the last time I saw her before that. That's why I thought she would be so upset by it. It was completely unexpected as far as I was concerned."

"Did she give you any indication that she had done it, before the confession?" he asked.

"No," she said.

"From everything she had told you, did it surprise you to hear she had confessed?" he asked.

"Yes, it did. And now that you mention it, I never believed she had a thing to do with it."

"Neither did I," he said. "Thanks for your time, Nora. You've been very helpful."

Dave went straight into Dan's office when he got back to the station. Dan was reviewing an arrest report of a local drug dealer. He told Dave about the file when he sat down.

"I think I want to talk with this guy," Dan said when Dave walked in. "Maybe we can learn something about where he gets the drugs. How the distribution works, if he will talk. I'll ask the DA if we can offer to deal."

"Good idea. Do you think he'll talk?"

"Don't know," Dan said. "And even if he does, he may not get his stuff from our Williams County guys. But, worth a shot if the DA will play ball."

"Okay, go for it," Dave said.

"But that's not what you wanted to talk about," Dan said.

"No, it isn't. I found Doris Lewis' hair dresser and talked with her. She sees Doris every Saturday for a couple of hours. They talk all the time. She tells me that she had no idea that Doris had anything to do with his death until after she confessed. Her assessment was that she was distraught over his death and was heartbroken."

"Could have been guilt," Dan said.

"Maybe, but she also didn't seem to think there was anything on her mind the day she supposedly killed him," Dave said. "I would think if she had intended to go up and confront him with something that would lead to that, it would have been on her mind a few hours before."

"So, she confirms what we already thought," Dan said. "Which gets us confirmation but leads nowhere."

"Very astute," Dave said.

A couple of weeks later, Paul Adams name showed up on Dave's caller I.D. as the instrument jarred him from deep concentration on a field arrest report of a man with a gun threatening his ex-wife.

"Sheriff Harbinger," he said into the phone.

"Paul Adams, Sheriff. The AG has given us the go ahead to make arrests at the pick ups next week," he said. "I want to bring them all into your facility for booking, even the ones from Williams County. Will you be okay with that?"

"Sure, Paul. Will you be looking for assistance on the arrests from us as well?"

"Maybe there in Springfield. I'll be contacting the Springfield Chief for assistance and if he can't provide it I'll get back to you," he said. "Regardless, you can expect a bunch of people and attorneys in your station next week."

"Do you plan to arrest just the people making the pickup?" Dave asked.

"No. We will grab them and the person we think they are picking the package up for. The plan is to follow the pickup to wherever they pass the package off. Then we'll arrest both."

"Okay, I'll make sure my people are ready," Dave said as Paul signed off.

"How's your work load?" Dave asked Jan as they were enjoying steaks at Outback that evening.

"Manageable. I'm starting to get more sent my way. I'm still the new kid, you know."

"Well, new kid," he said. "It looks like you may be short a couple of judges next week."

"Oh," she said. "Well, we do what must be done."

"I'm thinking it's time to get some more of the cars ready to cruise," Dave said changing the subject. "Cruise nights at Cliff's start up week after next. The Bird is all ready, but we need to get on the others. Want to do a couple tonight?"

"Sure," she said. "Sounds like fun. I want to learn what to do so that we can do them together."

"What a woman," Dave said.

As they drove home from dinner in the BMW they planned out the order of the cars to get ready for summer. In addition to the Superbird, the '64 GTO had been taken out of winter storage for D to drive while he was home on spring break a few weeks ago. Other than those two, all of the collection needed to be brought back out of hibernation for the summer ahead. Dave had a rule that every car had to be driven, otherwise they would deteriorate and things would go wrong that wouldn't be caught and fixed. He didn't want to get behind on maintaining the cars because with thirty four of them if he got behind he didn't think he would ever catch up.

At the front of the storage building were the two cars that were ready to go. Next to them were four empty spots. It was Dave's way to keep track of when a car had been driven to always park the most recent at the front. In addition to reminding him which car was driven last, it required him to move cars around that may not have been started in a while.

Jan wanted to do the Cuda so she pulled the cover off and started the routine. Dave pulled the cover off the car next to it, which happened to be the '70 Corvette. As they were working they heard a car pull to a stop outside. They thought it must be Chris and kept on working. The man door at the front opened and in walked Bobby.

Dave introduced him to Jan.

"I'm glad to meet you, Bobby," Jan said. "But I need to get back to the house."

She smiled warmly and left.

"She's okay, Bobby," Dave said.

"She da judge," Bobby said. "But wow, you scored dude."

"Thanks," Dave said. "What's up?"

"Gotta tell ya," Bobby said. "Really think you all wet on ma dudes man. Been listenin an watchin, man, aint nuthin, man."

"You really think so?" Dave asked.

"Yeah, really do," he said.

"Let me ask something else," Dave said. "Are you guys paying people off?"

"Don't know," Bobby said. "We send packs out every month, don't know what or to who."

"Where do you get the packs?" Dave asked.

"Juan or Alfonso give em to us, we just mail em."

"You don't know what's in them," Dave confirmed.

"Nope, just wanted to let ya know what I learned, gotta go."

Bobby left. Dave finished up the two cars they had started and drove the Corvette home. There was a four car garage at the house and they only had the three cars so the Corvette could park in the garage for a few days. It was not uncommon for Dave to have a car from the collection at home.

"What was that about?" Jan asked when he walked in.

"He wanted to tell me that he thinks my idea about the gang wasting the sheriff is all wet," he said.

"That helps, huh?"

"Another confirmation that I have no idea what happened," he said. "Thanks for bailing by the way, I think it made him more comfortable when you left."

"I thought it would," she said, "now let's go get comfortable."

Chapter 31

Dave had everything ready for a busy day on the fifteenth of the month. He told Bob and Dan that he wanted them to be in the station when all of the suspects were brought in. That way they could be most assured that one of the three of them could be available to witness the booking of all suspects. It could be a long day because they had no way of knowing when people would pick up the packages. The distance to Jackson also added time to the process. There were a lot of unknowns and he wanted to be ready. They expected to hold everyone overnight for bond hearings before a federal judge who had been scheduled to be in town the next morning. Dave had prepared his staff for the process of booking and transporting multiple suspects for an overnight stay in the jail. Bob was holding four patrol officers in the station to act as transport. Only Dave, Bob and Dan knew who to expect to be booked.

At a little after four in the afternoon, the dispatcher said that a state police unit was in route with two male suspects, ETA of ten minutes. Dave checked to make sure two interrogation rooms were available. He asked two booking clerks to get ready.

In less than ten minutes the station door opened and two state police officers escorted two men into the station. One of the men was Judge Quincy and the other Dave recognized as the boy Chris had said was his grandson. Dave showed them into the two rooms he had set aside. One of the officers told Dave the AG people were expected any minute to oversee the bookings. A couple of minutes later four men from the AGs office came in the door. They divided into pairs and a pair went into each of the rooms Because the identification of the boy showed him to be a minor, his parents were called and no further action taken at this time. The boy was asked to wait in one of the chairs that lined the hallway by the interrogation rooms. The booking of the judge continued with Bob as an observer.

About ten minutes later the dispatcher called to inform Dave there were two suspects, one male and one female, in route from Williams County with an ETA of forty minutes. And shortly thereafter another male suspect from Williams County with a forty minute ETA.

Bob came out of the room a short time later.

"The Judge is not saying anything," Bob said. "I get the feeling he either thinks we have nothing on him or that he will just take his punishment. Either way, I don't see getting anything from him. There is one wrinkle though, he has requested his attorney be present for any questioning. He says his attorney is Randy Sherwood."

"That is a wrinkle, to say the least," Dave said. "I'm thinking he may be looking for another attorney. Did the kid say anything?"

"Told the arresting officer that he was just picking up his grandpa's mail," Bob said. "Says grandpa pays him to do it for him."

"That should be enough," Dave said. "I assume they will release him when his parents get here."

Another call from dispatch. Springfield police have two more suspects coming in, one male and one female, ETA fifteen minutes. It was important to keep the suspects separated from each other to assure they could not conspire or create stories. They could use Dave, Bob, and Dan's offices as well as the interrogation rooms and the conference rooms. After five, when the rest of the staff gone for the day, other offices would become available. Dave was confident they could handle the situation.

The next two suspects in the door were Randy Sherwood and the woman Jan had identified as his personal secretary. Dave pointed to the interrogation room the boy had been in and the officer escorted Randy in and closed the door. The woman was asked to wait in the hallway. Her escorting officer sat between her and Judge Quincy's grandson.

The door to the station opened again. This time four men in suits came in. They stopped at the reception desk. The receptionist directed them to Dave.

"What can I do for you," Dave asked as they approached.

"We're from Witman, Wallace and Sherwood," the lead man said. "We understand you have arrested Mr. Sherwood."

"No," Dave said. "We have not arrested Mr. Sherwood, the state police have. If you would like to have a seat, I'll let them know you are here."

"We demand to see Mr. Sherwood, right now."

Dave turned and walked away. He didn't look back. He walked to his office, went in and closed the door. Dan, who had been close by, motioned for the four guys to sit. They did.

A few minutes later Dave called Bob and asked him to let the AG guys know that Mr. Sherwood's attorney had arrived.

At five o'clock most of the office staff was leaving and Dave came out of his office to stay up on what was going on. He was walking toward Bob, who had taken a seat at the reception desk when the next suspect was brought in. It was Megan Barker. She was not in handcuffs but looked like she was tied in knots. Her face was distorted and her eyes looked like she had cried all the way from Jackson. Dave took her hand as they met near the door. He walked her to the conference room.

"Dave," she said in a low shaky voice. "They arrested me, read me my rights and brought me here. Why here? Are you behind this?"

"Megan," Dave said calmly. "No, I am not behind this. You should not say anything to me or anyone else without an attorney."

"Dave," she pleaded. "Help me, you need to get me out of this. Daddy would have wanted you to."

"Megan, as I said. Don't talk without an attorney."

"At least call John for me. He'll get me out of this."

"Why did they say you were being arrested?"

"They said I was taking bribes. Why would anyone bribe me?"

"Did they say you could have an attorney present during questioning?"
he asked

"Yes."

"Did you say you wanted an attorney present?" he asked.

"No. John is a Major in the sheriff's department, why would I need an attorney? Would you call John for me?"

"Megan, please don't say anything else. Just answer a question for me. Once again, do you want an attorney present during your questioning?" Dave looked at her sternly and nodded his head.

"Yes," she said hesitantly. "But why, John will take care of this...."

Her voice trailed off, she looked at Dave. Dave said nothing.

"Oh," she said, looking even more scared. "They're arresting John, too."

"Megan, please don't say anything more. Just wait, you have said to me that you want an attorney present. Do you have an attorney, do you want me to have someone call your attorney for you?"

"I don't know," she looked scared now. "I don't know if we have an attorney. Maybe Sam Johnson?"

"I'll have a call placed to Sam Johnson. I'll stay with you if you like, but please don't talk about this."

"Why?" she said, confused. "Why can't I talk with you about this?"

"Because I'm an officer of the law and everything you say to me goes into the record," he said. "There's no way around that. You could incriminate yourself, and you may already have."

She looked startled, folded her hands under her chin and looked at the tabletop.

Dave called Jan on his cell phone. She was still in her office. She said she knew Sam Johnson as a very good criminal attorney and would ask him to come right. Dave told Megan her attorney was on the way.

Dave sat with Megan, neither of them talked. In a few minutes Dave heard movement in the corridor which he assumed was John being brought into one of the other rooms. He didn't know if Megan understood that but if not he wasn't going to tell her. After about fifteen minutes the door opened and two of the AG guys came in. They put legal pads on the table and sat down across from Megan. Dave sat beside her.

"We understand that you have waived your right to have an attorney present," one of them began.

"Wait," Dave interrupted. "Mrs. Barker told the arresting officers that she did not require an attorney, but upon my confirmation of that she changed her mind. I called her attorney, he is on the way."

"Very well," the AG guy said. "We'll wait for him."

They left and Dave and Megan sat some more. When the attorney arrived, he asked if he could talk with Megan alone. Dave agreed and left them.

Since he had been in the conference room with Megan, Paul Adams had arrived and taken full control of the operation. He had been in Jackson assisting with the arrests there. Now that all of the suspects had been brought in the processing was moving toward the bonding stage. The suspects were to be held overnight to appear before a judge the next day for a bond hearing. The only exceptions were Judge Quincy's grandson and the secretaries of Randy Sherwood and the Lincoln County Elections Chair. The three of them were thought to only be following orders to pick up mail.

When all of the subjects had been processed and taken to their respective overnight accommodations, the team got together in the conference room for a debrief session.

"Okay," began the lead AG guy. "Here's what we have. For the most part the subjects kept silent. We have an admission from Judge Quincy's grandson that the Judge hired him to pick up the mail from the subject PO box. We have the same admission from Mr. Sherwood's secretary. The wife of the Lincoln County Board Chairman admitted that she knew she was picking up money but had no idea who it was from. She thought it was campaign contributions. So we have eleven people being held on the federal charge of accepting bribes through the mail or accessory there to. Anything else?"

"Yes," Dave said. "Prior to her attorney's arrival, Megan Barker indicated to me that she knew her husband was taking bribes. He took out his note book and read his conversation notes: "Me: did you say you wanted an attorney present? She: No, John is a Major in the Sheriff's department, why would I need an attorney? Now would you call John for me? Me: Don't say anything else. Just answer, do you now want an attorney present? She: Yes, but why, John will take care of this. Oh, they are arresting John, too."

"That would indicate that she knew John was taking bribes and that the box she was picking up at the post office was the bribe money," said the AG. "Good work Sheriff. Thanks, anyone else got anything?"

No one else did and they called it a wrap.

It was after midnight when Dave got home. Jan was already in bed.

"Long day, huh?" Jan asked as he crawled into bed next to her.

"I'll say, how about you?" Dave asked.

"Not too bad, but it's better now," she said.

Chapter 32

Dave did not attend any of the bond hearings but heard that bond was posted for all eleven of the suspects. The bond amounts varied with the wives getting the lowest and increasing up to the four judges having to post the highest bonds. He was told that a couple of the suspects had to spend another night in jail while they waited for their bond funds to be raised.

Things fell into a routine for a while. The day to day activity of the job and getting the crops planted took Dave's attention away from the still open and troubling case of Sheriff Will. Although he felt good to have helped with the payoff and corruption case, it really didn't fix the real problem of having a drug farm operating just across the county line.

Dave and Sheriff Alexander had become the best of friends after John was determined to be the leak in the Williams County department. John had been placed on administrative leave pending his trail. Rob told Dave that he really didn't think the leak was in his department and was glad that Will and Dave pushed the issue. He said he never hesitated to share everything with John because he trusted him. If Dave and the DEA had let it drop he would have continued to be blind.

Jan and Dave were full swing into car show and cruise night season. Naturally, Chris was right there too, and D when he was home from school. They would sometime invite a friend or two of Chris or D to cruise nights as well. The friends were invited drive one of the cars from the collection. Dave felt it important to the hobby to get as many young kids interested as possible. He did take precautions, such as dictating that the kids drive in between he and Jan and never drive over the speed limit. And, most importantly, never get to the speed limit very fast. He found that any nineteen or twenty year old boy, or girl, would gladly abide by the rules in order to get to drive a '40 Ford Street Rod or a '69 Camaro Z28 into a local cruise night.

A cruise night at Cliff's on a beautiful early summer evening found them there with five cars from the collection. Dave in the '63 Corvette split window, Jan in the '64 Corvette roadster, D in the '68 Shelby GT500KR, Chris in the '69 Z28 and one of Chris' friends in the '30 Model A coupe. They were all parked in a row along the back of the restaurant and sitting in lawn chairs behind the cars. A fellow enthusiast with a '70 big block Chevelle was parked next to Dave. Dave knew him by sight and his first name only, which was Jake.

"So, how does it feel to be Sheriff?" Jake asked.

"Not much different than being a patrolman, except every problem in the department is mine."

"Well congratulations on being elected," Jake said.

"Thanks."

"A real shame about the way the job came open though," Jake said.

"Yeah."

"Can't believe his wife did it," Jake said.

"Me neither," Dave said.

"You know, she almost ran into me that very day," Jake said.

"What day?" Dave asked.

"The day the Sheriff died," Jake said. "It was a Saturday, right?"

"Yeah," Dave said.

"I remember it because when I heard he had died, I thought that was the very day she almost ran over me," he said.

"Tell me about it," Dave said.

"Well, I work at the plant out by the interstate. I was working that Saturday and when I got off work I was on my way out of the parking lot. The light had just turned green and I started to make my left to come back into town and here she comes pushing the yellow right in front of me. It really wasn't that close, but if I had put my foot in it as soon as the green came she would have broadsided me," he said. "Anyway, she went right by me and onto the north bound ramp."

"What makes you think it was Mrs. Lewis?"

"Ain't no other pink Cadillac in town," he said.

"What time do you get off work on Saturdays?" Dave asked.

"Punch out at 3:20, on the dot," he said.

"How long do you figure from the time you punch out till you saw Mrs. Lewis?" Dave asked.

"Saturdays are light. Not many people, parking lot is pretty empty. I'd say no more than five minutes, maybe seven at the outside."

"Jake, could you testify to what you just told me?" Dave asked.

"What? You mean in court?" he asked.

"Yes, maybe," Dave said.

"I thought she confessed," Jake said.

"She did, but I'm not so sure," Dave said. "Can you testify?"

"Sure," Jake said.

Dave took Jake's contact information down for future use. He made notes about the conversation they just had in his note book.

The next morning Dave drove over to Aunt Dar's house once again. But this time he didn't go in, instead he parked in front of her house and walked to the hairdressers. He clicked his stop watch as he started walking and clicked it off when he got to the salon. It had taken him nine minutes. He reset the stop watch and walked back to his car. Again the trip took him just over nine minutes.

He got into his car, reset the stop watch and clicked it. He drove to the traffic light at the plant just before the interstate taking the most direct route. As he stopped at the intersection he clicked the watch off. The watch showed twenty nine minutes. He turned around and drove back the way he had come, clicking the watch again as he started. When he was back in front of Aunt Dar's house he clicked the stop watch off, it read thirty one minutes.

Dave turned around in Aunt Dar's driveway, clicked the stop watch again and hit the flashing lights and siren. Once again he drove back to the plant intersection but this time in full pursuit mode. He clicked the watch when got there and read sixteen minutes.

Dave pulled off to the side of the road, he put pencil to paper and calculated the times. His notes said that the hairdresser told him Aunt Dar left there at 3:12. It took him nine minutes to walk from there to her house, and she always walked. Dave was sure that he walked faster than Aunt Dar, so the nine minute number should be a conservative estimate. That means that Aunt Dar probably got home at 3:21 at the earliest or more likely 3:25. If she had left home immediately and drove straight to the interstate that adds about thirty minutes, putting her there at about 3:51. Even with lights and siren it had taken him sixteen minutes, or there at 3:37. No where near the 3:25 to 3:27 time that Jake had seen her there.

Dave sat looking at his notes. Another clue that proves she didn't do it. Is there one out there somewhere that will tell him who did?

Dave was headed for the station when his cell phone rang. He hit the hands free button and said hello.

"Dave, it's Paul Adams, we may have found something important."

"I'm listening," Dave said.

"One of my people was looking through the pictures we took that day when we tailed Juan to the restaurant," Paul said. "They compared them to other picture we had taken and found a match. That Williams County Major's wife went into, and back out of the restaurant while Juan was there."

"Megan Barker?" Dave asked.

"That's her, ninety-eight per cent sure," Paul said. "What do you make of that?"

"I don't know. Have you told DEA?"

"Not yet," Paul said. "I left a message for George Hoffman, but he hasn't got back to me yet. Do you think she was there to see Juan?"

"I don't know," Dave said. "I can't think why she would be. Juan had to be dealing with her husband, didn't he?"

"Maybe she was acting as the go between," Paul said. "You know, keep arms length from the bad guy so to speak. I'm not sure how well that would work out, though, she didn't seem too stable to me."

"Yeah, I know what you mean," Dave said. "Say listen, Paul, do you think the AG would entertain the idea of a plea bargain? We may be able to get her to talk, if we go about this right. And the deeper we get into this the more she seems to be involved."

"I'm ahead of you Sheriff. Already asked and waiting for a response. I think they'll go for it. Do you want to be involved in the questioning?"

"Yes, I do."

"I'll let you know when I hear from George," Paul signed off.

Dave got to his office and had no more than sat down when the phone rang. His caller ID said George Hoffman. Dave picked it up.

"DEA is on the ball today, Paul Adams and I were just talking about you," Dave said.

"Yeah, I got his message but haven't got back to him yet," George said. "I got a hot one. Our friends down Mexico way sent a shipment this way yesterday that came across the border this morning. We figure it to be about ten to twelve hours away. Do you think we can get Williams County involved?"

"I think so," Dave said. "John is on administrative leave, and Sheriff Alexander isn't going to be telling him anything."

"How sure are we that he's the only one?" George asked.

"If not we'll find out, don't you think?" Dave said.

"I guess, I just hope we can get them this time," he said. "I've got a guy on the way down there now to do a stakeout. He'll let us know when the shipment arrives. Can you provide a few uniforms and maybe a paddy wagon?"

"Sure, We'll get ready with whatever you need. How many you what?"

"Can you have four units near the county line from about midnight on?" George asked.

"Sure, and I'll be one of them. See you then."

Dave called Jan to let her know that it was going to be another late night for him. She asked if he could meet her for supper? He agreed and they set a time and place.

"Can you tell me what's up?" Jan asked during salad.

"Going to pay a visit to our friends in Williams County," he said.

"Do you expect it to go well?" she asked.

"Yes, I do. At least if it doesn't we'll know we haven't solved the problem yet."

"There is that," she said.

"Listen," she said seriously. "I was going through the files of my predecessor and found some troubling irregularities. Seems he was letting a lot of drug offenses fall through the cracks. Things like issuing warrants and never calling them in and setting hearings for reschedule but never rescheduling them. Far too many to be normal mistakes. And, even more troubling to me is that most all of the defense attorneys involved are from my old firm."

"Like the four guys who showed up for Randy," Dave said.

"No, partner level," she said. "Not who you would expect to be handling such cases. I'm thinking this goes farther than just Randy. And, by the way, I'm pretty pissed that I was a part of a firm that would do that."

"Calm down, Judge. The feds have Randy cold, I don't see him getting away with anything."

"Don't be so sure. He'll claim they were paying his fee and then attorney client privilege kicks in. But I think this may go farther than we know. Be careful out there."

"I will," he said.

Chapter 33

Dave, Dan, Bob and Brian set out for the county line area around eleven o'clock. They were in separate vehicles. Bob had also arranged for the department van which was outfitted as a prisoner transport vehicle with one of Brian's guys, named Steve, at the wheel. The plan was that they would each find a spot to pull off the road as if they were looking for speed violations. Then they would wait for George's signal to move in. It was a radio silence operation since they assumed the drug farm had scanners monitoring all of the police frequencies.

About a mile from the county line on the state highway Dave backed into a deserted gas station in the classic speed trap mode. He had only been sitting for about five minutes when his cell phone rang.

"Dave Harbinger."

"Dave, it's George. My guy is in the grove of trees you used and is watching with night vision equipment. He just saw a dark colored van with Texas plates pull into the farm drive. All of my units are in place. We have three state police and four Williams County, including Sheriff Alexander, in place standing by. Are you and your guys in place?"

"Yes, four squads and a paddy wagon within two miles, standing by."

"Good," George said. "We're going to wait a few minutes, hopefully give them time to unload and get the goods into the building. I'll let you know when we're ready to move."

Dave waited. Once George gave the go ahead, he would call Dan and Brian on their cells with the go signal. Dan would call Bob. Brian would call Steve in the paddy wagon. In about fifteen minutes George called again.

"Change of plans," George said. "The van came back out of the farm and went into the Juan's drive. We're going to wait a bit longer and take both locations. I had the search warrant drawn up to cover both the farm and the house so we're good to go on both. Instead of the farm, I want you and your guys to hit the house? I'll be going in with you and have reassigned two of the state boys with us. Josh Trubaldi is taking charge at the farm with Sheriff Alexander and his team."

"Got it, I'll alert my team."

Dave called each of the guys and filled them in on the change in plans. Five minutes later the call came in and they moved in, no lights or sirens, but very fast.

When Dave got to the driveway to Juan's house the gate was laying on the ground. It was bent in a couple of places as if some vehicle had pushed it in. Dave drove up the drive with Brian close behind him. As they approached the house there was a van in the circular drive by the front door, two state police cars and a dark colored SUV surrounding the van. George was by the front door, he waved Dave and Brian around to the rear of the house as Bob, Dan and Steve came up the drive one after the other. Dave popped his trunk and grabbed the shotgun. Brian pulled the shotgun from the holder in his squad, they both chambered a round. Dave flipped the safety off.

The house was large. Dave ran the length to the rear quickly and quietly. Brian had gone around the other side and as Dave came around the back, Brian was coming around the other corner. There were no side doors but the rear of the house was one large mass of windows and sliding glass doors. The house had a walk out basement with a large concrete patio area and a deck above that. There were two glass doors spaced across the back at ground level. Access to the deck was by way of an elaborate split staircase. Dave motioned for Brian to stay on the lower level as he slipped up the steps. He stopped when he could just see over the deck and waited. He could see Brian down below watching the lower level doors. They had their shotguns at the ready. There were no lights on in the lower level but the main floor was brightly lit.

After a few seconds he heard the commotion in the house as George and the others exercised the search warrant. To his relief there were no gun shots. Suddenly the door directly in front of him opened and a dark skinned man stepped out onto the deck. He had a automatic hand gun in his right hand.

"Freeze," Dave shouted as he pointed barrel of the shotgun at the guys chest. "Police, drop the weapon."

The man turned toward Dave's voice raising the gun. Dave fired. The man did just as Dave had commanded, he dropped the weapon, as he fell to the deck.

Brain had started toward Dave but Dave waved him back down. The situation was not yet secure, Brian returned to his post watching the lower doors. Dave kept his eye trained on the man now lying on the deck. He wasn't moving. The gun was out of his hand. Dave waited.

After what was probably only a couple of minutes that felt like an hour, he heard a voice inside the house yell "Clear." It was followed by several similar responses.

"Dave, are you clear?" he heard George ask from inside the house.

"Clear," shouted Dave.

Dan appeared in the doorway the man had come from. Dave relaxed, they both approached the man on the deck, Dan kicked the gun away. The man was dead.

Dave handed his shotgun to Brian who had come up the stairs behind him. He inhaled and wondered if he had been holding his breath the entire time since the man came out the door.

"You okay?" Dan asked.

"Yeah, what we got inside?" Dave asked as they went in the back door followed by Brian.

"Three subjects secured, no one else in the house," Dan said.

They walked into the large living room. There were three men in hand cuffs sitting on the floor.

"Do you know any of these guys?" George asked.

"Alfonso Ramirez," Dave said pointing to one of the men who had a scar on his left cheek. "Saw him on a security camera at a gas station and interviewed him about that."

"This is Juan Martinez," George said pointing at the second guy. "We don't know the third guy but we think he's the van driver. Come check this out, Dave."

George walked toward another room and Dave followed. They went into a large bedroom in the front of the house. The bed was huge, bigger than a king size. Along the wall opposite the bed was a large entertainment center with every known electronic device. Above the entertainment center were six monitors which were apparently connected to security cameras. One of the monitors showed a group of officers, including Sheriff Alexander, inventorying what looked to be a large amount of cocaine or other drug. To the side of the picture were four men sitting on the floor in handcuffs. Dave noted that Bobby was not one of them.

"Here's what I wanted you to see," George said pointing to what should be a closet door in the corner of the bedroom.

Dave walked to the door. Yes it was a closet, but it was larger than most bedrooms. The interesting thing about it was in addition to clothes racks and dressers it had a vault door to the rear. The door was open. Dave looked in. There was shelving on either wall and in the rear of the vault. Ten shelves high, every shelf was stacked with what appeared to be one hundred dollar bills. In the middle on the floor were two large suit cases. One was open and about half full of hundreds.

"I guess we caught Juan putting up a shipment of cash," George said.

"There must be several million in here," Dave said.

"I'm sure it's all legit," George said with a smile. "But we'll count it anyway. I'll get a team down here."

Dave started back out of the room when something caught his attention. There was a video cassette sitting on a VCR player in the entertainment center. With DVDs, flash drives, TIVOs, on line video, who has VCRs anymore, he thought. He took out a handkerchief to avoid finger prints and carefully picked up the cassette by the corner. As he turned it over he saw a small label with a pencil mark that said "Barker."

"George, look at this," he said.

"What do you make of that?" George asked as he looked at the label.

"Is this covered in your warrant?" Dave asked.

"Any and all property therein," George answered.

Dave hit the power button on the VCR and pushed the tape in. It took some figuring to get the image to appear on the TV screen but when they finally figured it out it jumped to life in a full sixty inch display. What they saw was a standard porn film of two people engaging in sex. The location of the film was the room they were in, on the huge bed with a camera angle to the side and slightly toward the foot of the bed. They were both completely naked and the man was on his back with the woman on top. She was facing the camera. The man in the film was Juan Martinez. The naked woman on top of him was Megan Barker.

Dave hit the stop button and ejected the tape. George took the tape out and handed it to Dave.

"This is evidence," George said. "Keep it safe for me."

Chapter 34

When Dave got home it was almost four in the morning. Jan woke up as he was getting undressed.

"What time is it?" she asked.

"About four," Dave answered.

"Everything go okay?" she asked.

"I guess. I killed a man," Dave said.

"What?" Jan sat up, suddenly looking wide awake, "who?"

"Don't know who he was," Dave said. "I was watching the back with Brain. A guy came out with a gun. I identified myself and told him to drop it. He didn't. He started to point it in my direction so I shot him. Center mass, shotgun from about twelve feet. Dead when he hit the ground most likely."

He crawled into bed next to her. They hugged and kissed.

"Are you all right?" she asked.

"Yes, just very tired and drained."

"Did you get them dirty?" she asked.

"Sure did. Drugs and their money stash," he said. "Legal search warrant and all. I think the cartel may be looking for a new location."

"Good," Jan said. "I'm glad you're okay. I worried about you."

She snuggled up against him.

He thought he would lay awake for hours, but the next thing he knew it was ten in the morning. Jan had been able to get up, get dressed and leave without waking him.

"Must have been a long night," Cheryl said as he walked by her desk. "Bob and Dan haven't come in yet."

"It was. Any calls?"

"No, it's been very quiet," she said.

Dave sat behind his desk and tried to process what he had learned. Specifically about the death of Sheriff Will. He knew that Aunt Dar didn't do it but Pop had seen her. Jake also saw her but not at the time it could have been her. He looked back through his notes. He saw the note from when they were talking to Pop, *Mrs. Lewis' pink Cadillac* it said. He got up from his desk and headed out the door.

"I'll be gone for several hours," he told Cheryl as he passed her desk.

About an hour and a half later he walked into Pop's.

"You remember me?" Dave asked Pop.

"Yep, Lincoln County Sheriff's department. What can I do for you?"

"Couple of questions," Dave began. "When we talked before you told us that you saw Mrs. Lewis' pink Cadillac go up toward the cabin on the day Sheriff Lewis was killed. Is that correct?"

"Yep."

"But you didn't say it was Mrs. Lewis, why?" Dave asked.

"Cause it weren't her," Pop answered nonchalantly.

"What do you mean, how could you tell? Could you see her face?"

"I know it weren't her because she always drives with her nose against the windshield, pert nert," he said. "Never seen anyone who crowds the steering wheel more. She has the seat as high as it will go and as far forward. Don't know how she does it. Whoever went by here in her car that day was far back in the seat. Had a hat on like she wears, but it weren't her."

"Was it a dark haired woman driving?" Dave asked.

"Couldn't tell. Couldn't make out who it was, but it weren't her," Pop said.

"Thanks, Pop. You've been very helpful."

Dave headed back to Springfield.

When he got back to his office he pulled out his note book and looked up the contact information he had noted for Jake at the cruise night. He dialed the cell number Jake had given him.

"Jake, it's Dave Harbinger. A quick question, did you see who was driving Mrs. Lewis' Cadillac that day we talked about?"

"No, not really," Jake said. "All I remember was they had on a big hat."

"Dark haired woman?" Dave asked.

"Couldn't say," Jake said.

"Okay, thanks," Dave hung up.

Dave made notes and was thinking about this new information when his phone rang. The caller ID told him it was George Hoffman, DEA.

"Hi, George," Dave said answering.

"Got an ID on the dude on the deck," George said.

"Okay," Dave said.

"He has been positively identified as one Pablo Ramirez from Guadalajara, Mexico," George said.

"The hit man," Dave said.

"Yep. That cartel is going to need a new enforcer, I guess. Guadalajara police send their regards, by the way."

"Thanks, George. Any news from the bond hearing?"

"Bond denied everyone due to flight risk," George said. "Looks like our drug guys are going to be in the slammer till the trial."

"Any chance I could see the interrogation report on Juan?" Dave asked.

"Not happened yet. Maybe I can get you in on it. I'll check and let you know."

"Thanks, George," Dave said and signed off.

It was almost three in the afternoon. Dave walked out of his office.

"I'll be out the rest of the day," he told Cheryl as he walked by.

He drove home and changed into civilian clothes. He got in the Corvette, which was still parked in the home garage, and headed back into town. He parked in front of Aunt Dar's and walked to the door and rang the bell.

"Hi, Davey," she said as she opened the door and stepped back so he could enter. "More questions?"

"Yes, but I'm not here as the Sheriff. I'm here as a close family friend."

"What does that mean?" she asked.

"Look, Aunt Dar. I know you didn't shoot Uncle Will. I can prove it. I think I know who did and I think you're playing a protection game. I want to help. I want to find a way to make this as easy as possible on everyone. But I need your help to do that."

She looked at him. A tear came to her eye and she nodded slowly.

"How long has Megan been a drug addict?" he asked.

"A couple of years, we.." she stopped herself. "Oh, my God. How did you know?"

"Tell me about the day Uncle Will died. I know she took your car. Tell me the story of what happened."

"Can you help her?" she asked.

"I will do all I can. But I have to know the truth."

She hesitated.

"Your confession will be thrown out. It will be proven false. We have the evidence, including an eye witness who saw her driving your car."

She still didn't say anything. Dave sat and waited.

"Well," she started slowly. "When I came back from the hairdresser that day, her car was parked in front of the house. I came in expecting to find her here but she wasn't here. I finally looked in the garage and found that my car was gone. I didn't know what to think. I waited, thinking she had gone to the store or something and would be right back. I tried her cell phone but it went to voice mail."

"Did you leave your car keys here?" he asked.

"I always leave my keys on the hook beside the door to the garage," she said.

"Does Megan have a key to your house?" he asked.

"Yes, of course," she said.

"When did she come back?" he asked.

"I don't know. She hadn't come back when I went to bed at about eleven. I thought she had just borrowed the car for some reason and must be planning to bring it back the next day. When I got up the next morning, my car was in the driveway with the key in it and her car was gone."

"Did you ask her about it?" he asked.

"Yes, of course. I called her and she acted like she had no idea what I was talking about. She said she had not left her house all day."

"What do you think happened?" he asked.

"When she is high she loses all control. Sometimes she has no idea what she is doing," she started crying. "It's like the drugs just take over and she isn't even there. Will and I were trying to help, but she didn't seem to want help."

"When I first told you that Uncle Will was murdered, you seemed relieved. Was that because you had not put it together that Megan could have done it?" he asked.

"Yes. After you left I figured it out. I tried to get her to talk with me, but she would have nothing to do with it. She kept saying I had no idea what I was talking about."

"So you decided to confess to protect Megan," Dave said.

"Yes," she sobbed. "I didn't want anyone to know about her drug problem and that it could lead to her killing her father."

Dave patted her on the shoulder.

"Tell me, how did you know she was an addict?" she asked.

"I didn't," he said. "I guessed, and you told me."

She looked into his eyes with hers full of tears and nodded.

"I guess I'm glad you did, Davey. Can you help her?"

"I'm going to do my best," he said. "Are you going to be alright?"

"Yes, I think I am now," she said. "Thank you for helping me."

As he drove back home he thought about all that Aunt Dar had been through and marveled at how much stress and pain she must have endured, all alone.

He drove the Corvette into the collection barn and parked it at the front. He took out his cell and called Jan.

"I was just thinking about you," she said answering.

"Are you on the way home?" he asked.

"Yep, be there in about ten minutes, are you there?" she asked.

"I'm at the farm. If you'll pick me up I'll buy you dinner."

"Deal. See you soon."

"Can't wait."

Over dinner in a quiet corner of a very nice and very expensive restaurant Dave told Jan all he had learned.

"You certainly are the super sleuth," she said.

"I guess. But I don't feel good about it," he said quietly.

"It's not your job to feel good. It's your job to get to the truth and uphold the law," she said. "Besides you have to feel relieved that Dar will be cleared."

"I guess," he said.

"So, what's next?" she asked.

"I need to talk to Megan," Dave said. "But, based on what Dar told me, I don't think it is going to lead anywhere."

"You think she really doesn't remember?" she asked.

"I don't know. But I have to try to find out. So, let's talk about you, what's the judge doing these days?"

"Divorcing people and trying to collect child support from deadbeat dads mostly," she answered. "I'd say those two things are eighty percent of my calendar."

"Sounds like fun. Being a judge is so exciting."

"Being a judge is six hours of reading and four hours of listening to people argue every day," she said. "I can't believe I let you talk me into this. Being a bum was so much more fun."

"But think about that black robe. Sexier you can't get."

"You are a very strange man," she said as she shook her head slowly.

Dave called Arlington County the next morning to let them know he had evidence that Mrs. Lewis did not do it. He talked with Sheriff Allen. He told him that he would soon relay the information to him. But he was still working a lead that may have an impact and was not ready at this time. Sheriff Allen said that he would inform the DA that there was new information coming and that they should hold off on any further action against Mrs. Lewis.

Dave went back into his notes to review what he knew and what he didn't. His interest now had shifted to Megan. His notes told him that Uncle Will had seen a car registered to the drug farm on the afternoon he had picked Corey up from a ballgame the week before he was killed. He saw in his notes that Corey told him Uncle Will had planned to go to an out of town ball game on that Saturday but canceled out.

Corey and John were out of town at an away game on that Saturday, Dave said to himself. *That means Megan was home alone. Or was she?*

Dave called Megan and asked when he could come for a short visit. She said she would be home all afternoon and it would be fine for him to come by. After lunch Dave drove down to Jackson.

Chapter 35

John answered the door when Dave rang the bell.

"Hi, Dave. Megan said you were coming by."

"Hello, John. I have some questions about her dad. I'd like to talk with her alone if you don't mind."

"Not a problem," John said. "I was just on my way out anyway. I'll get her. Come on in."

John showed Dave into the kitchen and Dave sat at the table. John went up the stairs and came back in a couple of minutes.

"She'll be right down," he said. John went out the door to the garage and Dave heard the door opener whirl.

"Hi, Dave," Megan said, as she came into the room. "Want anything, coffee, tea, water?"

"No thanks, Megan, I'm fine. Please sit down, I have some very hard questions for you."

She looked a bit concerned as she sat at the table across from him.

"First of all, are we here alone? I don't want anyone else to hear what I have to tell you. I'm here to help," he said slowly.

"We're alone," she said, looking a bit scared.

"I have questions about the day you father was killed," he said. "I know that John and Corey were out of town that day and that you stayed here."

"Yes, I remember. Corey had an away game," she answered.

"Do you remember when they got back home?"

"No. It was the middle of the night, I was asleep," she said.

"What time did they leave?" he asked.

"In the morning, maybe nine?"

"And what time did Juan come over?" he asked.

"What...." her face went white, she folded her arms. She shook all over.

"Megan, I know you're having an affair with him. Is he giving you drugs?"

"I," she stuttered. "I don't know what you're talking about."

"Look, you need to be honest with me," he said slowly. "Juan made a video tape of you having sex in his bed. I have the tape and I plan to keep that our secret if you cooperate."

"John and Corey," she looked frantic. "How, what ..."

Dave could see her mind was spinning. He was afraid she was about to completely loose control. He got up, walked around the table and hugged her where she sat.

"Megan, listen to me," Dave said softly. "I'm here to help. Calm down, try to relax. I know what's going on with you and Juan, but I don't think anyone else does. Not John or Corey, not your mother, not anyone else. Just me. Now, let me help you get out of this."

She seemed to calm down some. She stared to cry softly.

"No one else knows?" she asked through tears.

"No, just me," he said. "I haven't told anyone."

He waited, holding her in his arms, letting her calm down. After a couple of minutes she slowly pushed him away, picked up a napkin off the table and wiped her eyes.

"Okay," she said.

Dave sat back down across from her.

"Do you get your drugs from Juan?" he asked.

"Yes," she said.

"Does he give you drugs in return for sex?" he asked.

"It didn't start out that way, but that's the way it is now," she said.

"How did it start?"

"I knew he was a drug guy. John asked me to be the go-between on their dealings," she said softly. "At one of our meetings I asked if I could buy drugs from him? He said I could, so the next time we met he sold me some meth. I liked it and kept buying more. One day he said there was a way to get it without paying, and that's how it started."

"How long has it been going on?"

"About three years," she looked down at the table.

"Does John know about your drug use?" he asked.

"Yes, but he thinks I buy them."

"How long had your dad and mom known?"

"Maybe a couple of months before dad...." she trailed off.

"Tell me what happens when you get high?" he asked.

"I love it," she said, "I feel so alive, so powerful, so sexy. I'm on top of the world."

"Do you remember everything after you come down?"

"Sometimes, other times I don't remember anything at all."

"That Saturday morning, did Juan bring you drugs?"

"Yes, and they were great."

"What did he bring?" he asked.

"I don't know, several different kinds I think, I don't remember too much."

"Tell me what you remember."

"I remember he gave me some pills and we had sex while I was getting high," she said. "Then I woke up the next morning."

"That's all you remember?"

"Yes."

"You don't remember driving up to Springfield and getting your mother's car?" he asked.

"I know she thinks I did," she said. "But I don't remember anything after the sex with Juan."

"Do you remember finishing the sex with Juan and him leaving?" he asked.

"No," she said thoughtfully. "I don't, I remember we were having sex and then I woke up the next morning."

Dave was quiet. They sat looking at each other across the table for a long time.

"Do you think I killed Daddy?" she asked.

"It looks that way," he said softly. "But you didn't know what you were doing."

"What's going to happen, am I going to jail?" she asked.

"I don't know."

"You won't tell John about the sex?" she pleaded.

"I'll do everything I can to keep that our secret. But I don't know."

She looked away.

"I trust you, Dave," she said.

He left.

When Dave got in his car he took out his note book and recorded everything Megan had told him. His number one question was what drug Juan could have given her that would cause her to do such a thing. It seem evident that that was what happened, but was it possible? He headed back to Springfield wondering.

That evening Dave called his brother at home.

"Hey little bro," Kent said. "What's up?"

"I have a medical question for you, Kent. Can a person be drugged and caused to do something they would not normally do?"

"You mean like a drug induced-hypnosis?" Kent asked.

"I don't know, maybe. I have a suspect who may have done something at the suggestion of someone else by being drugged. I'm wondering if that is possible."

"Highly improbable," Kent said. "People who are susceptible to hypnosis will normally not do anything that they would normally not do. Some drugs may help someone be hypnotized easier, but I don't believe a hypnosis as we normally understand it can be accomplished only by a drug."

"So in order to cause someone to do something you would have to be a hypnotist, but even then you could only get them to do something they would normally do," Dave said.

"Yes," Kent said. "I know there have been some studies about how to take over the human brain and control things like drug addiction, and emotional fears but I don't think there's anything to do what your talking about."

"Drugs can make you forget what you have done, though?"

"Oh, yes. There are many drugs which will cause complete memory loss of anything the subject experienced while under the influence of the drug."

"How long will a given drug influence someone?" Dave asked.

"There are to many variables to generalize," Kent said. "Type of drug, dosage, size of the individual, and on and on."

"A period of say, eight hours, would be possible?" Dave asked.

"Easily. I would say the norm would be from an hour or two to twelve hours."

"Thanks, Kent." He talked with his brother about other things for over an hour. They didn't talk often, so they always had catching up to do.

"You looked troubled," Jan said after Dave finished his phone conversation with his brother.

"Yeah," he said. "I think I know what happened the day Sheriff Will was killed. I just can't figure out how he did it."

"Who's the he?" she asked.

"Juan Martinez. He is really smart. You can tell that just by what he has accomplished and the way he acts. But I'm just not seeing how he did it."

"I'm sorry, I don't think I can help you. I'm on the side that applies the law to what they did, not figuring out how they did it. I'm afraid you're going to have to find someone else to give you that answer."

"Yep, I have an idea who that might be," he said as they got ready for bed.

The next morning as he walked into the station, Dave asked Dan Muscovy to come into his office. They both got coffee, closed the door and sat in their usual positions to talk things over.

Dave laid out the whole story of everything he knew and what he suspected happened. Dan listened quietly, drinking his coffee.

"So," Dave said when he had finished. "What do think?"

Dan was quiet for a minute then set his coffee cup down on the edge of Dave's desk and leaned back.

"Sheriff," Dan began. "Let me tell you a story. The story is about a robbery at gun point of a convenience store. The main suspect, we'll call him Johnny, was identified by the store clerk even though he wore a ski mask. The clerk also gave a description of Johnny's car, including license number. The store cameras were broken so all there was to go on was the clerk's description. The young sheriff's detective in our story, we'll call him, Dan Muscovy, knew the parents of eighteen year old Johnny. Johnny told the detective that he was no where near the store and that the store clerk was an enemy of his and out to get him. Johnny's story checked out that he and the clerk had issues. The clerk also had a long rap sheet and was constantly in trouble. Muscovy believed Johnny and set out to prove he was being set up. But, lo and behold, a gas station about a block away did have a working camera pointed at the street and when he checked the date and time of the convenience store robbery he saw Johnny's car drive by. And he still had on the ski mask the clerk described."

Dave nodded slowly.

"Sheriff, our job is to look at the evidence and let it lead us to the truth. The truth as the evidence shows, not as we think it should be or want it to be."

"You think I may be trying to believe what I want to believe." Dave said.

"You have far more reason than Dan had to believe Johnny," Dan observed.

"Keep going," Dave suggested.

"Just for argument, let's say that there is more to the relationship between Megan and Juan than just drugs. Let's say she really had fallen for him, and even was in love with him. Let's say that her father was about to put Juan away. What would that do for your scenario?"

"Good point," Dave said. "If she was in love with him, she may feel a want, or even a need, to protect him. Not only for love but for her drug supply."

"Even to the extent of killing her own father. A man she wasn't getting along with. A man that was threatening her happiness in love and drugs." Dan offered.

"If that were the case," Dave said. "Juan may not have even had to suggest anything, she may have done it on her own to protect him."

"Sad, but true," Dan said slowly.

Dave massaged the back of his neck with both hands as he grimaced with his eyes closed. Dan was right. It was not what he wanted the evidence to show. But it was looking him right in the face. He needed to grasp the reality that was right in front of him. As much as he wanted it to be different, the facts show that Megan was not forced into anything. She acted alone. Premeditated, murder in the first degree.

Chapter 36

The newspapers were full of stories of the corruption in the courts and political circles in the two counties. There were also stories about the drug farm and the raid on the cartel's local operation. Dave read all the stories with interest, but knew there was more to come. He had more to tell but was not looking forward to breaking it on those involved or the public.

The county court system in Lincoln and Williams Counties was in a near panic mode. Judges in both counties had been arrested on bribery charges. In keeping with the *innocent until proven guilty* adage they still held their positions. But due to the pending charges both counties had withdrawn all of the case load from the charged judges. This pushed the case loads onto other judges, causing delays. The delays were expected to continue for some time. It was a long process to bring a case against a judge to trial in federal court.

Jan's case load had almost doubled overnight. She was being required to spend much more time in her office preparing for court sessions. When she came home she always had a brief case full of docket files she needed to review. This meant less frequent leisurely dinners out and almost non-existent evenings at home with nothing to do. The weekly cruise nights, however, were still on the schedule every week. "Priorities must be maintained," she said.

The Lincoln County Board unanimously voted to remove the Board Chairman and the Head of Elections from their positions. An interim chairman had been appointed by the board until the next election. The board had also appointed a new Head of Elections. The Williams County Board had taken similar action to remove the charged individuals from power there.

The law firm of Witman, Wallace and Sherwood, and Randy Sherwood personally, were charged in federal court for accounting irregularities, money laundering and mail fraud. Randy Sherwood was under review by the state bar association for accepting cash for the purpose of money laundering, accepting cash without providing services in kind and mail fraud. If the charges are upheld, the firm could lose it's license and be shut down. If the charges against Sherwood were upheld he could go to jail and lose his license to practice law.

The shooting of Pablo Ramirez was reviewed and Dave was cleared of any wrong doing. Brian's testimony that he heard Dave identify himself and order the subject to drop the weapon was important. Brian also said that Dave did not move from his position near the top of the steps until Dan came out the door. Dan testified that when he got to the door, Dave was still in the position from which he had apparently fired. Dan said he was the one who kicked the gun away from the subject. The review board had no trouble reaching their decision.

All of the drug gang members arrested at the farm were charged with possession with the intent to deliver. Juan and Alfonso, in addition to the drug position charges, were charged with money laundering, receiving drug funds, mail fraud and income tax evasion. The van driver was a Mexican national on a tourist visa and was immediately deported.

It was mid-afternoon. Dave had spent most of the day trying to figure out his next step to deal with Megan Barker. Arlington County was asking for the information he promised. He knew what he had to do, but kept finding things to check on before he did. He knew it was time to take action and get it over with. His phone rang.

"Dave, I have tentative approval for you to be in on the questioning of Juan Martinez," George Hoffman's voice said on the phone. "But the DA wanted to know what you want to learn?"

"We have an open investigation into the murder of Sheriff Will Lewis," Dave said. "The sheriff's daughter, Megan, is a prime suspect in that investigation. Martinez was her drug supplier and saw her often. My interest is to question him about what she may have told him."

"I'm sure they will have no problem with that," George said. "Tomorrow morning at nine in the federal lock."

"I'll be there," Dave said.

With that, he shifted his focus to work up the questions he needed to ask Juan Martinez. He didn't expect to learn much, but there was a good chance he might be able to get a better handle on the type of relationship they had. He hoped it would make him feel better, but he wasn't very confident.

At eight forty five the next morning he was sitting with George Hoffman, the District Attorney and two DA staff attorneys. They were in a conference room drinking coffee while they waited for the questioning of Juan Martinez. Shortly after nine, the door opened and in came a man, that Dave recognized as being from Whitman, Wallace and Sherwood, Juan Martinez and a uniformed agent. The attorney introduced himself as Robert Moretti and said he represented Mr. Martinez.

"This proceeding will be very short," Moretti said. "Since I have told my client to answer no questions."

Dave noted what he thought was complete distain for the attorney from Juan.

Dave looked straight at Juan and said, "You letting that wimp speak for you?"

"I speak for myself," Juan shot back with a degree of disrespect.

"Mr. Moretti, it looks like your client does not agree since he has already answered a question," Dave said.

Moretti leaned over and whispered something in Juan's ear.

"I'll talk if I want to," Juan shot back at him

At that point the DA took over and began a systematic questioning of Juan Martinez. He asked about the drug farm operation, the staffing, the connection with the Mexican Cartel, the stash of cash, the flow of drugs, and so on. Juan answered some questions at the discomfort of Moretti, but mostly denied any action and sat quietly.

After about an hour the DA said that there was another matter outside the scope of their investigation of which Mr. Martinez may have information. He turned it over to Dave.

"Mr. Martinez, I am investigating the death of Sheriff Will Lewis. We think Megan Barker, the Sheriff's daughter may have information about the reason the Sheriff died." Dave began, "I am aware that you know Megan Barker and would like to ask you some questions about her to help with our investigation. Is that alright?"

"Is my client suspected of participating in a crime?"

"No," Dave answered. "Our sole interest is Mrs. Barker."

Moretti whispered into Juan's ear. Juan nodded.

"I have no objection to asking Mr. Martinez about his relationship with Mrs. Barker," Moretti said.

"Very well," Dave continued. "How long have you known Mrs. Barker?"

"Bout three years," Juan said.

"You know her socially?" Dave asked.

"Yeah," Juan smiled.

"Did you see her at her home on the day that her father died?" Dave asked as he read the date from his notes.

"Yeah, I was there that morning."

"What time did you leave?" Dave asked.

"Noon, I guess."

"Did she give you any idea that she was going to go see her father that day?"

"No," Juan answered.

"Did she tell you how she felt about her father?"

"She didn't like him," Juan said.

"Did she say she wished he was dead?" Dave asked.

"No, I don't think so," he said.

"Did she tell you she planned to go up to his cabin that day and murder him?" Dave asked.

"What murder?" Juan asked. "The old man killed himself."

"Why do you say that?" Dave asked.

"It was in the papers," Juan said. "Shot himself with a shotgun."

"How could he do that? The shotgun barrel is too long."

"He put the gun in a vise and pushed the trigger with a yard stick. It was in the papers," Juan said.

Dave was quiet for a second. The whole case flashed in his mind. He had been right all along about the drug gang, now he knew that Juan was the murderer. *But what about Megan, was she involved or not?* Now, he was getting close, but still had some loose ends to tie up.

"Mr. Moretti," Dave said. "I apologize, what I told you before is no longer true."

Dave paused, Moretti looked confused. Juan looked defiant.

"I have no further questions at this time," Dave concluded.

Dave left in a hurry. On his way back to Springfield he placed a call to Aunt Dar.

"Aunt Dar, have you heard from Megan lately?" he asked when she answered the phone.

"Why, yes, Davie. She called this morning and is coming up to spend the afternoon with me. She should be here in about twenty minutes."

"Good," Dave said. "I need to talk with her, it's very important. Would it be alright if I stop by in an hour or so?"

"Sure. We'll see you then."

Dave drove straight to Aunt Dar's. There was a burgundy Chrysler 300 in front of her house. Dave went up and rang the bell.

"Hi, Dave," Megan said as she opened the door. "Come on in."

"Well, I've been in the car for a while and would like to stretch my legs a bit. Do you think your mom would mind if you and I take a walk around the block? We need to talk."

"I'll let her know," she said as she went back inside.

Dave walked back down to the driveway and waited. It was only a minute before Megan came down the steps and joined him. They began walking up the sidewalk toward the end of the block.

"Megan, I have new information about the death of your father. I can't say what it is, but it is very important. But, in order to learn exactly what happened, I need more. I think you may be able to help. Will you?"

"Of course, Dave. I trust you and will help if I can."

"I need to know what you knew about your father's investigation of the drug gang. Did he tell you what he had found out?"

"Some. He told me that he knew Juan was providing my drugs and he had enough on him to put him away."

"How did he know that Juan was your drug source?" Dave asked.

"I'm not real sure, but I think daddy may have seen Juan leaving my house, or maybe he was following him when he came here," she said.

"Did he say what information he had that would put Juan away?"

"No."

"When did he tell you that?"

"A few days before he died. When he called to say he was going to the cabin instead of Corey's ball game."

"Did you tell Juan what your dad had said?" Dave asked.

She didn't answer.

"Megan, I need to know. I can't help you unless I know everything."

"Yes," she said in a low voice.

"Why would you tell Juan?"

"He always asked about Daddy, and wouldn't give me the drugs until I told him," she said.

"When did you tell him?" Dave asked.

"That Saturday morning," again, her voice was soft.

"Did you also tell him your dad was going to the cabin?"

"Maybe."

"What do you mean, maybe?" Dave asked.

"Well, he gave me some new drug. We were in bed and he was asking questions," she said, "I'm not sure what I told him, I was drifting in and out."

"Did he ask where the cabin was?"

"He asked if I had it loaded in the GPS in my car?"

"What did you tell him?" he asked.

"I told him I wasn't like my mother who loaded everyplace she went into that thing."

"Megan, do you have your mother's house loaded in the GPS in your car?"

"Yes, what's that got to do with anything?" she asked.

They were back in front of Aunt Dar's. Dave thanked Megan for her help and headed back to the station. Once he was at his desk, he began work on the report that would explain to the world what had happened to Sheriff Willard Lewis.

Epilog

Dave's report read:

Juan Martinez murdered Sheriff Willard Lewis. His motive was that Sheriff Lewis had been following him and knew he was providing drugs to the sheriff's daughter. The sheriff confronted his daughter and told her he was going to file charges in the next week. Sheriff Lewis knew the filing would make his daughter's drug problem public, which caused him anguish to the extent that he canceled out on his grandson's baseball game to go to his cabin. Juan forced Mrs. Barker to tell him about the pending charges by withholding her drugs until she did. She also told him that the sheriff was at his cabin. This occurred when they met that Saturday morning. Juan drugged Mrs. Barker and took her car. Mrs. Barker's car had her mother's house loaded in the GPS and he followed it to her house in Springfield. He used her mother's house key that Mrs. Barker had on her key ring to gain access to her Mother's house. Mrs. Lewis was not home. Megan had told him that Mrs. Lewis loaded everyplace in her GPS, so he figured the pink Cadillac would have the cabin loaded. He found the Cadillac in the garage and the key hanging on the hook by the door. He put on the mother's hat which she always had on the car seat and drove to the cabin. He found the Sheriff asleep at this desk, slipped in, took his shotgun and shot him at close range when the sheriff woke up. He drove the Cadillac back to Springfield, left it in the mother's driveway, without her knowing. Since Megan's car was parked in front of Mrs. Lewis' house, Mrs. Lewis thought Megan had barrowed the Cadillac for some reason. Juan drove back to Mrs. Barker's house got his car and left. Mrs. Barker was still drugged and didn't wake up until the next morning. When her mother asked her about the car, she denied everything. Megan's husband and son did not get back home until two in the morning, after Juan was gone."

Mrs. Barker confirms providing the information to Juan Martinez. Sheriff Lewis' notes provide a license number of one of Juan's cars, at or near Mrs. Barker's home the week before he was killed. Mrs. Barker confirms that she was administered drugs by Mr. Martinez which rendered her unconscious from late Saturday morning until Sunday morning. Mrs. Lewis confirms that her car was missing from when she got home from her hair appointment at approximately one thirty until the following morning. Mrs. Lewis left her hair appointment at 3:12 in the afternoon, her car was seen getting on the interstate at approximately 3:27, not enough time for her to be the one driving. Pop confirms that Mrs. Lewis' Cadillac drove past his station going toward the cabin late in the day on Saturday and that Mrs. Lewis was not driving, because the driver was sitting to far back away from the steering wheel. He also confirms that the driver was wearing Mrs. Lewis' hat.

Most importantly while being questioned, Juan Martinez told investigators that the shotgun was in the vise on the sheriff's desk. The information of the location of the shotgun was known only to the crime scene investigators and the murderer.

Dave provided his report and the evidence to the DA in Arlington County. In his rush to get the paper work done he forgot to mention the sexual relationship between Megan and Juan. The paper work showed that Megan was a drug user and Juan was her supplier. Dave felt it important to get it submitted quickly so that the case against Mrs. Lewis could be dropped and a new one filed against Juan Martinez. When he realized his error, it had already been submitted, so he decided to just let it go.

The Arlington DA brought charges of first degree murder against Juan Martinez. The trial was held about six months after it was filed. By that time Juan was represented by a public defender since the firm that had been representing him had been shut down, having been found to have violated federal banking rules, and postal regulations. Juan was transported to the trial in Arlington County by the US Marshall's office since he was serving a twenty year prison term for drug trafficking, mail fraud and tax evasion.

Juan Martinez was found guilty by a jury of his peers of the murder of Sheriff Willard Lewis of Lincoln County. He was sentenced to life in prison without parole.

John Barker was found guilty of accepting bribes and dereliction of duty. He was sentenced to five years in prison and a twenty thousand dollar fine.

Each of the judges charged were found guilty and removed from the bench. They also received prison terms of varying lengths and fines.

The county board chairmen and election chairmen were found guilty of accepting bribes. The received prison time and fines.

Sheriff Will's tape recorder was never found.